A GIRL DURING THE WAR

Center Point
Large Print

Also by Anita Abriel and available from
Center Point Large Print:

The Light After the War
Lana's War

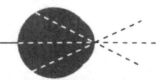

**This Large Print Book carries the
Seal of Approval of N.A.V.H.**

A GIRL DURING THE WAR

ANITA ABRIEL

CENTER POINT LARGE PRINT
THORNDIKE, MAINE

This Center Point Large Print edition
is published in the year 2022 by arrangement with
Atria Books, a division of Simon & Schuster, Inc.

The text of this Large Print edition is unabridged.
In other aspects, this book may vary
from the original edition.
Printed in the United States of America
on permanent paper sourced using
environmentally responsible foresting methods.
Set in 16-point Times New Roman type.

ISBN: 978-1-63808-282-8

The Library of Congress has cataloged this record
under Library of Congress Control Number: 2021952360

To my mother

CHAPTER ONE

Rome, November 1943

Marina Tozzi crossed Piazza di Santa Maria, hugging her parcel to her chest. The late-afternoon sun reflected off the gold-flecked tower of the Basilica di Santa Maria in Trastevere, giving Marina a glimmer of hope.

The Nazis may have made it impossible to get food, turning even the most honest Roman citizens into experts on the black market. They may have prompted all the young men to join the Italian army, leaving the streets filled with mothers missing their sons, young women longing for their husbands. But they couldn't dim the famous Roman light, the light that had drawn artists to the city for centuries.

Marina would know. Her father, Vittorio, was an art dealer who spoke endlessly of the great artists who once resided in the city: Caravaggio, Bernini, Michelangelo. Some historians claimed they had come because they had been sponsored by wealthy Romans, or had sought camaraderie with other artists at the workshops. But her father insisted it was for the light. Nowhere in Italy, not in Venice nor Florence nor Naples, was the light as spectacular as in Rome, strands of gold caressing the Roman Forum and the Colosseum, as if the whole city had been touched by God.

The piazza had been quieter in the two months since the Germans arrived but not entirely empty. It was against Romans' nature to stay indoors. Even with armed Nazi soldiers roaming the streets, friends gathered before curfew for a quick gossip. Marina watched her neighbors lounging on their balconies or standing under ancient arches that had survived the Allied bombs.

As she turned onto her street, there was a popping sound and Marina smelled an acrid odor, like the few times her father had left a pot of pasta too long on the stove and the bottom of the pot burned. After her mother died ten years ago, her father had taken over the cooking. Now twenty years old, Marina was eager to help him. But he still insisted on making the pasta himself. It was his great love, besides Marina and the art gallery. He was happiest when stirring a pot of pomodoro sauce, grating the Parmesan, adding oregano and a touch of olive oil.

The door to their house was flung open, the pungent smell coming from inside. She was about to run up the steps when she heard voices. They were shouting in German. Her stomach clenched, her fingers gripping the precious anchovies she'd procured for her father's favorite pasta sauce.

She had traded a silk purse for the fish at the market. Her father would be angry if he knew.

He didn't like Marina going without the little luxuries that were important to girls. But Marina wanted to surprise him. The gallery had sold a painting by a new artist that morning and her father had gone to deliver the money to the artist himself. Marina worked at the gallery too, while taking art history courses at the university. They were going to celebrate the sale that evening with pasta and a bottle of wine.

She stepped behind a bush, hoping that she was wrong, that the unfamiliar voice belonged to a neighbor. Then she saw them. Two German officers scurrying out the door like rats departing a sinking ship. Their pistols were at their sides, a thin line of smoke trailing from one of them. The men ran around the corner, their heavy footsteps clattering on the cobblestones.

Marina waited to make sure there weren't any more soldiers, then darted inside. The house appeared as she'd left it that morning. Her father's overcoat hung on a peg, and his boots sat beside a pair of slippers.

In the kitchen, the table was set with two place settings. Since the occupation, they only used the dining room to entertain clients. Somehow it was cozier to eat in the kitchen, as if the warmth of the oven, the familiar smells of garlic and olive oil would keep them safe.

The burnt pot sat on the stove. Perhaps her father got called away by a knock at the door, forgot the pasta was simmering, then after the visitors left went to his bathroom to wash and shave. That's where he was now. The Germans had simply been making their rounds. Her father was upstairs dressing for dinner.

She turned off the stove and ran up the staircase. The bathroom was empty, and there was no one in the bedroom.

The house had a basement where her father stored paintings. There was never enough room at the gallery, and he often brought pieces home.

She crept down the two flights of stairs, more carefully this time. The staircase to the basement was narrow, and she didn't want to risk twisting her ankle.

She turned on the bare light bulb at the bottom of the stairs. Five feet away, the body of a man lay on the ground. Blood seeped from his chest and his arms, and his legs lay at odd angles. The man was young, with a head of thick, dark hair. She didn't recognize him. Who was he, and what was he doing lying dead on the floor?

She glanced around the space and all thoughts of the man fled. Another body was propped up in the corner. It was hunched over, as if someone had kicked it. Blood pooled on the floor underneath, and it wasn't moving. Even with the face turned away from her, she knew it was her father. And she was almost certain that he was dead.

She rushed over and laid him on his back. His chest was perfectly still; there was no heartbeat. He was holding a small bag that fell to the ground. A wad of lire tumbled out.

Footsteps echoed on the basement staircase. Perhaps the Germans had come back. She scooped up the lire and hid under the stairs.

"Marina," a male voice called. The footsteps stopped at the bottom of the stairs. "I saw officers running down the street—is everything all right?"

It was their neighbor Paolo. Paolo was a widower like her father. He often joined them for dinner and talked obsessively about the war: the Allied landing in southern Italy in July and the uprising in Naples in September. The war was turning but not fast enough. Two months before, when German troops marched in and occupied Rome, no one knew how long they would be in charge. But the spirit of Roman citizens continued to burn like the candles at St. Peter's Basilica.

There would be no more dinner conversations with her father, Marina realized. No more pasta with anchovies. A sob caught in her throat.

"Paolo," she cried, stepping out from her hiding place beneath the staircase. "I saw German officers leaving the house, so I crouched in the bushes until they were gone. I searched the house and found . . ."

She waved at the bodies. Words failed her, and the sobs became an ocean of tears. Her body convulsed into shivers.

"My father and this man are dead," she said, when she could speak. She turned to Paolo, her eyes wide. "Who is he, Paolo, and what was he doing in our home?"

Paolo moved closer to the bodies. His face turned ashen; tears formed in his eyes.

"It's Enrico," Paolo said. "Your father had been hiding him in the basement. I warned him that it was dangerous—the Germans had started searching neighborhoods close by—but your father wouldn't listen."

Enrico was the artist whose painting her father had sold that morning. But he hadn't lived with them; he had a room near the gallery.

"You're wrong," she said firmly. "Enrico had his own place. My father was going there today, to take him the money for his painting."

"Vittorio lied to you." Paolo's voice was low. "Enrico fled the Jewish ghetto a few days ago. He was staying here."

Marina looked at Paolo sharply. The gallery sold paintings by well-known artists, but her father also loved to help beginners who showed talent. Sometimes if their paintings didn't sell, he quietly bought them himself. And plenty of hungry artists had joined them at their dinner table, but they were never invited to spend the night. Marina was a young woman; her reputation must be considered.

"What do you mean, he was staying in the basement?"

"Enrico was Jewish. When the Germans emptied the Jewish ghetto, he escaped and had nowhere to go," Paolo said. "Vittorio offered him the basement."

A few weeks before, the Germans had rounded up all the Jews in Portico d'Ottavia, the ghetto where Jews had lived since the sixteenth century. Twelve hundred Jews were put on trucks and taken to Tiburtina station, where a train waited for them. No one had heard from them since.

"I spoke with your father this afternoon. He sold Enrico's painting to a German officer. The officer didn't know Enrico was Jewish, but he returned to the gallery because he forgot his gloves and overheard Vittorio talking." Paolo rubbed his brow. Grief washed over his features. "Your father was worried that the officer might follow him home, but the German didn't come. Vittorio must have thought it was all right, that they were safe."

Marina realized she was still holding the wad of lire: the money for Enrico. She didn't want it. She wished she could toss it out the window, that it was a grenade and would fall on a German soldier.

"Oh, Paolo." She crouched down next to her

13

father's body. "It's my fault. I stopped at the market to buy anchovies for the pasta. We were going to celebrate the sale. If I hadn't stopped at the market, I might have been here when the Germans arrived. I could have warned my father, maybe he'd be alive."

"Or maybe you'd be dead too," Paolo returned. He looked at her kindly, his own misery set aside in order to comfort her. "Vittorio would have said that you were meant to buy the anchovies. That God was watching out for you."

Marina's head swam, and the room became a terrible blur. She put her hand out to steady herself and sunk to the floor. She felt as if someone had torn out her insides, as if her heart had been crushed inside her chest. She didn't want to think about God. She wanted to think only about what she had lost, the one person she could count on. The only man she loved and trusted.

"He can't be dead." She gulped, tears pressing against her eyes. "My father can't be dead."

"I'm sorry, Marina." Paolo patted her arm. "I loved your father; we were neighbors for thirty years. When my wife died five years ago, I asked him how he still managed to get up in the morning. He said the answer was helping others. Enrico wasn't the first Jewish artist who stayed in your basement. There were others."

Marina tried to remember if her father had

acted differently over the last few months. He often made more food than the two of them could eat, yet there never seemed to be any leftovers, she realized. Marina had assumed her father was anxious about the occupation, that cooking calmed his nerves. She never thought to wonder where the extra food went.

"My father was operating a safe house without telling me?"

Marina had heard about safe houses, of course. Hundreds of Allied prisoners of war who had escaped from southern Italy made their way through Rome on their journey to the Swiss border. Romans hid them in their homes. Without the safe houses, many of these soldiers would have been discovered and put in prison. But she'd also heard some were hiding Jews, many of whom were starving. Rationing was fierce all over the city, but it was worst in the Jewish ghettos. There, even pasta was impossible to find, and a loaf of bread cost three times the normal price.

Everyone knew operating a safe house was dangerous. Just the previous week, Marina and her father had been walking in Trastevere and saw German officers drag a man and woman into the street. They were shot in front of everyone, their bodies loaded into a German truck. Marina and her father watched long enough to hear a neighbor whisper that the couple had been hiding

Jews before Vittorio had quickly dragged Marina away.

How could her father do such a thing? Risk his life—her life—without telling her?

"My father and I didn't keep secrets from each other. How could he tell you and not me?" she demanded.

If she kept asking questions, maybe she could hold back the pain that shot through her like a fire burning out of control.

"I only found out by accident. I came over to return a book I had borrowed and found Vittorio and an artist in the living room. The man was holding a towel; he had just taken a shower," Paolo replied. "If he told you, he would have put you in danger. Vittorio loved you more than anything. He would have died himself before he let anyone hurt you."

"But he did die." Her voice broke.

Her eyes were wide and frightened. Her body felt as if it didn't belong to her—it went from being on fire to cold as ice.

"How will I live without him, Paolo? He's the only person who's been there my whole life."

"You will find a way, Marina. You must. But you can't stay in the house. I'd invite you to stay with me, but it's not a good idea for either of us." Paolo paused, considering. "If the German officers searched the house and noticed a young woman's bedroom, they may come back."

"Come back?" Marina was puzzled.

"They would assume anyone else in the house would be part of this—they could come back to arrest you and question you about other safe houses and their networks," Paolo explained.

"Even if I knew anything, I'd never tell them." Marina sat up straight. She had to find somewhere else to stay. Marina thought of her two best friends at the university, Selena and Inez, both art history students too. And there were other family friends from childhood. But if she was being watched by German officers, she would be putting them in danger.

"Is there somewhere you could go? A cousin in the country, a friend in Florence or Venice?" Paolo suggested.

The mention of Florence sparked Marina's memory. "My father's friend Bernard Berenson has a villa outside Florence. He's an American art collector," she answered. "My father saved his life a few years ago. He always said he would do anything for him."

Marina had last seen Bernard when he came to Rome a few years ago. He was older than her father, in his sixties. Marina remembered him being tall and thin, with gray hair and a distinguished beard. He was an intellectual and enjoyed discussing books and music as well as art.

Bernard would take her in, she knew. But she

couldn't leave the gallery. It was as important to her as it was to her father. He had been teaching her to run it. One day it would be hers.

"But I can't leave the gallery," she said stubbornly. "And all my father's things are here."

"You mustn't go near the gallery," Paolo warned her. "The rest isn't important. What matters is that you are safe. That's what your father would have wanted."

Tears rolled down her cheeks. Memories of her father flooded her mind: dressed in his black suit after her mother died, the only time she had seen him weep openly. The hours they spent together working at the gallery. The day she got accepted at the university, when he appeared with a new dress and a briefcase he'd bought her: something frivolous and something serious.

"I need his things," she said vehemently. "I've lost my father; I can't lose everything else too."

"One day you can come back for them," Paolo said. He looked old and gray, as if the events of the last hour had aged him. "The war won't last forever. You'll return to Rome."

"It's already evening," Marina remarked. "How would I get to Florence? It might be too late to leave tonight."

She had to find the courage to go. There would be no dream of running her own gallery, of continuing what her father started, if she was dead.

"There's no time to waste. You need to leave now—your life depends on it. You can catch a train to Florence," Paolo said.

"What if there aren't any trains?"

"You have papers, and the trains are still running," Paolo urged her. He reached into his pocket and took out a handful of lire. "Take this for the ticket. I'll send more money when you're settled."

"I can't let you do that." Marina shook her head.

"I'm fifty years old. My wife is dead, and both my sons died fighting in the civil war in Spain. I wake up every morning afraid that my neighbors have been shot by German soldiers, or that Allied bombs have destroyed the churches. And there's nothing I can do about it." He wiped a tear from his cheek. "Vittorio said the only way to keep going is by helping others. Let me at least do this."

Marina remembered the wad of lire she was holding. She knew there was more money hidden in an envelope in her father's study. It was for emergencies, but she was certain this counted as one.

She handed the lire back to Paolo and looked at his weather-beaten cheeks, the skin sallow from months without fruit and vegetables.

"It's not safe for you either." She frowned. "The Germans might search the whole neighborhood. You should come with me."

19

Paolo smiled thinly. "Don't worry about me. I can stay with a relative until things die down. The Germans will move on, there are plenty of houses in Rome for them to loot."

Paolo sat beside her. Marina leaned forward and kissed him on both cheeks.

"You were a good friend to my father and to me," she said. "I won't forget it. And I won't forget what the German officers did to my father and Enrico. One day I'll return and find them. They will pay for what they did."

Paolo stood and started up the basement stairs. He turned around.

"The best thing you can do is move forward. By the time you come back to Rome, I hope the Germans will be long gone."

Marina choked back her tears and kissed her father's brow. She hated leaving him. Upstairs, the sun cast patterns on the living room drapes. She had always loved this room. The furniture was simple. Deep leather armchairs, a table next to the window, a mantel with photos of Marina. It was the paintings on the walls that drew her attention. A still life of a bowl of pears that was so vibrant, Marina could almost taste the juice. A view from the Orange Tree Garden of Rome, showing the dome of St. Peter's Basilica bathed in a topaz glow.

The paintings reminded Marina of her mother, Gloria. Gloria had been an artist and died from influenza when Marina was ten. Marina had considered becoming an artist too. She'd spent hours in the attic, covering her mother's old canvases with paint. But she discovered she enjoyed the business side of art more. She loved learning how to spot a piece that would become valuable, working out why some paintings pulled straight at the heart.

She had developed an eye that was as discerning as her father's. Marina's great love was Renaissance art. Since the occupation, clients had brought in paintings to sell that had been in their collections for years. It was better to sell them than have them seized by the Nazis. Her father had been teaching her how to tell the real paintings from the fakes.

Her mind went fleetingly to Nicolo, whom she had met working at the gallery. He was the first boy she ever loved. She had believed Nicolo loved her too, until he betrayed her. She'd told Paolo that she and her father didn't keep secrets from each other, but she had kept her relationship with Nicolo secret from him. It didn't matter now. Nicolo was long gone.

She moved into the kitchen. She hadn't eaten all day, and she didn't want to faint from hunger on the train. She took a loaf of bread from the bread box and opened the fridge. Inside was a bottle of wine. Where had her father found wine? Fresh anger boiled up inside her. Until now she had hated the Germans for making life so uncomfortable. Professors at the university had lost their jobs; the curfew made it impossible to see friends at night; food had become scarce.

But now she hated them with a passion she had never experienced before. Her father had done the honorable thing. Great Jewish artists had existed for centuries. What if Enrico was the next Pissarro or Modigliani? Her father would have done the German officer a service by selling him the painting.

She hurried upstairs to her room and grabbed her papers, then threw a few things into the suitcase she kept under her bed. Downstairs in her father's study, the curtains were closed. A book of Donatello's sculptures lay open on the little table beside her father's armchair. Her father liked to flip through it after dinner with a digestif—a glass of amaretto or a Galliano served in the crystal snifter that had been a wedding present years ago.

Marina took the emergency lire from the desk drawer. It was quite a large amount and would last her for a while. A letter was folded inside the envelope. It hadn't been there before. She read it out loud.

My dearest Marina,
If you are reading this, something has happened to me. To be honest, I'm not

surprised. The war has ruined so many lives. It has ripped apart countries, separated loved ones, left young women as widows and children as orphans. How could I expect to be different?

But I have led a long and good life. First, I was blessed with your mother. She made me happy for more than fifteen years. With her I learned what it means to love. And there was you. Not only were you a sweet and beautiful child, you have grown to be a young woman whom I love and admire.

Our mutual love of art is the greatest joy of my life. You already know more than they can teach you at university, more than I can pass on to you at the gallery. You see through a painting all the way to the artist's soul. Accept and nurture that gift, and you will always be able to take care of yourself.

Remember too that we are Italians. Better yet, we are Romans. Rome has been here for centuries. The Germans can no more easily take away its wisdom, and its beauty, than they can extinguish its famous light. One day the war will be over and the streets will again be filled with laughter, the clink of glasses, the scent of perfume in a woman's hair.

You are young. There will be time in your life for everything: lovers, a husband, children, the career that you so desperately want. You will have it all, and I will be watching over you. No one deserves it more than you, my dearest Marina, because for twenty years you have made me the happiest father alive.

Be safe.

Your loving father, Vittorio

Marina folded the paper and slipped it back in the envelope. She wouldn't let herself cry. There would be time to cry later. She would walk into the piazza with the courage and strength of the lions that had once fought at the Colosseum.

She picked up her suitcase and walked out of the house, closing the front door behind her.

There was a train to Florence that night. She would be on it.

CHAPTER TWO

Florence, November 1943

It was almost 9:00 p.m. when the train rattled through the outskirts of Florence. Marina had been so nervous she kept a book in front of her the whole two-hour journey. She kept expecting a German officer to appear and order her off the train. But no one disturbed her. Now she closed the book and forced herself to relax.

At the train station in Rome, she'd called Bernard to tell him she was coming. A housekeeper answered the phone. Bernard was out, but the woman had promised to give him the message.

Bernard and her father had known each other for years; he was a frequent client of the gallery. Bernard was one of the world's leading authorities on Renaissance art. His collection included paintings that her father wasn't ashamed to drool over: early Titians, a Leonardo da Vinci, a Caravaggio.

Marina heard the story of how her father had saved Bernard's life a few years ago a dozen times, usually over dinner with a client or a new artist.

Bernard and her father had attended an auction

at a palazzo in Rome's Parioli district. Bernard had his purchase—a valuable book of early Renaissance sketches—under his arm when a thief approached them, brandishing a gun.

"Bernard was about to hand the book over when I stopped him," her father would say, his eyes dancing after a few glasses of wine. "Instead, I reached into my pocket and pulled out a knife. I brought the knife so close to the thief's face so quickly, he was practically blinded by the blade. The man ran.

"Afterward, Bernard couldn't decide whether to be furious with me or grateful," he continued. This was the part of the story he most enjoyed telling. "First, he yelled at me. 'Who brandishes a knife at a man holding a gun?' But I told him no thief would expect you to stop him with a knife. By the time he figured out I was essentially unarmed, he'd scurried away in surprise."

Bernard had vowed to her father that he would someday repay him. And if he couldn't repay Vittorio himself, perhaps he could help Marina.

She let the anger and pain wash over her again. Her father had tried to protect her, keeping her in the dark about Enrico. Just as she had been trying to protect him when she didn't tell him about Nicolo. But she couldn't think about Nicolo now. All she wanted was to keep the memories of her father fresh in her mind, to keep going over them as if they were a painting that the artist never wanted to finish.

The train pulled into Santa Maria Novella station in Florence, and Marina felt like she could finally breathe. She caught sight of the city—the red dome of the Duomo, the Pitti Palace large and imposing under a full moon—and almost wept with relief and exhaustion.

She and her father had visited Florence many times. He considered it second only to Rome as a center of art. Marina had stood in awe of Botticelli's *The Birth of Venus* and gazed for hours at Michelangelo's *David* and Donatello's sculpture of Saint George. She wondered how she would ever enjoy walking through the Uffizi Gallery and Galleria dell'Accademia again without him beside her.

The air in the train station was freezing, and she was glad she had grabbed her coat from the downstairs closet. Her teeth chattered, whether from the cold weather or the terrible day, she wasn't sure. She still couldn't take in everything that had happened. The grief washed over her in waves, and she could barely catch her breath. But she remembered what her father had said to Paolo: he had gone on living after her mother's death, and she had to do the same.

Now that she was in Florence, she realized she didn't know how to get to the villa. There were no taxis, and she doubted any buses operated at night. She still didn't know if Bernard had received her message.

Outside, a fair-haired man with patrician features stood next to a small car. He looked only a decade or so older than she was, and he wore an expensive-looking dark overcoat. He watched her with clear blue eyes.

"Are you Marina?" he asked, approaching her.

Marina stiffened. He had a slight accent that almost sounded German.

"It's all right," he said, as if reading her thoughts. He held out his hand. "My name is Ludwig Heydenreich. I'm a friend of Bernard's. He called and asked me to collect you. He's terribly sorry that he wasn't able to pick you up himself. He was visiting a client a few hours away and worried that he'd be late."

Marina didn't move. He was German. She couldn't shake his hand, and she certainly couldn't get in his car.

"I'm sorry, you must have mistaken me for someone else," she said, turning away.

It didn't matter that she had no other way to reach the villa. It could be a trap. Bernard had been out when she called. He might not even know she was here.

Ludwig followed her across the pavement. He reached forward and touched her arm.

"I promise you, I'm a friend," he tried again. "He gave me a description of you. We can find a

28

phone booth and call the villa if you like. Anna, the housekeeper, will vouch for me."

Marina stopped and grudgingly turned around. Ludwig looked nothing like the German officers who prowled the streets of Rome. His expression was kind, and his eyes crinkled at the corners when he smiled.

"How were you sure it was me?" she asked cautiously. "There are other women with light brown hair on the platform."

Ludwig dropped his hand and smiled warmly.

"None of them are alone, and none of them are so young and pretty." He pointed to her suitcase. "Please come with me. It's much too chilly to be standing out here. Bernard will be furious if I let you catch a cold."

Marina's stomach lurched. Only a few hours before, Germans had killed her father and Enrico. Their blood was all over the basement floor. The wind blew up from the Arno, and she wrapped her coat around her. If she didn't accept his offer, she might freeze to death before she ever reached the villa.

"Thank you." She nodded, handing him the suitcase. "You're kind to drive me at night and at such short notice."

Ludwig carried the suitcase to the sidewalk.

"I don't mind," he replied. "It's impossible to keep any place properly heated in Florence with the rationing. My car is probably as warm as my rooms. At least I'll have a half hour's conversation." He chuckled. "I love to read, but even the biography of a twelfth-century monk becomes dry when it's my only companion."

Marina found a blanket below the passenger seat and wrapped it around her knees. Ludwig was a skillful driver. He easily maneuvered the car through the narrow streets leading out of the train station.

"How do you know Bernard?" she inquired.

"Bernard and I have been friends for ages." Ludwig glanced over at Marina. "We met in the art world. I've been in Florence for six years, and before that I studied art history at the University of Hamburg."

"Are you an artist?" she asked, trying to be polite. He didn't look like the artists she knew in Rome. Even when they came to dinner their shirts were rumpled, paint on their fingernails. He was well-groomed, and his shirt was perfectly pressed.

"I'm an art historian. I was in Rome only last week on business. The conditions were shocking," he reflected. "It's different in Florence. There are food shortages and a curfew here, but the citizens are mainly left alone."

Marina didn't want to talk anymore. It was all too raw, as if she had recently ripped a bandage from a wound that hadn't begun to heal.

They drove silently. Despite the dark, Marina

noticed a change in the landscape as the narrow houses on the outskirts of Florence turned into rolling hills that Marina knew in the sunlight would be green as emeralds. Olive trees and grapevines lined the road.

Ludwig pulled into a driveway that climbed high into the hills. On either side of them, gardens terraced downhill. Marble statues lined the path, which ended in a stone fountain in front of the door. The villa itself was a three-story stone structure painted yellow, dotted with green shutters. The entrance was completely covered in ivy.

He turned off the engine, and cold air rushed through a crack in the window.

"Thank you for bringing me," she said.

Ludwig jumped out to open Marina's door.

"I'll see you in," Ludwig offered, grabbing her suitcase. "You and Bernard must have a lot to catch up on. Although I wouldn't mind warming up by the fireplace. That's one good thing about living in Tuscany: firewood is still delivered to your door."

He rang the doorbell, and a light flickered on. A woman in a black maid's uniform opened the door.

"I'm here to see Signor Berenson," Marina announced. "My name is Marina Tozzi. I believe he's expecting me."

The woman nodded toward Ludwig.

"Signor Berenson is upstairs. You can wait in the study, and I'll tell him you're here."

Ludwig followed Marina down the hallway. The villa was even more beautiful than she remembered from when she'd visited years ago: parquet floors rested beneath wide arches, chandeliers and vases of flowers in nearly every room. She wondered where one got flowers in the winter during the occupation.

The study had bookshelves that reached the ceiling. There was a desk with a Tiffany lamp and leather armchairs. One wall was taken up by a fireplace. After a few minutes, Bernard appeared. He looked almost the same as he had a few years ago, although his cheeks were a little more gaunt and his beard was now completely gray.

"Marina, it's lovely to see you." He took Marina's hand and stepped back to admire her. "You've changed. Last time I saw you, you were barely fifteen. Now you must be twenty. You've grown into a beautiful young woman. I'm terribly sorry I wasn't at the train station. My housekeeper called me with the message, but I was hours away. I didn't want to risk keeping you waiting." He looked at her kindly. "It must have been a harrowing journey."

Marina was about to answer when a woman in her fifties entered the room. She had olive skin and wore a velvet smoking jacket and red satin shoes. Marina was puzzled. Bernard was married. Marina had seen a photo of his wife—she was British with pale skin and fair hair. This fascinating-looking woman was someone completely different. She had dark, flowing hair and a wide mouth. Whomever she was, she must have been away the last time Marina visited with her father.

"I'm Belle," she greeted Marina. "Bernard has been telling me all about you and your father. Bernard counts him as one of his dear friends." The woman was even more dazzling when she smiled. "Please, sit down. You look exhausted. Can I get you something?"

The scent of Belle's perfume, light and airy as if she had come from a dinner party, combined with her mention of Marina's father was too much. Marina thought of everything that had happened that day and was overcome by a feeling of desperation so heavy it threatened to smother her.

"If I could have a hot drink, I'm very cold," Marina said.

The room tipped and Belle's voice came from far away. Marina put her hand out to steady herself. But only the floor was in front of her as she crumpled to the ground.

Marina opened her eyes. Sun streamed through the window and caught the side of a yellow pitcher. She blinked, wondering why her father had put a pitcher next to her bed, then sat up, worried that she was late for work.

But the room was unfamiliar. Instead of the single bed she'd had since she was a child, she lay on a king-size mattress with ruffled bedding. A Chinese armoire stood opposite her, and the ceiling was painted blue, with fat white clouds.

"You're awake," a female voice said.

Marina turned and noticed a woman sitting next to the bed. She dimly remembered meeting her. Her face was powdered, and she wore a strange outfit: riding pants and a hat adorned with silk flowers.

"Where am I?" Marina asked.

"Villa I Tatti," the woman replied. "I'm Belle da Costa Greene, we met two days ago when you arrived." She chuckled. "It wasn't a long meeting. You fainted after I said hello."

It all came rushing back to her. Her father's murder, the train journey to Florence, meeting Ludwig at the station. Then nothing.

"I've been here two days?" Marina asked anxiously.

"You had a high fever," Belle confirmed. "Don't worry, we fed you soup, and I made my special hot chocolate with molasses and brandy." She smiled wickedly. "It's much too potent to drink for pleasure, but it's strong enough to bring you back from the dead."

"Thank you," Marina said uncertainly. "I didn't mean to inconvenience anyone."

"I hardly thought you developed a fever on purpose," Belle responded. "Bernard tried to call your father in Rome, but he didn't answer."

Marina gulped. She sat back against the pillows.

"My father is dead. He was shot by the Germans for housing a Jewish artist," she began. Her eyes filled with tears, and her whole body shivered. "That's why I came. I had nowhere to go."

Belle nodded.

"We thought it was something like that. Bernard was so worried, your father was very important to him," she said darkly. "You kept calling for him in your sleep." She put her hand on Marina's. "I'm very sorry. My father ran off when I was fourteen, and I haven't seen him since. Your father is the first man you ever love. Losing him is the most painful thing imaginable."

"I feel like I'm stuck inside a bubble," Marina admitted. "It's so small and tight, I'm afraid I'll suffocate."

"You did the right thing by coming here. You need food and rest, and we have plenty of room," Belle assured her. "It's not like before the war when the house was full of guests. You should have seen our dinner parties. Sitting there talking about art and literature as if we could set the world on fire. Since the war, we rarely have overnight guests."

"Are you a collector too?" Marina asked.

"I'm a librarian," Belle replied.

Marina took in Belle's carefully made-up face and extravagant outfit. The pointed boots with gold buckles, the bangles dangling at her wrist.

"A librarian!" Marina said in surprise.

"Just because I'm a librarian doesn't mean I have to dress like one." Belle laughed. "I've been lucky in my career. But we'll talk about that another time. What's important is to make you strong. Anna will bring up breakfast, and you can take a bath. The bathtub used to be in the grand suite at the Hotel Cipriani in Venice. It's so deep, you won't be able to get out."

After Belle left, Marina entered the bathroom and gazed at her reflection in the mirror. Her father always said her eyes were her best feature: they were warm and brown and full of mischief. Now they seem shrouded by a haze of grief.

Her cheeks were too thin and the bones on her shoulders stuck out. The worst part was her skin. She remembered a handsome young man at university once complimenting her on her creamy complexion. What would he say if he saw how deathly pale she was now, how the skin on her neck was almost gray?

After the bath, she pulled on a robe and climbed back into bed. Outside the window, the hills were turning orange and the trees had lost their leaves. Now she could see the full scope of the gardens' beauty: manicured hedges and stone fountains and trellises that in the summer would be in full bloom. Whomever Bernard hired to design the gardens had taken the task very seriously.

Marina waited for breakfast and wondered what she was going to do with her future. Until now, her life had formed a simple straight line. She would finish university and join her father full-time in the gallery. Eventually, she would marry a man who shared her interests and would be a good father.

There was a knock, and Anna entered. She set a tray on the table next to the bed.

"Thank you." Marina nodded. "It smells delicious."

"Signora Belle said now that you're better, you must eat all day," Anna replied. "She made the porridge herself. Don't tell Lucia, the cook. She's very proud; if she knew Signora Belle was in her kitchen, she would be furious."

Anna left, and Marina inspected the tray. There was a bowl of porridge and a glass of milk. She ate a spoonful and stopped. Her mind went to the breakfasts her father prepared in Rome before they left for work. He'd stand at the stove, stirring the porridge while Marina buttered slices of bread. They'd talk about a new artist at the gallery, or a client who was impossible to please. Despite the war, Marina had been happy.

The spoon clattered to her plate. She sat against

the pillows and tried to breathe. It was impossible that she was there, lying in that glorious bed, able to take a bath and eat and drink when her father had been gunned down in their basement.

It was another week before Marina left the bedroom. Even then she started slowly, taking walks around what was called the Green Garden, so named because the terraced lawns contained no other colors. Bernard had instructed the landscape architect, Cecil Pinsent, to create a garden that belonged at a Renaissance villa. The entire grounds of Villa I Tatti were almost impossibly beautiful. A covered walkway led to a separate library with stained glass windows. There was a stone pergola flanked by statues and views of the hills that made Marina's heart lift. Red-roofed houses and churches surrounded by stone walls more than a thousand years old stretched out beyond.

She explored the grounds over the next month, slowly regaining her strength. The grief overtook her at various times; she never knew when it would come. Sometimes her father's death felt far away; at other times the bodies in the basement were as clear and close as if she had discovered them moments ago.

During her time at Villa I Tatti the weather remained almost freezing, but she still spent some of her time outside. Bernard and Belle were both very kind, but she felt awkward inside the villa. She wasn't used to being idle. She missed the familiarity of the art gallery, the energy of the university.

As Marina strolled across the lawn farthest from the villa, she noticed a young woman about her age. She was hunched under one of the hedges. Her hands clutched her stomach as she groaned.

"Are you all right?" Marina asked as she approached.

"I didn't know anyone was here." The young woman straightened up. "I'm sorry, I live next door."

She pointed to a villa on the adjoining property.

"Would you like me to walk you home?" Marina asked. "You sound like you're ill."

"No! I can't go home," she said sharply. "I mean, my mother sent me to borrow some flour. She's baking bread, and she ran out." She looked at Marina sheepishly. "I must have some kind of a stomachache. Suddenly I felt sick."

"I'm Marina." She held out her hand. "It's nice to meet you."

The girl shook Marina's hand. She had wild dark hair, as if someone took a brush to it and forgot to comb it out. "My name is Desi Pirelli. Are you the girl staying at Villa I Tatti?"

"Yes, I'm from Rome." Marina hesitated. She still didn't know how to talk about her father.

"I heard my mother talking about you," Desi commented. "My mother is friends with Belle." She laughed. "Everyone is friends with Belle, she's like some wonderful jewel you can't resist. I'm very sorry about your father. That must be awful for you."

"Thank you." Marina nodded briefly. "I'm lucky to be here. My father and Bernard were good friends. He and Belle have been so welcoming."

"It sounds like your father was very brave. You must be brave also, to come to Tuscany by yourself," Desi commented. "I hope you like it here. At least the rationing isn't so bad in the countryside. Thank God for our cows and chickens. We'll never run out of milk and eggs. And my mother is always baking bread. That's why she sent me to borrow the flour. Bread fills you up."

"I could eat eggs every day," Marina said companionably. "My father and I often ate frittatas at trattorias on the weekends. We both ordered them the same way, with zucchini and extra butter and mozzarella cheese."

"You'll have to share the recipe with my mother, she loves to cook," Desi said. "It keeps her mind off the German soldiers who patrol the neighborhood; I even saw them on our vineyards. They're not supposed to be on private property, but how do you stop a man carrying a rifle?"

"It must be so hard to live with every day," Marina said.

"Last week a Jewish family was taken from their villa in the middle of the night." Desi's mouth trembled. "No one knows what happened to them. Now my mother keeps a pistol next to her bed, and she showed me where the sharpest knives are kept in the kitchen. She moved them from the drawer to the pantry. If any German enters the house, I'll stab them through the heart."

Marina's mind flashed to her father and Enrico. Again, she wished she had come home while the German officers were there. She could have grabbed a knife from the kitchen and stabbed them in the back.

The light returned to Desi's eyes.

"You and I are young; my mother says fear is for old people. We have to believe in the good things: wine, food, and love. Without love, none of this would exist." She waved her arms at the landscape. "Not the birds or the squirrels or the sheep."

"I think you mean sex," Marina said, laughing.

"Sex and love arc the same thing." Desi shrugged. "A woman can't have sex without love."

Marina's mind went to Nicolo, the joy of his kisses. She had been in love. She had reprimanded herself for falling for him so easily.

But Nicolo had been handsome and charming, and he had sworn he had feelings for her. Marina wondered if she would ever trust a man again.

"You're right about that." Marina nodded.

Desi clutched her stomach again and let out a moan.

"You have to do something for that stomach-ache," Marina said. "Lean on me, and I'll take you home."

"All right, but you mustn't tell my mother," Desi warned. "She'll ask the doctor to make a house call, and it will be so embarrassing."

Desi's villa was smaller than Villa I Tatti but very pretty, with a large terrace that overlooked the rolling hills. Stone columns reached up to a second floor, where the windows were covered with lace curtains. A vineyard and a separate garage lay beyond.

They entered the kitchen through a back door. A long table and counter were strewn with pots and pans. A woman with reddish hair stood at the stove. She turned.

"Desi, there you are," she said. "You missed breakfast. I have to go to the barn and talk to the cows. We need more milk."

"My mother believes if she talks to the cows, they'll produce milk whenever she likes," Desi explained to Marina. She turned to her mother. "This is Marina, she's staying at Villa I Tatti."

"Of course it helps to talk to the cows. They

want to be loved like anyone else," Desi's mother insisted. She wiped her hands on her apron. "Belle mentioned a young woman was staying at the villa. I'm terribly sorry about your father. Please call me Catarina."

"Thank you, it's a pleasure to meet you. You have a lovely home," Marina replied.

"I adore this house. But it's like a difficult child. It's unbearably hot in the summer and freezing in the winter," Catarina said. "Luckily we have fireplaces in every room." She went to the icebox and took out a square package.

"I made some cheese for Belle. Perhaps you can take it to her." She handed it to Marina. "The milk is from Greta. She produces the best milk in Tuscany."

Marina placed the package in her bag and followed Desi through the house. Marina was about to compliment the design when she noticed a young man standing in the living room, his arms filled with wood. He brightened upon seeing them.

"Marina, this is Carlos," Desi introduced them. "His family lives next door, and they practically own the whole forest. Carlos brings us firewood so we don't freeze to death."

"I've seen your closet," Carlos said to Desi with a grin. "You own enough coats to survive comfortably in Siberia."

"Carlos loves to tease me about how many

clothes I have," Desi explained. "I don't see why. Before the war he dated girls who bought their dresses in Paris and Milan."

Desi's cheeks turned pale again. She obviously wasn't feeling well. It was better that Marina leave and they finish the tour of the house another time.

"I'd better go," Marina cut in. She nodded to Carlos. "It was nice to meet you."

"Please come back," Desi said as she walked her to the door. "It's wonderful to have a new friend."

Marina walked through the gardens to the villa. It was late morning, and the house was quiet. Bernard was on a trip, and Belle was probably upstairs in her bedroom.

Marina put the cheese in the fridge in the kitchen. She remembered Desi saying she was coming to Villa I Tatti to borrow flour. And yet her mother had never asked about the lack of it.

She unwrapped her scarf and walked up the staircase. At the top, she stopped to admire the view out the window. She hadn't noticed the forest before, but now she saw it formed a ring around the hills, like a wall protecting some medieval village. She wondered how one family could own all those trees.

Her step quickened as she reached her room. For the first time in weeks, she felt as if the terrible weight that pressed on her shoulders was lifting. Desi was her age and lonely. Marina still couldn't see what the future held, but it would be nice to have a friend.

CHAPTER THREE

Florence, November 1943

A few days later, Marina sat in her bedroom, reading a book about the old masters. Books about art were scattered around the villa: large tomes in the living room with pictures of the very paintings that hung in frames on the walls. Most of the books in the study were about various artists, and in her room there was a mix of books and magazines and a few recent novels that Belle must have placed there for Marina.

Some of the books were coauthored by Bernard himself. Bernard was a very important figure in the art world. His opinion held such value that it could change the worth of a painting. Before the war he had been involved in millions of dollars' worth of sales, and his private collection contained works from all the greats: Raphael and Tintoretto and Michelangelo, plus a selection of ancient Chinese texts and Persian paintings.

Marina closed the book and paced around the room. Her energy had returned, and she was restless. Now coupled with the grief of mourning her father, there was the pain of missing her old life. She missed her classes at the university, she missed strolling around the city. The seven hills of Rome provided many opportunities to go for exercise: hiking to the top of Capitoline Hill and taking loops around the Borghese Gardens, and even walking up and down the Spanish Steps to stretch her legs. In the last few days the weather had grown too cold to walk in the gardens and Marina missed the fresh air.

Her thoughts were interrupted by a head poking through the door.

"Buongiorno." Belle entered the room. "I hope I'm not disturbing you."

"Not at all." Marina shook her head. She moved to the sitting area near the fireplace and gestured for Belle to join her.

"Please sit down. I was just doing some reading."

Belle glanced at the closed book on the table.

"Thank goodness you're interested in art." Belle smiled. "Bernard's collections are like other people's children. They're always underfoot, and there's no way to escape them."

"It was the same for me growing up," Marina commented. "Art was as necessary to my father as oxygen. He taught me to love it too. I was going to take over the gallery one day, it was the most important thing in my life."

"I'm sure you miss everything." Belle studied Marina carefully. "You look better. Your cheeks are filling out, and you have more color."

"I feel better." Marina nodded. "You and

Bernard have been so patient. I don't know how to thank you." She hesitated. "I don't know what I would have done, but I know I can't stay here forever."

"Of course you can." Belle waved her hands. "I told you, before the war the house was full of guests. Once, a man came down for breakfast and Bernard and I didn't know that he was here. Anna had showed him up to his room the night before, while we were out. Bernard had forgotten that he'd invited him to come and stay."

"You're very kind. At the very least, perhaps I can make myself useful. I need to do something productive"—Marina frowned—"but I don't know what."

"That's why I came to see you, actually," Belle said. "Bernard wanted to ask a favor."

"A favor from me?" Marina asked.

Belle stood up.

"It's easier if he shows you." She motioned to the door. "He's going to join us in the library. Follow me."

They walked down a back stairway to the garden, then along a pathway to a long building. Belle entered first and turned on the lights.

Marina couldn't help but gasp. The vaulted ceiling was made of mosaic tile and the floor was polished wood. Long tables were scattered around the room, and there were light-colored rugs and a stone fireplace. Several seating areas were furnished with upholstered chairs. Bookshelves lined the walls, and a circular staircase led up to two higher levels, which were also filled with books.

"Bernard likes to say he bought Villa I Tatti because he wanted a house that came with a library," Belle said mischievously. "He's assembled one of the finest private collections in Europe. There are over one hundred thousand books, and that doesn't include the ones waiting to be cataloged."

On one side of the room there was a row of glass cabinets. Each cabinet held leather volumes.

"These books are kept under glass because they're so fragile, if you breathe on them, they might disintegrate." She walked to a bookshelf. "Bernard plans on donating the villa, including the library and its contents, to Harvard. I'm going to donate my books and letters to Harvard too. That's what we wanted to talk to you about. When I curated J. P. Morgan's library in New York, I was in charge of buying and selling his collection of illuminated manuscripts. These shelves contain hundreds of letters I sent and received throughout my career." She paused, seeming slightly embarrassed. "There is also personal correspondence."

"Personal correspondence?" Marina repeated.

"It's no secret that Bernard is married. He's been with his wife, Mary, for more than thirty years. But Bernard and I have been together for twenty years." She waved her hand. "Don't worry, Mary and I have become friends. Mary has a fulfilling career in London as a historian. And to be honest, Bernard and I wouldn't have gotten married even if he were free. I've never quite seen the point of marriage." She shrugged. "Bernard and I are like bookends. We both want to fill our lives with the same things: great art and interesting people and love."

The door opened, and Bernard entered. He wore a navy suit with a pocket watch sticking out of the blazer pocket.

"Marina, I'm glad you decided to join us this evening. I hope you're feeling more like yourself. I'm still getting over Vittorio's death. He was one of the finest men I knew, I'm so sorry for your loss." He approached her. "I'm glad Belle is showing you the library. It's my favorite place at the villa."

"I've never seen anything like it. Belle said you had a favor to ask. I'll do anything," she answered. "I'll be much happier if I'm productive. I'm not used to having nothing to do. In Rome, I opened the gallery every morning by myself. My father liked to start the day with an espresso at a café and a chat with friends," she recalled fondly. "And he believed in taking the full Roman lunch hour, which often stretched into the midafternoon."

"Then I have just the thing," Bernard replied. "Belle told you about my agreement with Harvard? My vision was that future generations of scholars would come to Villa I Tatti and take advantage of everything it has to offer. They'd walk in the gardens, read in the library, and have long conversations about art over dinner, well lubricated by a cellar of fine wines. Like the literary salons of Paris in the 1920s." His eyes twinkled merrily. "But with walls covered in paintings by the great Renaissance artists." His tone became serious. "But with that monster Hitler running loose through Europe, who knows what the future holds? Already the Louvre's masterpieces have been spirited away, and the pope won't let German soldiers cross the red lines painted around the Vatican. It might be wiser to transport the collection's most valuable books and paintings to America in the near future."

"But how would you get the pieces out of Italy?" Marina inquired.

"Gerhard would help," Bernard said.

"Gerhard?" Marina questioned.

"Gerhard Wolf, the German consul to Florence. He and Ludwig both love Renaissance art with the fervor most men reserve for romance," Bernard said. "You'll meet him; he's a frequent dinner guest. Recently, Gerhard confided that Hitler is intent on transporting the contents of the Italian museums to Germany. Hitler insists that it's to keep them safe from Allied bombs, but I'm quite certain they'll never be returned. I wonder if you could go through the collection and decide which pieces should be sent to Harvard now."

"You want me to decide?" Marina said in awe.

"I happened to talk to your father a few weeks before he was killed. He told me that you've been studying Renaissance art at the university. He said you've become quite the expert and you have a sharp eye for which pieces are important," Bernard said. "It's a gift, you know, and quite rare."

Marina was touched. Her father had praised her skills to one of the greatest art collectors in the world.

"I don't know much about antiquated books," Marina said modestly.

"I don't expect you to know everything," Bernard commented. "But I'm too busy to take it on, and we're running out of time."

"In that case, I'd be honored to help." Marina nodded.

"Good," he said with a smile. "I can pay you—"

"Staying here is more than enough payment." Marina stopped him.

Bernard didn't try to argue.

"I'm glad that's settled." He glanced at Belle. "If you'll excuse me, I have to see a client. I'll leave Belle to show you around."

She and Belle climbed the staircase that led to

a second level and a small kitchen, where there was a sink and water glasses.

"I hope you won't mind if I sometimes work beside you," Belle said. "I'm going through the personal letters I was telling you about to get rid of the ones that might be too shocking." She smiled. "Otherwise a Harvard scholar who thinks he's going to read about the authenticity of a painting by Leonardo da Vinci might instead find a detailed account of a romantic night under the stars in Capri. Not that it would be of any interest. I just don't want them being read after Bernard and I are gone. Love between two people is the most natural thing in the world, but it can be hard for others to understand." She stopped. "That's enough of a lecture for one day. Bernard is thrilled you're taking on his project. I'm having a small dinner party tonight. I'd like you to come."

Marina wasn't sure she was ready to attend a dinner party.

"I have some letters to write. I'll eat in my room tonight," Marina said, clutching for an excuse. "I'd be happy to go to the kitchen and prepare a tray for myself."

"Are you sure?" Belle pressed her. "It's only a few neighbors, it will be good for you to meet new people."

A glimmer of tears pooled in Marina's eyes. She didn't want to meet new people. She wanted her father, and Paolo next door, and the shopkeepers she passed on the way to the gallery. She wanted the heady excitement of being with handsome young men without worrying they were going to betray her.

She blinked rapidly. Tears wouldn't help, and at least now there was a way to occupy her days with art.

"Of course, I'll come if you want me to," Marina said. She glanced down at her dress. "I only packed a few dresses, but . . ."

"I'll ask Anna to bring you some dresses. I have a closet full from when I was younger." Belle studied Marina's waist and smiled happily. "I was never as slender as you but I was slimmer before I came to Italy and started eating pasta."

Marina chose a red crepe gown. It reminded her of the dress she'd worn to celebrate her father's birthday in September. His birthday fell during the first week of the German occupation. Every year they ate at the same restaurant in Piazza del Popolo, and her father had refused to allow that year to be any different.

He'd worn his navy suit, and Marina had put on a red dress, and they ate seafood ravioli. At the end of the meal the owner, Lorenzo, had brought out the almond sponge cake he served every year, and her father had gasped as if he were surprised. Everyone laughed, and Lorenzo joined them for a glass of wine and a toast.

It was only when they were walking home and Marina heard heavy footsteps behind them that she felt the first chill. It was as if the warm summer weather had turned to autumn in the space of the day. The German soldiers behind them had reminded them sharply of the curfew.

That was only two months ago, but everything had changed since then. She still couldn't believe that her father was dead, that they would never again celebrate his birthday together.

The other guests were mingling in the living room when Marina descended the staircase.

"Marina, you look lovely," Belle greeted her. "The most wonderful palette is a young face. All it needs is a touch of powder." She led her farther into the room. "Let me get you a drink, and then I'll introduce you to everyone."

Marina was wearing the perfume she had bought when she had been seeing Nicolo. She had never used perfume before, and rubbing the scent on her wrists and neck had made her feel sexy and mature. It had sat on her dressing table since she sent Nicolo away, but for some reason she'd packed it in her suitcase. It felt good to wear it now. She wasn't a girl with a father to watch over her anymore; she was a young woman alone in the world.

Bernard found her. He held a cocktail glass in one hand and a cigar in the other. His beard was combed, and he wore a black dinner jacket.

"Marina, I was just telling Ludwig some stories about your father." He sipped his drink. "One of my favorites is about a client who traveled from Venice to see a painting in his gallery. The client had only one day and night in Rome. The first evening Vittorio sent a note to the client's hotel. Vittorio couldn't meet with him; you had some kind of school performance that he refused to miss. The following morning, Vittorio brought the painting to the client's suite. Then he offered to drive the client to the artist's workshop outside Rome to meet the artist in person. The client so enjoyed their excursion, he bought three paintings. Later, I said to Vittorio, wouldn't it have been simpler to be late for the performance? He explained that was out of the question, telling me if I had children I would understand."

Marina couldn't keep the tears from her eyes. She tried to swallow, but there was a lump in her throat.

"I miss him very much," she said, her hands brushing her wet cheeks.

"He'd be proud of you," Bernard offered.

"I don't see why," Marina blurted out. "I could have tried to go after the German officer who killed him. . . ."

The unbearable anger at being unable to avenge his death boiled up inside her.

"It's easy to think like that during wartime," Bernard reflected. "Mussolini has failed his citizens. He sided with the Germans early in the war simply because he thought they would win. Now he's in exile in Salò. And Badoglio is even worse, having fled to the south like the coward that he is. Only Pope Pius XII was brave. He warned that if German troops come near the Vatican they'll be shot."

Marina was grateful to Pope Pius XII. He openly defended the Jews against Hitler. He even allowed Allied prisoners of war to hide within the walls of the Vatican, until it became too dangerous for everyone involved.

They were interrupted by Belle. Her wrist rested on the arm of a man Marina recognized as Ludwig. His patrician features were well suited for formal attire. He looked almost handsome in a white dinner jacket and black bow tie, a yellow pocket square peeking out. His fair hair was brushed to the side.

"I hope Bernard isn't monopolizing you," Belle said lightly. "I know you met Ludwig when he delivered you to our door."

"You make it sound as if I were the stork dropping off a baby," Ludwig joked. "I felt terrible that night."

"You did?" Marina asked.

Ludwig had been so kind, driving her all the way from the train station in the cold. She had wanted to thank him, but he hadn't come back to the villa until now.

"My car was so cold," he explained. "I came by the villa a few days later, and Belle said you were still in bed recovering. I hope you're feeling better."

"I'm fine. I'm the one who owes you an apology," she assured him. "You rescued me from the train station, and I was quite rude." She smiled. "I should have known that any friend of Bernard's could be trusted."

Ludwig shook his head.

"On the contrary, you were smart. It's difficult to know who's on the right side during a war." He took her hand and held it briefly. "I'm glad I passed the test. You look lovely tonight, and I hope to get to know you better over dinner."

"You said you were an art historian," Marina recalled. "Do you work at a museum?"

"I'm head of the Kunsthistorisches Institute in Florence. It's the oldest institute of art and architecture in Italy. We house pieces from antiquity to the modern era. Our library has more than three hundred and sixty thousand volumes." He smiled. "Many more than my friend Bernard has here. It might seem like a lot, but it's never enough for me."

"I've never heard of it," Marina said in awe. It was hard to imagine a building that could house 360,000 volumes. Even Bernard's library with its circular staircase and three floors of bookshelves housed only 100,000 books.

"Most people find it quite boring. We're not the sort of place tourists flocked to before the war," he said good-naturedly.

Marina noticed a young man with a mop of curly dark hair enter the room. He was very handsome with narrow cheekbones and large green eyes. A scarf was wrapped around his neck and he wore a signet ring on his left hand. He looked familiar, but she couldn't place him.

"Carlos, come join us," Belle called, waving him over. "Marina, this is Carlos Adamo. He lives nearby. I thought I'd invite a few people your age."

"We already met in the Pirellis' living room," Carlos said. He smiled at her warmly and held out his hand. "Desi wanted to come, but she's not feeling well."

"Carlos works in his family's lumber business," Belle explained. "Before that he was an art student in Florence." She glanced at Carlos. "Though I heard a rumor that you were also an artist's model. Don't worry, I didn't tell your mother. She would have gone straight to the priest and stayed in the confessional for days."

"When we are young, we try many things." Carlos shrugged.

"Said from the wise age of twenty-three." Belle laughed. "I'm sure you and Marina will have lots to talk about."

Voices outside made Marina freeze. She could swear they were speaking German.

The mood in the room changed. Everyone stopped talking, and Bernard started toward the door.

"You stay here," Ludwig offered. "I'll go."

Marina tried to stay calm, but her heart raced. What if German officers had returned to the neighborhood in Rome and questioned Paolo? But that was impossible. Paolo would never betray her. And the Gestapo had more important things to do than trail after the daughter of a Roman citizen who operated a single safe house.

Ludwig returned a few minutes later.

"They were German soldiers. There have been reports of partisans around here." Ludwig addressed Bernard. "I told them that I would vouch for you myself. I'm sorry they disturbed the party."

Marina knew from reading the newspapers that the partisan network stretched from Naples in the south all the way to the Swiss border. The partisans were originally formed by members of the Italian army when Italy changed sides from the Axis powers to the Allies.

The first partisan uprising was in Naples the past September, when for four days the locals used guerrilla warfare to fight the Nazis. They managed to stop thousands of citizens from being deported, but there was enormous bloodshed, and innocent people died. The thought of gunfire erupting in the pretty Tuscan villages made Marina feel sick.

"I understand why young men become partisans," Ludwig ruminated. "They're fighting for what they believe in and for their own personal freedom. It would be nice if war didn't exist, but that's not the reality."

The group moved to the dining room, but Marina couldn't relax. She sipped her wine and hoped no one noticed that she wasn't eating.

The soldiers' visit had brought the war closer once again, as if it were lurking behind the silver drapes, settling itself on the table next to the soup bowls and butter plates.

"Bernard and I were talking earlier about love," Belle was saying. Diamond earrings dangled from her ears. "If you could only have either love or beauty in your life, which would you choose? I picked love, but Bernard disagreed. He thinks love can cause pain, while beauty gives pleasure and requires nothing in return." She stopped for a moment. "I have to admit, he has a point."

"I disagree with Bernard," Carlos piped up. "I think Belle is right."

Marina hadn't noticed Carlos since they entered the dining room. He sat at the other end of the table. Even from a distance, there was something magnetic about him. He had an easy confidence that reminded her of Nicolo. And she couldn't deny how attractive he was. She'd never met anyone so handsome.

"On what grounds?" Belle inquired, obviously pleased that he agreed with her.

Carlos took his time answering.

"If you don't experience love, you're missing out on one of life's great mysteries," he said. He seemed to be looking straight at Marina. Her cheeks flushed, and she glanced away.

"No one knows what draws two people together," he continued. "It can be as simple as a smile. But when the attraction is there, it's impossible to resist. It becomes more important than anything."

Belle finished eating her soup. She put down her spoon and smiled at Carlos.

"You make a good point, but I still think that Bernard makes a better argument. It's easy for you to say now. You have youth and beauty, all you're missing is love." She picked up her wineglass. "Answer again in a few years. You might feel differently."

Belle turned her attention to Ludwig.

"What about you, Ludwig? You're unattached. Which is more important: finding the woman of your dreams or discovering a priceless piece of art?"

Ludwig picked up his butter knife and spread butter on a dinner roll.

"Art, without a doubt. Our time is fleeting,

while a painting brings joy for centuries," he reflected. "The war makes me even more certain that I'm right. Great art has to be preserved, or we'll sink back into the Dark Ages."

Marina noticed Carlos studying her. His gaze was somehow unsettling.

After dinner, they moved to the living room. Marina sat near the fireplace, taking in the beauty of the room: French doors leading onto the terrace, elegant sofas and thick rugs. Bernard was right, the beauty of one's surroundings was important.

Carlos approached her. He held a glass of port, which felt incongruous. Like her, he seemed too young to be drinking port.

"You hardly touched your food at dinner," he said, sitting on the sofa beside her.

"I wasn't that hungry." Marina shrugged.

"Perhaps you would have been hungry if you hadn't been chatting with Ludwig before dinner." Carlos's voice was casual. "He's German, you know."

Marina's cheeks colored, and her eyes flashed in anger. The warm feelings she had for him at dinner dissolved.

"That's ridiculous. Why shouldn't I talk to Ludwig? Belle and Bernard invited him," she said sharply. "And I don't answer to you. You don't know the first thing about me."

"Belle and Bernard have to stay friendly with

everyone. But I would have thought that with what happened to your father . . ."

Marina tensed. He must have heard her story from Desi. She didn't want to think of her father at that moment, not with a room full of people.

"I didn't ask what you thought," she said. "Ludwig has been a great help to me, more than you've been in any case. The institute that he runs is Italian; it has nothing to do with the Nazis. None of us can help what country we're born in. I've spent the last month trying to recover from my father's murder. I am completely gutted, and at times, the pain has been so bad that I've wanted to take my own life. If you think there's a single day when I don't hope to make sense of his death, you're mistaken."

Carlos took a while to answer, and fresh rage boiled up in Marina. She opened her mouth to keep talking, but he stopped her.

"I apologize; you're right. I don't know anything about you," Carlos conceded. His gaze lingered over her features, and his voice became gentle. "I do know that you're very beautiful. In my experience, beautiful women don't know the power they have over men."

Carlos's eyes were intent on her. She stared back at him and then looked away.

"Apology accepted." She nodded. "Tell me about yourself. Do you enjoy working in the lumber business?"

Carlos hunched forward. He sipped his port.

"I wanted to be an artist, but my father refused to support me. And I didn't want to join the Italian army." He sighed. "I'm against fascism, and I would never do anything to support the Nazis. But it's almost impossible to sit in a warm house, drinking port, while soldiers are dying on battlefields."

"I can see that," Marina agreed. "I feel the same. I want to do something so that my father didn't die in vain, but I don't know what."

Carlos's mind seemed to be somewhere else.

"I should go." He stood up. "Desi really enjoyed your company the other day. You should visit her at the villa, she could use a friend."

"I'll take her a cup of soup tomorrow," Marina ventured. "Thank you for the suggestion."

The guests left, and Marina went up to her room. The evening had been better than she had expected, but she was glad it was over. Bernard was so caring, and Ludwig had been interesting to talk to. Only Carlos had flustered her. The way he gazed at her across the dinner table, the way he dared to act so familiar. She finally let herself remember Nicolo and how he had hurt her.

Nicolo had been the first man she'd loved, the first man she'd kissed. Her father knew nothing about it. To her father, he was simply the lanky young man he'd employed the previous summer when he came down with a bad case of gout.

Marina had been immediately drawn to Nicolo as they worked together in the gallery's back room. Everything about him was attractive. His wavy brown hair that smelled of lemons, his large dark eyes. The way he stood just a little too close to her.

They started getting espresso or gelato together after work. It was nothing scandalous. The sun was still out, and she was never late for dinner. One evening he insisted on walking her home. They stopped to admire a garden, and he drew her close and kissed her. She felt the kiss from her mouth all the way to her toes. She walked around the next week as if she had been kissed by a film star.

Even her father noticed the change in her. She practically skipped up the steps when she arrived home at night.

For almost a month, Marina let herself be kissed. Sometimes when Nicolo embraced her, his hands would stray to her thighs or even her breasts. She never allowed him to go further, but she was surprised at how much she enjoyed his caresses. No one had ever told her about the electricity that seemed to course through her body when he touched her. The way she couldn't wait for them to be alone together, the way his kisses made her feel alive.

One day she noticed the fifty lire note she had put in the cash register was missing. She could easily have spent it on lunch and forgotten. But the next night the register was short again. She was tempted to ask her father. Sometimes he took a few hundred lire from the till to buy a client lunch or dinner. But he usually left a piece of paper listing the amount.

The alternative was too awful to consider.

Marina told herself she was imagining it, and for a few days she didn't say anything. Nicolo brought her little gifts: flowers, a loaf of panettone. At the end of the month, Marina did the books, and she couldn't ignore it any longer. They were short almost one thousand lire. Nicolo had been stealing from the gallery for weeks.

That night after closing she accused him of taking money from the cash register. At first he denied it. He even said that Marina was jealous because she'd seen Nicolo walking with another girl.

Marina threatened to tell her father unless he admitted the truth. Finally he confessed. Then he put his head in his hands and wept. His mother was ill, and he had to pay for her surgery. He was falling in love with Marina and couldn't be without her. She had to let him stay on; he would never do it again.

Marina felt his arms around her for the last time. For one moment she let herself believe him. People made mistakes, and he said he was falling in love with her.

But the gallery and her father were too important. She had to fire him. Reluctantly she held her hand out for his key. Then she gave him two hundred lire from her own pocket and told him if she ever heard from him again, she would go straight to the police.

She never told her father. Instead she made up a story that Nicolo quit because he needed to leave Rome. Vittorio prided himself on his ability to judge a person's character with ease. He would have been embarrassed to have hired Nicolo in the first place.

Marina would stop thinking about Carlos. Even though she felt an attraction to him at dinner, and he seemed to take an interest in her, it would only lead to trouble.

The following day, she would start her work in Bernard's library, and in the afternoon, she would go and see Desi. It felt good to help, even if just a little.

She unzipped her dress and wiped the powder from her neck. Somehow, she had to figure out how to do more.

CHAPTER FOUR

Florence, November 1943

Marina spent the next morning going through Bernard's collection. There were so many items in the library, she didn't know where to start. Paintings and sketches by the great Italian Renaissance artists: Raphael, Bellini, Giotto. There were shelves of illustrated books and a small selection of books on Asian and Persian art. Marina had never come across anything like this collection, and she doubted herself. What if she chose the wrong books or paintings? Ones that Bernard had included simply because they caught his eye or he got a good price but weren't inherently valuable.

Then she remembered why her father had faith in her. It wasn't because she could recite everything her professors taught her about the value of a certain painting. It was because Marina seemed to understand the artist's inspiration by studying his work. Michelangelo was contracted to create a male figure to stand in the middle of the Duomo in Florence. He chose David from the Old Testament because David had been a hero. Even if Marina had no idea that David had been sculpted by Michelangelo, she would have recognized the sculpture's heroic stance.

For centuries, visitors came from all over the world to see the statue, and Florence was forever associated with *David*'s youth and beauty and courage. All she had to do was trust in herself, and she would make the right decisions.

Later in the morning, Belle joined her and sorted through her own letters. She perched on the spiral staircase with boxes of letters at her feet and read them out loud, laughing and smiling as if she had discovered old friends. Marina learned a lot about Belle by listening. She may have dressed outrageously and flirted with every man in the room, but she was also ambitious and dedicated to her work.

From the way Belle effortlessly handled the servants, Marina had assumed she grew up in luxury. But Belle's earliest letters after her father left were about her mother having to work two jobs and never having enough to eat. Even with her brothers and sisters pitching in, none of them could afford to stay in school.

When Belle was twenty, she got a job in Princeton's Pyne Library. One of the Princeton students was the nephew of the renowned financier, J. P. Morgan. Her letters from that time were full of flirtations: with professors, with a curator at the library, even with an Arabian prince. But Belle never wavered from her goal, which was to assemble for J. P. Morgan one of the greatest collections of illuminated manuscripts, and in doing so, make a name for herself in the world of rare books. The descriptions of her flirtations at Princeton were nothing compared to the excitement in a letter to her mother announcing that J. P. Morgan had hired her to manage his personal library in New York.

" 'It's not the library building that excites me,' " Belle read out loud. " 'Though you should see it! It takes up a whole block on Madison Avenue. J. P. had it built to resemble a Greek temple, complete with two marble lionesses guarding the entrance. But it's the amount of space inside the library that's truly thrilling. I told J. P. I'm going to fill it with rare books and illuminated manuscripts so that he's the envy of every collector in America. Do you know what he said? He looked at me over his glasses and said he wished he'd met me thirty years earlier; then he would have tried to make me fall in love with him. I told him I was glad he hadn't. Because then I wouldn't have taken the job.' "

Marina dragged herself away at lunchtime, but she couldn't wait to return and hear more. For a moment, she wondered what it would be like to lead a life like Belle's. She stepped through the years as confidently as Anna Pavlova performing the "Dying Swan." Even when making difficult deals with important collectors, she commanded their adoration and respect.

But Marina was different. Marina took everything seriously: art, love, family. Up until now, she had always worked toward a goal: to keep her father happy when he had lost so much, to make a name for herself in the art world. She didn't want to change who she was; there had to be a new way to feel worthwhile.

It was noon when Marina walked to Desi's villa. She brought a jar of Belle's soup. Perhaps it would make Desi feel better.

As Marina approached the house, she heard a sound coming from the garage. The garage door was open, and she peered inside. Desi was stepping out of the driver's seat of a Fiat. She glanced up in surprise, and the car keys clattered to the floor.

"Marina! What are you doing here?"

"I brought you some soup." Marina held up the parcel. "Carlos came to dinner last night. He said you still weren't feeling well."

"I'm not." Desi colored. She picked up the keys sheepishly. "I just came from the doctor."

Marina frowned. "You said your doctor makes house calls."

"It wasn't far. The doctor lives in the next village," Desi replied.

"Couldn't your mother have taken you?" Marina asked. "I'm sure she doesn't want you driving if you're sick."

"She's gone for the day," Desi admitted. "She didn't know I was going."

Marina studied Desi curiously. Her cheeks were flushed, and there were circles under her eyes.

"How long have you been sick?" Marina inquired.

"A few weeks." Desi shrugged. "The doctor said there's nothing to worry about. I'm not going to die." She tried to laugh. "Though tell that to the German Volkswagens I passed on the way home. Come inside, I'll make us both milk with honey. All I need is a bit of fattening up and some rest."

They moved into the kitchen. The counters were spotless, and there was a covered pot on the stove.

Desi went to the icebox and poured two glasses of milk. She added honey and handed one to Marina. Desi was about to sit down when suddenly her cheeks paled. She excused herself and rushed from the room.

When Desi returned, her eyes seemed even bigger, and her hands were trembling. She didn't look sick, she looked frightened.

Marina finally understood.

"You're not sick, you're pregnant."

Desi pulled out a chair. She bit her lip and wound her hand through her hair. She reminded Marina of a small child on her first day of school.

She nodded. "Yes, I'm pregnant."

Marina remembered Carlos delivering the wood to Desi's villa, him saying the previous night at dinner that Desi needed a friend.

"Is it Carlos's?"

Desi's eyes went wide.

"Of course not! I've known Carlos since he wore a little sailor suit and used to eat all the plums in our garden." Desi shook her head. She smiled defiantly. "Plus, I'd never date anyone that good-looking. Carlos is a loyal friend, but he can be quite self-centered. Dating him is a recipe for a broken heart."

"Then whose is it? If you love each other, you can get married."

"We do love each other," Desi said seriously. "I never knew I could feel like this. But he doesn't know about the baby, and we can't get married."

"Is it because of your age? You're young, but it's different if you're having a baby," Marina said. "If you get married soon, you don't even have to tell your parents you're pregnant. You can say you want to get married so quickly because of the war."

Desi stirred her glass of milk. Her eyes were watery, and she pushed back her hair.

"The other day, when we met, I didn't tell you about my brother, Donato," she said finally. "Donato was fighting in the war. He died last year in Morocco."

"He was part of Mussolini's army?" Marina questioned.

Desi's eyes were so big they hardly seemed to fit in her small face.

"His regiment was stationed in Casablanca. He

bought food and clothing on the black market and gave them to Jewish families who had nothing. His fellow soldiers discovered what he was doing, and he was shot."

Marina put down her glass. The terrible sadness welled up in her again. So many lives ruined by the war.

"I'm very sorry," Marina said. "I never had brothers or sisters."

"None of us left the house for weeks," Desi admitted. "My parents blame themselves. They shouldn't have let Donato fight; he was so young. There were ways to stop him—they could have said he had to work in the vineyards like Carlos's parents. Carlos and Donato were best friends; the three of us grew up together. Carlos was always in our house, eating in the kitchen, playing in the garden. My parents were devastated. They're so protective since Donato was killed; I'm all they have." She gulped. "They treat me like Rapunzel in the fairy tale."

"That's still no reason not to get married," Marina reflected. "Your parents could love the baby's father too. And they'd have a grandchild to look forward to."

"A grandchild, now? With German soldiers roaming the countryside?" Desi shook her head.

"So what will you do?" Marina asked.

"I'll go away before the baby is born," Desi said stoically. "We're Catholic. It's against my parents' beliefs to have a baby out of wedlock. I'll go away and have the baby by myself."

"Surely the baby's father can help?" Marina suggested. "You can run away together and return after the war."

Desi finished her milk. She stood up and placed the glass in the sink.

"I'll tell the father eventually," she said. "But I can't do it yet. And to be honest, I have to get used to the idea myself. I only turned twenty in July." Her voice cracked. "I've never been responsible for anyone but myself. What if I'm not a good mother?"

"You'll be a wonderful mother. For now, there's nothing you can do except take care of yourself." Marina stood up and hugged her. "I'll do anything I can to help."

"You help by being here." Desi hugged her back. "It's good to have a friend."

After Marina finished the milk, Desi showed her around the villa. A grand staircase led to a landing with a wood floor and floral rug. Desi's bedroom had a canopied bed and a little sitting area with views of the vineyards. At the end of the hall sat a room with a closed door. Marina guessed it had belonged to Donato.

"The villa is a hundred years old," Desi said, leading her downstairs. "It even has its own chapel. My mother goes every morning and prays. It doesn't seem to do any good, but she says God works in mysterious ways, that he's taking care of us, we just can't see it. I think she's just afraid that if she stops going something terrible will happen again."

"What does your father do?" Marina asked.

"He runs the family wine business. Before the war, he was training Donato." Her eyes pooled with tears. "He was going to take it over when he was older."

They talked for a while, and Marina was struck by how much she enjoyed Desi's company. When Marina hugged Desi goodbye, she promised to return soon. She crossed the garden quickly. A thick fog covered the hills, and even with her coat, she was cold.

Voices drew her to the drawing room when she returned to Villa I Tatti. Bernard was sitting on an armchair opposite a man of about forty with dark hair and brown eyes. He wore a navy coat and leather gloves.

"Marina, come join us," Bernard greeted her. "I'd like you to meet Gerhard Wolf. He's the German consul in Florence."

Gerhard stood up and offered his hand. "It's nice to meet you. Bernard has told me so much about you. I hear you're an expert on Italian art."

"Hardly an expert," Marina rejoined. "I worked with my father at his art gallery in Rome. Now I'm helping Bernard catalog his collection."

"The collection is in good hands," Bernard

told Gerhard. He turned to Marina. "Gerhard is a greater art lover than any of us. He received his doctorate degree in art from the university in Drcsdcn and has been in Florence ever since."

"Ludwig and I came to Florence around the same time," Gerhard explained. "We have different roles, but we take them very seriously."

"Your roles?" Marina questioned.

"To protect Florence's precious artworks," he explained. "Whatever happens in the war, the art must remain untouched."

"What about people? Should innocent people be killed?" Marina blurted out before she could stop herself.

Gerhard smoothed his gloves.

"I don't blame you for being angry," he replied. "I don't agree with Hitler on anything, and I'm sickened at what's happening around Europe. I only joined the party in name to keep my position. I'm hoping that by staying in Florence, I can stop the worst from occurring." His smile was sincere. "In fact, I came today to apologize for German soldiers intruding on your dinner party last night."

"I'm sorry, I didn't mean . . . ," Marina stumbled awkwardly, but Gerhard stopped her.

"You don't have to say anything. I don't have children, but my nephew is staying with me in Florence. It's good for young people to speak their minds."

He stood up. "I should go." He addressed Bernard. "Please thank Belle for the dinner party invitation. I'm sorry I couldn't attend, but I'd be delighted to come another night."

Gerhard left, and Bernard turned to Marina.

"You mustn't worry about Gerhard, he really is our friend." He studied Marina. "But I'm glad you arrived; there's something I want your opinion on. A collector offered me a sketch by Ghirlandaio. He insists it's from the late fifteenth century when Ghirlandaio had his studio in Rome, before he came back to Florence. I have a feeling that it's not authentic, but it wouldn't hurt to see it through another set of eyes."

"You want me to look at it?" Marina gasped.

Ghirlandaio was one of the preeminent artists of the early Renaissance. Pope Sixtus IV commissioned him to paint a fresco at the Sistine Chapel and Michelangelo served as his apprentice.

"The collector took me to lunch at the Grand Hotel." Bernard offered her his arm. "It was very flattering, but why would he ply me with steak and a bottle of Masseto Merlot if the sketch was real?"

For a few moments, Marina forgot about Desi being pregnant. One of the most important art collectors in the world wanted her opinion.

Her heart was full. She took Bernard's arm and followed him to the library.

CHAPTER FIVE

Florence, December 1943

A few mornings later Marina came downstairs to find Belle in the living room. She was poring over one of Bernard's beautiful art books.

"You caught me." Belle looked up and smiled wickedly. "Other people's vices are drinking too much or smoking. I miss looking at art. Before the war, Bernard and I traveled, visiting museums. The Tate Gallery in London for the Turners, the Prado in Madrid for the Goyas, and the Louvre in Paris for practically every important piece that's not in Italy." Belle laughed. "Now everything at the Louvre has been carted away so the Nazis can't find it. And Leningrad, where Bernard and I once spent an entire day at the Hermitage, has been under siege for eight hundred days. I have to satisfy my craving for art by looking at books."

"I know what you mean," Marina reflected. "My father started taking me to the Vatican Museum when other little girls were learning to play on swings. For my fifteenth birthday he arranged a tour of Villa Medici for my friends and me." She smiled. "My friends didn't mind. They loved the statues of naked men."

"You must miss Rome," Belle said, reclining against the cushions.

"I loved everything about my life," Marina reflected. "The galleries in Trastevere, the outdoor cafés in Piazza di Santa Maria. I even loved the tourists who crowd the Spanish Steps. They reminded me how lucky I was to live in Rome." She gulped. "I miss my father and working with him at the gallery the most. My mother died ten years ago; my father and I were very close."

"Of course you were." Belle squeezed her hand. "One day you'll meet a man who takes his place. He won't be the same, of course; Bernard is the opposite of my father. But he'll occupy your heart. In the meantime, you have friends and your work. And you have yourself. I learned a long time ago to be my own best friend."

"You and Bernard have been so good to me," Marina said.

"Bernard is relieved to have someone knowledgeable helping him. And it's purely selfish on my part," Belle said airily. "It's wonderful to have someone young to talk to, it makes me feel young too." She smiled. "I wish I could spend all day telling you stories about my past; you're a wonderful listener. But this morning I have to run some errands. I'll be back this afternoon."

Marina went into the kitchen to make a cup

of coffee. She wanted to work in the library, but first she had to mail a letter to Paolo. She hadn't written to him since she arrived, and she wanted to let him know she was safe and well. The post office was nearby in Montelopio. She put on a coat, retrieved a bicycle from the garage, and started toward the village.

Montelopio was filled with winding passage-ways and cobblestone streets. It had a main square and alleys that were too narrow for cars. The village was surrounded by walls, and the views—of rolling vineyards and swathes of fir trees—stretched on forever.

After Marina had mailed the letter, she stopped to buy small gifts for Bernard and Belle. When she returned to her bicycle, the tire was flat.

"You're not going to get far with that," a male voice said. She looked up and saw Carlos standing over her. He was dressed in a thick sweater and wool pants. A scarf was wrapped around his neck, and he wore wool gloves.

"Carlos," she greeted him. "What are you doing here?"

"I was delivering wood to the local hotel."

"It's nice to see you, but I have to go." She turned away. "My tire is flat, I have to get it fixed."

It was too cold to be standing outside, and she wouldn't be going anywhere until she fixed the tire.

Carlos walked after her.

"Where are you going?" he asked, catching up with her.

"To find a hardware store or a garage. It's probably a nail. I can take it out with the correct tool, and then I have to find someone with a pump."

"You didn't ask for my help." He frowned. "I have tools in my truck."

For some reason, she didn't want Carlos to do her a favor. She remembered the way he made her feel at dinner and then Desi saying that he was self-centered. Dating Carlos would lead to heartbreak. It was better to stay away.

"Thank you, but I don't need your help." She kept walking. "I can figure it out myself."

"Marina, please stop," he tried again. "I didn't mean to offend you at the dinner party. I said I was sorry. Why don't we start again?"

Carlos was right; he had apologized for what he had said. But only after she got angry at him.

He was being kind, she reminded herself, and there might not be another way to fix the tire. Perhaps she should give him another chance.

She turned and faced him. It wouldn't hurt to be friends, as long as she didn't let her guard down.

"All right, you can look at the tire," she agreed. "Thank you for offering."

Carlos inspected the tire. It was completely flat. "It can't be fixed," he said. "We'll put it in the back of the truck, and I'll drive you to the villa."

Marina decided to accept his offer. It would take ages to walk back to Villa I Tatti, and it was too cold to be wandering on the side of the road.

She sat as far from him in the truck as she could. He drove slowly, stopping for a shepherd leading his sheep across the road.

"I thought you'd drive very fast," she commented. "Most young men in Rome treat any chance behind the wheel as an opportunity to prove they're a race car driver."

"In Tuscany, a car is mostly used to deliver things." Carlos glanced at her. "I'm supposed to make a delivery on the way home. Is it all right if we stop?"

Marina nodded, and Carlos turned onto a road lined with pine trees. At the end was a small farm.

"Why don't you come in?" he suggested. "It's too cold to wait here."

Instead of entering the farmhouse, he walked around to a barn. He knocked twice and slid open the door.

A stall for horses with bales of hay greeted them. A ladder stood in the corner. Carlos put his hand on the rung and motioned for Marina to follow him. Suddenly she heard a voice coming from the top of the ladder. The sound nearly made her lose her footing.

"Carlos, you came!" A boy of about fourteen greeted them when they reached the top. He had curly hair and wore a sweater that was too big for him. "What took you so long? I've been starving."

"You're always hungry. A full-time cook couldn't keep you satisfied," Carlos rejoined. "Eli, I'd like you to meet Marina. She's from Rome."

"You came all the way from Rome to see me?" Eli's eyes widened. He stepped forward and took Marina's hand. "I've read that Roman women are the most beautiful. Now I know it's true."

"Spoken with the infinite knowledge of a fourteen-year-old." Carlos grinned. "We're here to see your mother."

A young woman stood over a cot. She gathered a wide bundle and walked over to them.

"Carlos, you shouldn't be here," she said. "German soldiers were spotted in the village."

"They probably came to flirt with the women. I told Guido at the hotel not to hire such pretty waitresses," Carlos responded. "Sara, I'd like you to meet a friend, Marina Tozzi."

Sara wore a navy skirt. Her fingers were long and thin, and Marina could see her shoulder blades under her blouse.

"It's nice to meet you." Marina nodded.

Sara was quite pretty. She had high cheekbones and deep-set brown eyes.

"I'd offer you something to drink, but I don't have anything," Sara said awkwardly.

"You do now." Carlos held up his basket. "Coffee and milk. And biscuits."

"I hope not the ones with raisins," Eli piped up. "The raisins get stuck in my teeth."

"Stop being choosy, this isn't the Grand Hotel in Florence." Carlos handed him the biscuits. "Now go downstairs, we want to talk in private."

A whimpering sound came from the bundle. Marina caught sight of a round face. The baby looked about six months old. She had blue eyes and a shock of black hair.

"This is Francesca, the most beautiful baby in Tuscany," Carlos introduced them. "Francesca is destined to marry an Italian prince and live in a palazzo."

Marina tried to hide her dismay. How could a woman and two children live in a loft above a barn?

"We're Jewish," Sara said, as if reading her thoughts. "My husband was sent to a labor camp a few months ago, and last month we were forced out of our apartment. Carlos arranged for the family who owns this farm to take us in. They don't have enough to feed us. Carlos brings food and clothes for the children."

"Eli's sweater is too big," Carlos said. "Next time I'll shrink my sweaters in the wash. My mother kept all my baby blankets. Blue suits

Francesca." He stroked the blanket. "It brings out the color in her eyes."

A mattress was pushed against the wall, and blankets were piled in the corner. There was a makeshift table and a couple of chairs.

"It must be so cold," Marina said. "And how do you cook?"

"I don't cook. Carlos brings bread and milk and hard-boiled eggs. We haven't been here long. The cold isn't so bad." Sara paused as if she were trying to believe her own words. "We're lucky to have found somewhere safe."

"We'll find a better place soon," Carlos said confidently. "Eli already put in a request. He wants a dartboard so he can practice. And a fireplace for all the wood I'll bring. The house will be so toasty, you'll have to walk around in your underwear."

"We've never accepted charity before." Sara straightened her shoulders. "My husband, Benito, was an instructor at an art school. Then Jews weren't allowed to teach. When the Germans occupied Florence, they took our apartment and closed our bank account." She looked at Carlos. "We're fortunate we had Carlos to help us."

"I owed Benito," Carlos said. "He's the only instructor who believed I had talent as an artist. And I'm the lucky one, I get to hold this beautiful baby."

Francesca started crying and Carlos took her in

his arms. She made a sucking sound, her mouth searching for something to eat.

"I should feed her." Sara held out her hands.

"You eat first." Carlos waved at the basket of food. "Marina and I will sing to her."

They talked while Sara and Eli ate their meal. Marina was impressed with the way Carlos handled the baby. He was gentle with her, cooing her name and cradling her with his hands. Eventually it was time to leave. They said their goodbyes, and Carlos promised to return with more supplies soon.

"Next time take me into the village," Eli urged, when they climbed down the ladder. "I want to learn to shoot Germans, so I can keep my mother safe."

"No one is shooting Germans." Carlos ruffled his hair. "The best thing you can do for your mother is to stay inside, out of trouble."

Carlos opened the passenger door, and Marina stepped into the truck. She waited until they were driving before she said anything.

"Why did you take me there?" she asked, puzzled.

Carlos turned onto a small road and pulled over to the side.

"The other night at the dinner party, the German soldiers said there were reports of partisans in the neighborhood. They were right. There are partisans around here." He turned off the engine. "There's one in this truck."

Marina placed her hand on the dashboard. She shouldn't be surprised. Why else would Carlos be helping Sara and her children? But it still filled her with dread.

Her mind went to Desi. Desi and Carlos had been friends since they were children.

"Is Desi a partisan too?"

Carlos shook his head.

"Of course not! I would never involve Donato's little sister," he responded. "Desi knows nothing about it."

"You shouldn't be telling me this. You barely know me," Marina insisted. "How do you know you can trust me?"

"You said at the dinner party that since your father died you've felt helpless. That you want to do something to avenge his death but you don't know what."

Marina had told Carlos that she didn't want her father's death to have been in vain. But more than anything, her father had wanted her to stay safe. How could she accomplish both things at the same time?

Carlos kept talking. "The partisans need someone like you to help them."

"Someone like me?" she repeated.

"There are safe houses from here to the Swiss border. Jews and prisoners of war are hidden in some of the villas," he explained. "Other villas house partisans themselves, plus guns, ammunition, food, clothing. Those supplies cost money. People give us things to sell on the black market, mostly items from their homes. Lately we've received paintings, old books, statues. Some might simply be family heirlooms. Others could be extremely valuable. It's impossible to know." He looked at Marina. "Someone with your art expertise could tell us."

Marina's thoughts swirled. She tried to arrange them in an orderly fashion, like when she used to set up the chessboard so she and her father could play.

"Surely the person who gives you the items would tell you their value," she suggested.

"Not everyone knows. And not everyone is truthful," Carlos responded. "Especially when it means an entire family crossing the border to Switzerland."

Marina took in the meaning of his words. She gaped at him in astonishment.

"You mean people pay you to escape?" she gasped. "What about the families who can't afford it? Are they just abandoned?"

"Of course not." Carlos's tone grew impatient. "Look at Sara and her children. We try to help everyone. Supplies aren't free, they have to be paid for somehow. One can hardly walk into a bakery and offer a gold candlestick in exchange for a loaf of bread, or give a shoemaker a painting for a pair of boots. We need money."

She thought of the lire Paolo had offered her back in Rome, of her stay at Villa I Tatti when she couldn't afford to go anywhere else.

"I understand," Marina acknowledged. "But it still doesn't feel right. There must be another way to get money other than selling things on the black market."

"What do you think we are, a charity group with wealthy benefactors?" he spat. "Most partisans don't have money of their own. Some are peasants, they can barely read or write. Others are university students without twenty lire to their name, disillusioned by Mussolini's promises," Carlos said. "And there are young people like you and me, whose loved ones have been murdered." He turned to her. "Before Donato went to fight, I believed the war was far away, something in the newspapers and on the radio. Then I started getting his letters: Jews in Morocco were forced to live in ghettos; they were starving, and there was typhus and cholera. German soldiers dragged Jews into alleyways and shot them. They separated parents and children first and killed the parents while the children watched.

"After Donato was murdered, I couldn't spend my time cutting down trees so the SS headquarters in Florence stayed warm. I had to do something. Being a partisan has given me a purpose. That's what you said at the dinner party. That you had to do something too."

Marina was about to agree, but something stopped her. She barely knew Carlos. How could she trust him? She had trusted Nicolo, and she had been wrong. The interest he had showed in her was only a way to get what he wanted. What if Carlos was the same? And yet, she admired what he was doing for Sara and her children. . . . And he had been so gentle with Francesca. She had seen a new side of him.

"What you are doing for Sara is wonderful, but I still don't understand how you could take me to the barn without knowing me better," she reflected. "The other night you were upset that I talked to Ludwig simply because he was German. Now you're asking me to be a partisan."

"I apologized for that. Something did happen to change my mind," Carlos said. "A few days ago, I was delivering firewood to Bernard and Belle. I overheard Bernard saying how lucky he was to have you cataloging his collection, that you have an instinct for recognizing valuable art. I realized you were the perfect person for the job."

"You eavesdropped on their conversation?" Marina said in shock.

"Partisans do whatever they need to gain information. Do you think we discover when a train will be blown up by politely asking a German officer?" He shrugged off her surprise. "Listening is a key part of the job."

Marina still wasn't convinced. She believed in

what the partisans were doing. But some of the things Carlos said didn't sit right with her. She felt uncomfortable talking about selling things on the black market.

She wondered if it had been the same for her father. He hadn't been a partisan; he had merely been trying to help Jewish artists. Had her father quarreled with other Romans who ran safe houses? Or did the real partisans think he took too many chances, allowing a Jew to live in his basement, even though German officers frequented the art gallery? She desperately wished her father were here. They could have discussed Carlos's offer together.

Carlos sensed her hesitation. His voice softened, and he briefly touched her hand. There was a pinprick of desire when they touched. By the expression on his face, he felt it too.

"I'm not suggesting you become a partisan. The partisan work is dangerous; I would never involve you in deadly missions. And partisans have to move around the countryside. Sometimes I use my father's business as an excuse to be gone for a few weeks at a time. I'm only asking you to lend your expertise to the partisan cause."

"How would it work?" she asked cautiously.

"There are some unused rooms in my parents' attic. I'd bring the items there," he said. "You'll give me your opinion, and I'll take them away. No one will know; it will be perfectly safe."

"I can't do anything to put Bernard or Belle at risk," she said. "They've been so good to me."

"They won't have anything to do with it. It will be our secrct."

Marina gulped. She was tempted to say yes. But there was so much to think about. She didn't want to put anyone around her in danger.

"Thank you for thinking of me." She nodded. "I need some time to decide."

Carlos placed his hands on the steering wheel. He turned on the engine.

"Of course," he said. "I should get you home. Neither of us will do any good if we freeze to death in the cold."

They drove silently to Villa I Tatti. Marina rubbed her hands together to keep warm. There was a new energy between them, something disorienting and oddly close, and she didn't know how to fill the silence.

The truck pulled into the driveway. Carlos turned to her. His eyes were the color of emeralds, and his smile made her whole body feel warmer.

"Please think about it, Marina. Nazis are deporting Jews from all over Europe. They're put on trains and sent somewhere in the east." He waved at the countryside. "There are three deportation centers right here in Tuscany. One is in a villa in Oliveto Citra. We need money to help them escape." His voice became urgent. "And there are families like Sara and her children.

Without enough supplies, they'll starve or freeze to death."

Marina opened her door. The war seemed to settle over her as if it were the fog covering the hills, filling her chest like a terrible cold.

She stepped down from the truck. "I promise I'll give you my answer soon."

Marina strode past the villa to Bernard's library. She went to the sink and poured a glass of water. Her father had risked his life to save Jews, and she wanted to do the same. But she still had doubts. It didn't seem right to accept payment from people trying to flee. And then there was Carlos himself. They would have to work closely together; she had to completely trust him.

She had trusted Nicolo once too.

She put down the glass and walked to the bookshelf. She heard something behind her and turned around. Bernard appeared in the doorway.

"I came to get some books," Bernard said, glancing at Marina curiously. "You seem upset. Is something wrong?"

She tried to compose herself.

"Sometimes it helps to talk to someone," Bernard encouraged her. "Belle and I bounce everything off each other. Sometimes the simplest problems are easier when they're shared. For instance, not being able to fix the faucet in the bathroom because our usual plumber is fighting at the front, or missing out on a piece of art I desperately wanted by a few hundred lire to another bidder at an auction."

Suddenly it was all too much. Eli, with his youthful energy, stuck in the loft; Francesca, her small mouth rooting for something to eat. Marina wondered how a baby would survive the winter. She couldn't reveal anything about Sara, or about Carlos's request, but perhaps she could tell Bernard how she was feeling.

She told Bernard how grateful she was to him for her work but explained that she still wanted to do more. She wanted to do something to help.

"I was already mainly living in Italy during the last war. But when America joined the Allies, I wanted to enlist," Bernard said when she had finished. "Friends from home arrived in Europe in their smart uniforms, and I felt so guilty, sitting in my villa in Tuscany. But I was too old, and I had a weak heart; the army wouldn't have taken me even if I had tried. One day I returned to the villa from an auction in Florence, and Belle was in the study, crying. When I entered, she jumped up and kissed me." He smiled. "She'd been reading about the casualties at the Sixth Battle of the Isonzo and was so relieved that I couldn't join the army. If something happened to me, she said, she wouldn't recover."

"This is different," Marina said. "There's no one left who would miss me."

"We all need you," Bernard said. "You have to look at life as a jigsaw puzzle. If you remove your piece, what happens to the pieces around you?"

Bernard had a point. He was counting on her to catalog the important pieces in his collection, and Desi needed a friend.

"I hadn't looked at it like that," she said.

Bernard left, and Marina returned to the bookshelf. It was impossible to concentrate.

She finished her work and went into the kitchen, where she found Anna arranging some purple flowers in a vase.

"These flowers came for you. With a note." Anna handed her an envelope.

Marina opened it.

Dear Marina,
    The flowers are from my mother's hothouse. I hope you enjoy them.
                    Warmest regards, Carlos

Marina folded the letter. The violets were lovely; they smelled like Belle's perfume.

She recalled the night of the dinner party. Carlos said she was very beautiful, that beautiful women didn't know the power they had over men.

If she accepted Carlos's offer, she had to keep her distance. She had let Nicolo get too close, and he had broken her heart. She would listen to Desi's warning.

"Should I bring them to your bedroom?" Anna asked.

"No, thank you." Marina shook her head. "They're much nicer where everyone can see them."

CHAPTER SIX

Florence, December 1943

At noon the next day, Marina stood up and stretched. She had been in the library all morning, poring over the illustrations in Bernard's books. She felt the same as she did after a lecture at the university, or when her father received a new painting at the gallery: infused with energy and unable to sit still.

Most people didn't understand the power of art. It wasn't just the beauty of the paint on canvas, the curve of *Mona Lisa*'s smile, the color of Van Gogh's irises. It was the way art unlocked the viewer's emotions. She remembered the first time her father took her to the Sistine Chapel to see Michelangelo's frescoes. She looked up and saw her father's tears and wondered if he was missing her mother. He hugged her and explained he could almost see Michelangelo laboring over his work until his back ached and his fingers bled.

When she was older, Marina read that Michelangelo was so consumed with the frescoes, he didn't sleep for days. That's when she understood what her father was feeling. The artist's passion became as much a part of the painting as the brushstrokes.

One of the most exciting things about Bernard's collection was his own writings. He was donating first-edition copies of his two most famous books, *The Central Italian Painters of the Renaissance*, published in 1897, and *The Drawings of the Florentine Painters*, published in 1903. Skimming through the pages and discovering she and Bernard admired the same artists made her feel as if she belonged to a secret club. She imagined what it would be like to write her own book about art and have it read by university students and collectors. The idea made her swoon with delight.

The door opened, and Belle entered the library. She was elegantly dressed in a fur-lined coat, and her hands were hidden by a silver muff.

Marina looked up from the book she was reading.

"You seem preoccupied; I hope I'm not disturbing you," Belle said, joining her.

"I was reading some of Bernard's scholarly works." Marina pointed to the bookshelf. "I had no idea he'd written so many books."

"Bernard used to lock himself in his room and write for days." Belle picked up a copy. "Most women would have been jealous. When he finally emerged, his eyes were on fire, and he never looked so happy. That's what people don't understand about art and letters. They consume every part of you."

Belle's insights always surprised Marina. She

had a way of looking at things like no one Marina had met before. She was glad to have her as a friend.

"I came to tell you Bernard will be away for a few days," Belle said. "Bernard wanted to tell you himself, but he had to leave right after breakfast."

"Where did he go?" Marina asked.

"You mustn't tell anyone. He took the train to Switzerland."

"Switzerland!" Marina said, shocked. "I don't understand."

"Many Italian Jews are afraid the Germans will confiscate their art collections. They give them to Bernard, and he takes them to Switzerland for safekeeping until after the war," Belle confided.

"I thought Gerhard Wolf protected the art in Florence."

"Gerhard is the German consul; the SS doesn't answer to him exactly. German soldiers can search private homes," Belle said carefully.

"Isn't it dangerous to cross the border?" Marina questioned.

"Bernard carries an American passport, and his papers are in order, so the border guards mostly leave him alone," Belle commented. "It still makes me nervous. He hides the paintings in a secret compartment in his suitcase. If they were discovered, he'd be questioned and put in prison, or worse."

"Why does he do it?" Marina inquired.

Belle sighed. She twisted the silver muff.

"Bernard believes saving priceless art is worth risking his life. I tell him he's wrong. He's in his sixties." She gave a small smile. "There are so many more places we want to see, and we still have a good time together."

The worry lines around Belle's mouth relaxed. She changed the subject.

"I saw the flowers in the kitchen. Anna said they were from Carlos."

"They must be a thank-you for the dinner party," Marina said evasively.

"He already sent me a thank-you note." Belle paused a moment before continuing. "I've known Carlos since he was a boy. He's grown up to be so good-looking and charming. If I was twenty, I'd fall madly in love with him."

Marina shrugged. "I hadn't noticed," she said.

Marina went back to her work. All morning she had been trying to decide whether to agree to Carlos's request.

Her father wouldn't approve; her safety came before anything, although that hadn't kept him from harboring Jews.

The night before, she had tossed and turned, picturing Sara and her children in the barn. Marina slept on a feather bed and bathed in a bathtub brought from the Hotel Cipriani in Venice, while Sara had to wash with a bucket of ice-cold water.

Finally she made her decision. She would tell Carlos yes.

For the first time since her father's murder, she felt lighter, as if she could finally breathe.

She left Bernard's library and locked the door behind her. Carlos was probably out delivering firewood. She would tell him when he returned this evening. She was eager to check on Desi. Perhaps they could eat lunch together before Marina went back to work.

Desi was in the living room when Marina arrived at her parents' villa. She was wearing a coat, as if she were about to go out.

"Marina, I was about to come over," Desi greeted her. "I'm feeling much better. Carlos and I are going to Montalcino for lunch. We wondered if you'd join us."

Marina couldn't tell Carlos her decision in front of Desi. Desi didn't know anything about Carlos's work as a partisan.

"I can't." Marina shook her head. "I should keep working in the library this afternoon."

"Please, you must come," Desi urged. "Carlos has the afternoon off, and it will be fun. I've been cooped up here for days. And I finally have an appetite. I'm going to eat everything on my plate!"

Carlos appeared in the doorway. He nodded to Marina.

Desi turned to him. "I was just telling Marina she has to come with us."

"I can't," Marina rejoined. "Bernard expects me to work in the library."

"That's funny, I ran into Bernard early this morning before breakfast," Carlos remarked. "He mentioned that he hopes he's not working you too hard."

Marina colored slightly.

"Going through his collection takes up a lot of time," she said. "But I suppose I could take a break."

Desi looped her arm through Marina's. "Montalcino is one of the most beautiful villages in Tuscany. I can't wait to show it to you."

Carlos hopped into his truck. Desi sat beside him, and Marina squeezed in last. They passed cypress groves and rolling hills dotted with stucco villas. The road to Montalcino was so narrow, Marina began to feel carsick. Then the village came into view. A stone wall surrounded by rows of medieval turrets. There were cobblestone passageways with shingled houses and a small church that overlooked the valley. Old men with freckled hands played chess inside trattorias. A young mother walked down an alley, holding her son's hand and carrying a small puppy. It was so quaint and charming, and it reminded Marina of her old neighborhood.

"Montalcino is so high up in the hills, the

Germans haven't discovered it," Desi said after they parked in the piazza. "Up here, one forgets that there's a war."

Carlos led them to a café with checkered table-cloths and a brick fireplace.

"I don't want any wine, thank you," Marina said when the waiter brought a bottle. In Rome, she seldom drank during the day.

"You have to drink wine," Desi pleaded. "My only two friends in the world are together, so we should celebrate."

"I'll have one glass," Marina relented. "But only with the meal. I can't drink on an empty stomach."

The waiter brought plates of ravioli in pomo-doro sauce. Marina remembered all the nights she'd arrived home from class and found her father humming in the kitchen. She'd put on an apron and work beside him. He wouldn't let her near his sauces, but she was happy slicing tomatoes for the salad, grating Parmesan. She recalled the night of his murder; she had been so excited to show him the anchovies.

She put down her fork. Suddenly she wasn't hungry.

"Is your ravioli all right?" Desi asked, noticing her expression.

"It's very good," Marina said.

She felt Carlos watching her and forced herself to take a bite, washing it down with some wine.

The wine warmed her throat, and she let the waiter refill her glass.

"Carlos came for dinner every week when we were children," Desi mused. "After dessert, Donato and Carlos and I performed plays for our families. Carlos always let Donato play the prince; he was the villain."

"The villain had better lines," Carlos reasoned. "Desi was the beautiful princess. In every script, there was a sword fight to see who would claim her heart. I won every time. No one can beat me in a duel."

"When I was young, I always wished for a brother or sister," Marina admitted. Her head buzzed from the wine. "After my mother died, my father and I did everything together. Except for cooking. He used to sing while he was waiting for the pasta to boil."

"Your father and I would have gotten along," Carlos said. "I always make the pasta. It takes patience. The olive oil has to be added at the right time, and if it cooks too long, the pasta sticks to the pot."

"Carlos cooks the pasta because he wants to eat it before it's all gone," Desi said, laughing. She stood up and started toward the restroom. "Excuse me, I'll be right back."

Carlos turned to Marina.

"You should drink wine more often," he commented. "You're much more relaxed."

Marina stiffened instinctively and hunched forward in her chair.

"I don't usually drink wine during the day. I did it for Desi," she said sharply. "I didn't want to ruin her lunch."

"You should do it for yourself." Carlos touched her wrist. "You're even more beautiful when you're not worrying about something."

Marina inched away, pretending to study her plate. Her mind went to the first time Nicolo called her beautiful. They had been strolling through Trastevere, where many artists displayed their canvases. Marina decided to purchase a painting. The artist was merely a student, but she could tell he had talent. She went to get change for a twenty-lire note, and when she returned, Nicolo handed her the painting. He said beautiful women deserved gifts. At first, she refused. She paid Nicolo's salary, and she doubted he could afford it. But he was so hurt she accepted in the end.

She brought her mind back to the present. Was Carlos trying to charm her because she hadn't yet responded to his offer?

"There are more important things than a woman's looks," she remarked.

"You're right," Carlos said easily. He removed his hand. "Like her expression when she lets herself relax and enjoy a glass of wine. There's nothing wrong with being happy, even during the war."

After lunch, they strolled through the piazza. Desi entered the chemist, and Marina and Carlos waited outside. It felt so peaceful: the medieval walls surrounding the village, the rows of vineyards fanned out below them. And yet, Carlos had said there were deportation centers nearby. Looking around the quaint shops and cafés, she couldn't believe it was true.

"Are there really deportation centers near here?" Marina wondered out loud.

Carlos nodded. "There are three in Tuscany. They were originally for political prisoners who were considered enemies of Italy. But since the Germans arrived, they've been rounding up Italian Jews."

Marina took a deep breath. She rubbed her hands together.

"I've decided I want to help," she announced. "I'll value the art pieces."

Carlos glanced around to make sure no one was listening. He turned to her and his eyes were the brightest green.

"Are you sure?" he asked eagerly. "I'm expecting new items tomorrow."

Marina felt a surge of excitement. It felt good to have made a decision. To know that she was going to do something to make a difference.

"Perfectly sure." She nodded.

Carlos looked at her carefully. "You won't be sorry." His voice was thick with emotion.

"Together we'll be saving so many lives."

After Carlos drove them home and said good-bye, Marina and Desi sat in Desi's bedroom.

"It felt wonderful to go somewhere," Desi said, perching on the bed. "I'm glad you came with us. Carlos isn't easy to get to know sometimes, but he's really very sweet. He and Donato had a wonderful friendship." She paused. "I used to worry that I'd miss Donato too much if I spent time with Carlos, but it's the reverse. Being with Carlos makes me feel happy and carefree, like when we were children."

"Have you decided what you're going to do?" Marina asked anxiously. "Your parents will realize you're pregnant soon. You can't hide it forever."

"I took your advice and wrote the father a letter," Desi said. "But I haven't mailed it yet. I still don't know if it's the right thing to do."

Marina was elated that Desi had listened to her.

"I keep asking myself what I would gain by sending it," Desi went on. "There's a war on. Even if he accepts the baby, we can hardly run down to the priest and ask him to make us man and wife."

"Why not?" Marina asked.

Desi started to say something, but a voice called from downstairs.

"It's my mother." She stood up. "I'll be right back."

Marina sat at Desi's dressing table where she spotted a notepad and an envelope addressed to Peter Von Buren, 23 Piazza della Signoria, Florence.

Marina quickly glanced up from the dressing table as Desi returned. No wonder she hadn't told her who the father was. Desi's lover was German.

"My mother has some eggs and a casserole recipe for Belle," Desi said. "She wants to give them to you herself."

Marina followed Desi down to the kitchen. There wouldn't be any more time to talk in private. She would have to ask Desi about the envelope later.

That evening in her bedroom, Marina thought about the afternoon. It had felt good to finally agree to help the partisans. But sitting there in the quiet of her room, the light of the moon glinting through the window, she wondered if she had made the right decision. Never again would Villa I Tatti feel safe. She wouldn't be able to luxuriate in the bath with a book, or sit happily in the morning room with a cup of tea.

She thought about Bernard's clandestine trips to Switzerland and about the envelope on Desi's dressing table. The war was everywhere. Even the people closest to her were hiding something.

CHAPTER SEVEN

Florence, December 1943

Marina sat in the morning room, stirring honey into a bowl of porridge. Butterflies formed in her stomach; she couldn't manage more than a spoonful. All night she had lain awake wondering how Desi could have taken a German lover.

And then there was Carlos and the partisan effort. The first items were arriving that night. She was excited and nervous at the same time. She would have to trust her instincts.

A knock sounded at the door, and Marina waited for Anna to answer it. Bernard was still away, and Belle had left early. Belle's errands were becoming more frequent. That morning, Marina had peered out the window to see Belle getting into her car. Even for Belle she was peculiarly dressed, in a conservative suit and gloves, as if she were going to work in an office. And she took off quickly, glancing around to see if anyone was watching.

"Marina, you have a visitor." Anna stood in the hallway, Ludwig beside her. His nose was red from the cold, and he was dressed formally in a long wool overcoat and a felt hat. Marina glanced up in surprise. She was glad she had dressed before coming down to breakfast.

"Ludwig, it's nice to see you," Marina greeted him. She looked around the room, as if she had missed any other guests. "Bernard isn't here; he's away."

"Bernard sent me. We talked on the phone a few days ago," Ludwig explained.

"Can we offer you some breakfast, or coffee at least?"

"No, thank you. I've already had breakfast," Ludwig said, sitting opposite her at the breakfast table. "You seem to be settling in. Bernard said you're invaluable in the library."

"I'm enjoying it very much," Marina reflected. "Bernard's collection is fascinating. A single book of illustrations keeps me occupied for hours."

"I'm the same when I'm at the institute. I've been a terrible disappointment to my parents," Ludwig said. "My father wanted me to be an officer like him. And my mother still hopes I'll get married and start a family. It's getting too late for that; it seems I'll be a bachelor forever."

"Your father was a German officer?" Marina inquired.

Ludwig nodded. "In the First World War, yes. He's retired. He can't stand Hitler either. That's one of the reasons I was so glad to be able to study and work in Florence. Even years before the war, I dreaded what was happening in Germany. I hope you believe me."

"It's none of my business." Marina nursed her cup. "I shouldn't have said anything."

"It is your business. I want us to be friends." He looked at her evenly. "Don't worry, I truly mean friends. You're an attractive young woman, but I want you to know that you're safe with me." His expression relaxed, and he smiled. "I'm much older than you, and my track record with women is terrible. The last time I dated a woman, I bored her to death with details of the book I'm writing on Leonardo da Vinci. I finally had to admit I might never have success with women and bought a puppy instead. His name is Fra Angelico."

"That's quite a mouthful for a puppy!" Marina laughed.

She was relieved that Ludwig understood her.

She enjoyed Ludwig's company and valued him as a friend. It was nice to have someone new to talk to about art.

"Fra Angelico's first biographer described him as having a 'rare and perfect talent,'" Ludwig said slyly. "My puppy is the same. Except his talent is for digging holes in the garden instead of painting."

"I love dogs. I'd like to meet him," Marina said.

"I came to ask if you'd like to visit the Kunsthistorisches Institute," Ludwig continued.

"Bernard thought you might enjoy our collection. There are some fascinating works."

The whole day stretched ahead of her. She couldn't spend all of it in the library.

"Yes, why not?" She put down her coffee cup. "Is your book on Leonardo da Vinci part of the collection? I'd love to read it."

"Luckily for you, it's still with the publisher," Ludwig said, smiling. "I wouldn't want to bore you too."

The Kunsthistorisches Institute was located near the Ponte Vecchio. Marina hadn't been into Florence since she had arrived. As they drove through the streets, she wondered if the trip was a mistake. Her chest seized as she spotted German soldiers patrolling the sidewalks, whistling at Italian women.

But it was only one afternoon. And Bernard thought it was a good idea.

"The institute was started forty years ago by Baron Karl Eduard von Liphart. It's an independent organization; it has nothing to do with the Nazis," Ludwig said as he parked the car. "Baron von Liphart came to Florence in 1867 to view a new painting at the Uffizi Gallery. No one knew the artist. He uncovered the fact that it was a Leonardo da Vinci. Can you imagine the feeling? If I had been Liphart, I would have dropped dead with excitement."

He opened Marina's door, and she followed him inside. For a moment everything—Sara and the children, Desi's German lover, Carlos's partisan activities—dropped away. The ceiling seemed as high as the Vatican's, and the space stretched on forever. There were books everywhere, not just on shelves stacked high atop one another, but on tables and ladders, even heaped on staircases that led to the next level.

"I'm afraid my shelving skills can't keep up with my buying habits," Ludwig said sheepishly. "I had an assistant, but he joined the Italian army. Lately I've had to do everything myself."

Marina spent an hour examining works on Renaissance art and flipped through a couple of tomes on Pablo Picasso and André Breton.

"You can tell my great love is Italian architecture from the Renaissance period. Architects like Filippo Brunelleschi, Leon Battista Alberti, Andrea Palladio," Ludwig said, when Marina encountered a stack of books on the subject. "That's why this war has to stop. Can you imagine if bombs were dropped on the Vatican, the Duomo in Florence, St. Mark's Basilica in Venice? It would be the end of two thousand years of civilization."

Ludwig walked over to a drawer. He took out a small box and handed it to Marina. "Bernard and I were discussing the war recently. We both thought it was a good idea if you had this."

Marina opened the box. Inside was a small pistol.

"You and Bernard want me to carry a gun?" Marina was shocked.

The weapon was no bigger than a cigarette case. The handle was enamel, and it was set with mother-of-pearl.

"The black market has grown very active in Florence. One of the most valuable commodities is rare books. We're worried that someone might enter the library while you're there alone," he explained. "We want you to be safe."

"Villa I Tatti is in the countryside, and it's behind a gate," Marina said, frowning. "No one would intrude."

"I haven't heard of any break-ins in Tuscany," Ludwig confirmed. "But one can't be too careful." His eyes swept around the room. "A book of illuminated manuscripts is worth a great deal more on the black market than a pair of stockings. There are three different locks for the institute, and only I have the keys."

"I've never owned a pistol." Marina turned the gun over. "I don't know how to use it."

"This one is simple. I can give you a lesson before you leave," Ludwig offered. "Keep it in a drawer at the library. It will make Bernard and me feel better."

"Why didn't Bernard mention it to me?" Marina asked.

"We only thought of it a couple of days ago, and we didn't want to wait until he got back," Ludwig explained.

It must be important if it couldn't wait a few days, Marina thought.

"All right," she agreed. Keeping it couldn't do any harm, she decided.

"I'm glad that's settled." Ludwig smiled. "I want to show you one of my favorite books. I'm sure you know everything about Leonardo da Vinci's paintings, but this one covers his work as an inventor and architect. It's quite fascinating."

Marina sat at her dressing table and glanced at the box holding the pistol. The following day, she would take it to the library. For now she slipped it in her drawer and tried not to think about its implications. She spent so much time in the library, and there hadn't been any intruders. Bernard and Ludwig were probably worrying about nothing.

Belle called when Marina returned from the institute and said she wouldn't be home for dinner. She was picking up Bernard at the train station, and they were going to dine with Gerhard Wolf.

It was the perfect excuse to tell Anna she was going out to dinner. She and Carlos had made plans for him to pick her up and take her to the

Adamo villa. It wasn't far, but she didn't want to walk alone in the dark.

Marina studied her reflection in the mirror. She had dressed carefully in a navy wool dress with a thin belt. She looked almost like a schoolteacher, but that was her objective. She didn't want to do anything to encourage Carlos, especially since they would be alone.

She heard a car pull in and stop, and she peered out the window. Carlos jumped out and approached the villa.

Marina took one more look in the mirror. She wondered if she should have worn her hair back with a clip. It was too late now. She grabbed her coat and hurried down the staircase.

"There you are," Carlos said when she opened the door. "You should put on that coat. We're not driving far, but it's cold in the truck."

"I can decide when to put on a coat," she said stiffly, climbing into the passenger seat.

"I was only trying to be helpful," Carlos replied easily. He started the engine. "I don't want you to get sick."

Marina leaned against the headrest. She was being touchy because she was nervous. It was better not to speak about anything except the task ahead.

They drove the short distance in silence. Carlos's parents' villa was three stories with black wrought iron balconies and a tiled roof. It sat high on the hill with a line of pine trees on either side. The moon was full, and stars were thick in the sky.

"My parents are out, and the housekeeper has the night off," Carlos said as he led her to the back of the villa. "My mother loves to entertain and go to parties. One of her biggest disappointments about the war is that she can't give large dinners because of the rationing. We have the villa to ourselves; no one will see us."

How could Bernard and Belle still give dinner parties with the rationing? She would have to ask Belle. Marina had never seen so many rooms. It was like the palazzi in Parioli and Aventino. Every room was decorated with grand furniture and there were rugs and mirrors and expensive lamps. Back in Rome, she'd gaze up at the marble porticos and imagine what it would be like to live there when she had a successful art gallery. She'd have a husband and two children and perhaps a dog. The walls would be lined with her favorite paintings, and there would be a big kitchen and a garden. Her father would join them for Sunday lunches, and they'd sit for hours, drinking wine and talking about art.

The main floor of the Adamo villa had a salon with leopard-skin rugs and a lacquered armoire filled with Italian silks. In the dining room, a polished oak table and chairs upholstered in purple velvet waited for guests to come again.

They passed a music room with a gold harp and a game room with a billiard table and an ivory chess set.

Carlos led her up the staircase to the third floor. The ceilings were low, the hall spreading into a maze of rooms. Carlos entered the first one and led her toward a locked chest by the window, draped in velvet.

He crouched down and opened the lock.

"It's all in there." He motioned to the chest. "Take as long as you need, I'll wait. Let me know if you need anything, paper or a pencil or something to drink while you work."

Marina placed the velvet on the floor and laid the objects on top of it. The first items were ordinary objects a family might save: wedding china that was pretty but nothing special, candlesticks that were shiny but brass instead of gold. A few leather-bound books looked promising, and Marina went through them carefully, but they weren't rare—they were simply old.

Then she took out a painting wrapped in brown paper. It was no larger than a photograph one kept on a dresser.

The signature in the corner was so faint it was unreadable; she could just make out the date. She couldn't help but gasp.

"What is it?" Carlos noticed her expression.

Marina didn't answer. She had to study it more carefully. The painting was of a naked woman reclining against a red rock. In the background was a green hill and an olive tree. She recognized the scene. To her eye, it looked like an early sketch of the *Sleeping Venus* by Giorgione.

Giorgione was one of the most mysterious artists of the High Renaissance. Only a small number of his paintings survived, of which the *Sleeping Venus* was the most controversial. This sketch was dated 1501, almost ten years before the final painting. Even without the signature, she had a strange feeling that it was his.

There was a chance that it was a copy. But why would anyone make a copy of an early sketch instead of the finished painting? And there was something about the sheet where the *Sleeping Venus* was lying. A richness to the fabric that wasn't in the final painting. As if Giorgione had decided he didn't want the backdrop to overpower his subject.

"I think it's a Giorgione," she breathed. She couldn't keep the excitement out of her voice. "If I'm right, it's worth a fortune."

Carlos ran over and joined her.

"It's so small," he said dubiously.

"Giorgione came from a village near Venice—he didn't have access to big fancy canvases," Marina said. "He was very gifted. When he was quite young, he moved to Venice and apprenticed under Bellini. He was even an acquaintance of Leonardo da Vinci's. He died of the plague in

1510. The *Sleeping Venus* was his last painting."

Carlos glanced at her appreciatively.

"How do you know all that?" he asked.

"I studied him at university," she said, wrapping up the parcel. "You must take it to a reputable dealer. You'll want to get what it's worth."

When she had finished going through the chest, Carlos helped her drape the velvet over the lid and fasten the lock.

"I knew you were the right person for the job," he told her. His tone was elated, and his eyes sparkled. "Now we'll eat dinner. I'm starving."

They hadn't made plans to eat dinner together.

"You can take me home. I'll heat up a bowl of soup and some bread."

"You need more than a bowl of soup. We'll eat here. I made dinner—it's warming in the kitchen," he replied. "There's even dessert. The cook made a chocolate cake this afternoon."

Marina had told Anna she was going out to dinner. It might look suspicious if she made her own meal at home. And she hadn't eaten since lunch.

"All right, but I don't have much time," she lied. "Bernard and Belle will be back soon. I want to say good night to them."

The Adamos' kitchen had tile counters and a wood floor. Pots and pans hung above a round table.

Carlos moved easily from the pantry to the

stove, arranging spices and olive oil. Marina was going to offer to slice the bread but changed her mind. She didn't want to prepare the meal together, the way she used to with her father. It was better if she sat at the table and waited.

Carlos tossed salad in a bowl and added olive oil and oregano. A chicken was warming in the oven, and there was a platter of grilled vegetables.

"Thank God for Desi's mother and her chickens," Carlos said, placing Marina's plate in front of her. "I'm sorry there isn't steak; it's the best I can do."

"I don't have a huge appetite," Marina said. The chicken was cooked perfectly, and the vegetables were sweet and tender. "It's delicious," she said truthfully. "You're a good cook."

"I love to cook." He grinned happily. For a moment he reminded Marina of an innocent child. "When I was a boy I spent a lot of time with the cook. My mother was busy with social engagements, and my father was always working." He ate a bite of chicken and seemed to savor it. "Lara taught me to make the best marinara sauce in Tuscany."

Carlos poured two glasses of wine, but Marina took only a small sip.

"Tell me something about yourself as a child," Carlos said, drinking his wine.

"Something about myself?" Marina asked.

"All anyone talks about is the war," Carlos reflected. "Sometimes it helps to remember a time when life was different."

She wasn't comfortable talking about her father with Carlos. It was too personal.

"I'll go first," he prompted. "When I was ten, I got my first archery set. My mother made me promise not to practice in the villa. Of course, I didn't listen," he explained. "One day I decided to aim at an orange in the kitchen. The first two tries, I hit it directly. Then I got cocky." He grinned. "I lined up three oranges and put three arrows in my bow. The first two hit their mark but the third missed. It knocked over my mother's vase. I had to sell the archery set to pay for a new vase."

Marina laughed. She couldn't think of a funny story. Even as a young girl, she had been serious.

"My mother died when I was ten. My parents' marriage had been very happy. I never heard them argue, and they often gave each other little gifts: a smart tie for my father to wear at the gallery, a new paint box for my mother's paints. I thought all parents were the same: kissing each other when they left in the morning.

"One day I was at my friend Angela's house. Angela's mother was sitting in the kitchen, crying. I never heard an adult cry so hard; I was afraid someone had died. Angela whispered that it was because of her father. He made Angela's mother cry all the time. It finally came out that her father had been seeing his secretary on the side. Angela's mother threw him out, but even then, she kept crying. It took weeks for her to sit across from Angela and me at the dinner table and smile." Marina paused and ate a piece of chicken. "That's when I decided to have my own career. I never wanted my happiness to be dependent on a man."

Carlos sipped his wine and looked at Marina thoughtfully. "Being dependent on someone is part of falling in love."

Her mind went to Nicolo. It had been wonderful to meet someone who shared her passion, someone who understood art. But Nicolo stole money from the gallery and broke her heart.

"Love can't always be trusted," Marina remarked. "The only person you can count on is yourself."

Carlos cleared away the plates. He set down two slices of cake.

"Next week I'll have more items," Carlos said, handing her a dessert fork. "We'll wait until my parents are gone and do the same thing."

"Where do the items come from? Do the sellers get the money from the sale themselves and then decide how much to donate to the partisans?" Marina asked.

"It's different in every case." Carlos shrugged. "Sometimes people give us one thing to sell, others have an attic stuffed with boxes that haven't been opened in years. It all goes toward the same cause. To pay for false papers and guns and ammunition."

Marina was thoughtful while she ate her cake. Carlos hadn't really answered her question. She was about to ask something else when he reached out and touched her wrist.

"Think what you've accomplished tonight," he offered. "If the sketch is worth as much as you believe, Sara will have more blankets, and I'll be able to get tins of meat for Eli, who grows faster than he can eat. Someone else would have sold the Giorgione to a pawnshop for the price of the frame."

Carlos's praise made her feel warm inside. He valued her, and he wasn't afraid to admit it. Perhaps she could come to trust him. They worked so well together.

They finished their cake, and Carlos drove her back to Villa I Tatti. The lights were on upstairs. Bernard and Belle must be home.

"I'll see you to the door," Carlos offered, jumping out and running over to her side of the car.

Marina climbed out after him. She turned and held out her hand.

"That's not necessary," she said formally. "Thank you for dinner, good night."

Carlos took her hand. His palm was smooth on

top of hers and she felt a sudden bolt of desire.

"Next time I'll make something other than chicken. Veal and baby potatoes," he said, moving closer. His eyes were sleek as a cat's under the full moon. "Good work deserves to be rewarded."

Marina dropped her hand. She entered the villa and closed the door.

CHAPTER EIGHT

Florence, December 1943

The next morning, Marina started working straight after breakfast. She needed to occupy her mind with something besides thoughts about valuing the art for Carlos. The thrill of discovering the Giorgione had dissolved, and she felt somehow deflated. She didn't want to wait a week to discover new treasures; she wanted to do more now. At least going through Bernard's papers would keep her busy.

Belle was there when she arrived, holding a letter. A box sat at her feet. She didn't look up until Marina nearly tripped over her.

"I didn't hear you, I was reliving my youth," she said with a smile. She wore a sweeping black skirt, and her hair was held back by a pink scarf. "This letter is to a man named Aleister Crowley. He was British but spent a lot of time in India. I recognized it right away because I wrote it on a typewriter. Aleister couldn't read my handwriting; he complained it was dreadful." She waved the letter in the air. "It's terribly risqué. When I was in my twenties, I thought it was so mature to be writing about sex. Aleister believed he was the spiritual head of an obscure religion," she continued. "Later I found out he invented the religion. It was based entirely on sex. When the affair ended, Aleister sent back all my letters. I kept them to remind myself of how young and foolish I was." She folded the letter and put it back in the box. "Thank God one of my friends warned me about him. The worst kind of friend is the one who promises not to interfere."

"What do you mean?" Marina asked curiously.

"When you're young, you think you can figure out love yourself," Belle replied. "But love comes in many shapes. Some are real, others turn out to be mirages. I had a friend, Lucy, who knew Aleister for years. One day she said I had to stop seeing him. He was going to break my heart."

"You listened to her?"

Belle shook her head. "Not at first. I started finding things: letters from other women, a bottle of perfume that wasn't mine, and I realized Lucy was right."

"What did you do?" Marina asked.

"For the first month, I was like an opium addict going through withdrawals. Then I was cured." She sat next to Marina. "Everyone keeps secrets in a relationship. Bernard still doesn't know my exact age. And with the war, we hide things from each other." Her expression grew guarded. "But the one thing you have to be honest about is your feelings. If you can't tell someone you love them because you're afraid they don't feel the same, there's no point in being together."

"I'll remember that if I ever fall in love," Marina said, smiling.

Belle stood up, and the light from the window caught her earrings. They were topaz and looked beautiful with the pink scarf.

"What pretty earrings," Marina commented.

"Bernard bought them for me in Brazil." Belle touched her ears. "I decided to wear more of my jewelry. There's no point keeping them in their cases when German soldiers could confiscate them or they could be destroyed by bombs."

"Villa I Tatti is safe," Marina said uncertainly. "Gerhard and Ludwig are protecting you. Ludwig even sent German officers away."

"War changes all the time." Belle pulled on her gloves. "But you're right. I'm becoming an old woman with my worrying."

Belle left, and Marina turned to Bernard's collection. By the time she finished, it was lunchtime. She decided to go see Desi. She still didn't know whether Desi had sent the letter to the baby's father.

Desi was sitting in her bedroom when Marina arrived.

"I'm letting out my dresses," Desi said, smoothing the fabric. "I can hardly button them."

There was color in Desi's cheeks, and her skin had a warm glow.

"You look better," Marina commented. "The pregnancy is agreeing with you."

"I feel good. Today I ate breakfast, and I was hungry again an hour later," Desi said. "Yesterday I walked around the vineyards and wasn't tired. I've made a decision. I have a great-aunt on my mother's side. I met her once, years ago. She lives in the countryside, a few hours from here. I'm going to stay with her until after the baby's born."

Marina sat up straight. Her brow furrowed.

"Does your mother know?" she inquired.

"Of course not. She'd ask all sorts of questions." Desi avoided Marina's gaze. "I already telephoned my great-aunt. She's the black sheep of the family; she gave up religion long ago. She's happy to have me."

"You can't go," Marina insisted. "You need to be with familiar people when you have the baby. Your mother, the midwife, me."

"I don't see any other options," Desi said stubbornly. She pulled harder on the thread. "I told you, my parents are strict Catholics. My mother might appear open-minded, but she cherishes her relationship with God above anything. Once she finds out about the baby, she'll tell me to leave."

"What about the baby's father?" Marina asked. "You said you wrote him a letter. He might propose. You'll be together; you won't have to worry about your parents."

"I didn't mail it," Desi admitted. "I told you,

we can't get married. It would be for nothing."

"You can get married if you love each other."

"Perhaps if it wasn't wartime." Desi shrugged. "But not now."

Marina's eyes met Desi's. "Because he's German?"

Desi dropped the needle and thread.

"How do you know?" she gasped.

Marina told her about seeing the name on the envelope. "I didn't mean to snoop; I was sitting at your dressing table."

Desi's eyes flashed. Marina had never seen Desi angry before.

"You looked on purpose."

"I was curious," Marina conceded. "I only wanted to help you. I never suspected he was German. How did you meet?"

"At a wine shop in Florence," Desi began. Her eyes had a far-off expression, and she hugged her arms to her chest.

"I asked the sales clerk for a good bottle of Chianti. Our vineyards grow Sangiovese grapes; the wine ripens very slowly. Chianti is produced along the coast and has a fruitier taste. Peter overheard me. He suggested a bottle of Chianti Classico," she continued. "His family owns a vineyard in the Rhine Valley in Germany. They produce Riesling. He knew so much about wine; we couldn't stop talking." She folded her hands. "I didn't mind that he was German. Italy and

Germany were on the same side then." Her voice became anguished. "I should have paid more attention to what Hitler was doing, and what was happening to the Jews."

"Does he agree with Hitler?" Marina asked.

"Of course not!" Desi exclaimed. "But he's German. We could never get married."

"Perhaps not now, but the war can't last forever," Marina said. "He should know about the baby."

"What difference would it make?" Desi sighed. "I have to leave before my mother knows the truth."

"You'll have to tell your parents sometime," Marina reasoned. "You can't be gone forever."

"No one knows when the war will end. When it does, I'll find some kind of job. The baby and I will start a new life together," Desi replied. Her mouth was set in a firm line. "Besides, even if Peter didn't mind about the baby, his parents might not accept me. This is the only way."

Marina was silent. She couldn't lose her best friend. And what kind of life would it be for Desi, taking care of a new baby while living with a great-aunt she barely knew? But how could Marina stop her?

Suddenly she had an idea. But she knew Desi would never agree to it, so it would have to be a surprise.

"Why don't we go into Florence today before

you leave?" Marina suggested. "I'll buy you lunch, and we'll shop for baby clothes."

Marina stood up and took Desi's arm before she could protest.

"We'll take your car. I'll drive, and you can make a list of what the baby needs," Marina said. "I don't know how to knit, and all babies should have cute things to wear."

They drove through the Duomo neighborhood, past Santa Maria Novella. The Allied bombing in September had left gaping holes in the streets. Marina was grateful to see the Uffizi Gallery, as glorious as she remembered it.

Marina parked on a leafy street. Palazzi had been turned into elegant apartment buildings. She suspected that inside their gates they had gracious courtyards and green lawns. The sun made patterns on the leaves; a bird landed on a fountain. It was so pretty and peaceful. As if the war didn't exist.

"What are we doing here?" Desi asked, alarmed. "I thought we were going shopping."

Marina folded her arms. She turned to Desi.

"This is the address on the envelope," she said. "You're going to see Peter first. Then we'll go shopping."

Desi sat back in her seat, her eyes wide with horror.

"You tricked me!" she exclaimed.

"You were never going to tell him about the baby," Marina replied, her heart racing. She had never done anything like this before, but she didn't want Desi to have the baby all alone.

"It's his baby too," Marina continued. "You can decide what to do together."

"I can't believe you'd do such a thing!" Desi was almost shouting now. "You had no right; we've only known each other a short while. It's my life, and you shouldn't have interfered!" Her eyes flashed and she crossed her arms. "You can't make me go inside."

Marina hated to see Desi so upset. But she couldn't let her friend become estranged from her parents. And there was no one else to help her.

"I'm sorry. I should have asked you first, but I was afraid you'd say no," Marina said. "I don't want you to have to raise the baby by yourself if there's another way." She paused. "And I don't want to lose you as a friend."

"All right, I'll go in," Desi relented. "But you have to come with me."

"Are you sure?" Marina asked.

Desi opened the car door and gritted her teeth. "I'm sure. I don't have the courage to face him alone."

The apartment was on the third floor. A gilt staircase led to a door with a brass knocker. Desi's hands were trembling, and her eyes were

135

as big as saucers. She glanced at Marina for encouragement, then put her hand on the knocker.

A minute passed, and the door didn't open. Desi knocked again. This time, they heard footsteps.

A young man answered. He had blond hair and a slight build with a dimple on his chin. Marina could see immediately why Desi was attracted to him. He had the kindest eyes she'd ever seen. When he realized it was Desi, his face lit up as if he had received the most wonderful prize.

"Desi, what are you doing here?" Peter gasped.

"This is my friend Marina," Desi introduced them. "Can we come inside?"

Peter ushered them into the living room. It was very masculine, with dark sofas and a deep red Persian rug. There was a bookshelf full of books and a desk stood under the window.

"Please sit down." Peter waved at the sofa. "Can I get you something to drink?"

Marina shook her head. Desi said nothing. She sat down and looked at her hands.

Peter walked over to the desk. He picked up a pile of envelopes.

"I've been writing you letters, one for every day we've been apart." He handed them to Desi. "You told me not to contact you in case your parents found out about us. But I couldn't help it. Writing them was the only way to get through the days. I've dreamed about seeing you so many times, I'm afraid you're a vision." He sat down and took her hand in his. "I have to touch you, to make sure you're real."

Desi riffled through the stack. She glanced up at Peter in surprise.

"You wrote all of these?" she said in awe.

He nodded. "These are only half of them. The rest I tore up as soon as I wrote them. I didn't want to write about my own misery, I only wanted to say how much I loved you. Every moment apart was like a year. I've hardly slept, and I couldn't eat."

Desi's eyes filled with tears. Marina had never seen her friend look so beautiful, like the birth of Venus as she emerges from her shell.

"I wrote to you too, even though I was breaking my own rules. But I didn't send the letters," Desi volunteered. "The thing is . . ."

Desi stopped. She looked at Marina, and Marina nodded in encouragement.

"The thing is," Desi began again, "I'm pregnant."

Peter stood up. His brow furrowed, and his mouth was set in a firm line. He paced around the room, and for a moment Marina was frightened. What if Peter rejected Desi? She might not recover, and it would be Marina's fault.

Then he sat next to Desi and put his arms around her. He didn't say anything, but when he lifted his face it was wet with tears.

"We're having a baby," he whispered.

"I can't have the baby at home; my mother

would be furious," Desi said, as if she hadn't heard him. "So I'm going away for good. I'm going to live with a great-aunt a few hours from here. You don't have to worry about me, I'll take care of myself and the baby."

Peter rubbed his forehead. He looked perplexed.

"You never mentioned a great-aunt before," he said, sounding anguished. "I'd take care of you myself, but I can't."

Desi's face flushed. She inched away.

"I didn't expect you to," she said quickly. "Your parents would never allow it. I shouldn't have come at all. We'll go now . . ."

Before she could say more, Peter took her in his arms.

"It's not about my parents. I don't care what they think." He took a deep breath. "I have to leave Florence. I've been conscripted into the German army."

Marina gasped. The pain in Desi's eyes was as sharp as a knife.

"Into the army?" Desi repeated.

"I received the letter a few days ago," Peter said. "I've been lucky so far, but I can't avoid it any longer. Hitler has lost so many men fighting on the Eastern Front. If I don't go, I'll be tried and possibly executed."

Desi's mouth trembled, and tears glimmered in her eyes.

"When do you leave?" she asked.

"Tomorrow." He dropped his eyes. His voice was low. "I was going to write a goodbye letter. Even if I never sent the other letters, I couldn't disappear without an explanation." He gulped. "I take the train to Berlin in the morning."

"Even better that I go away then," Desi insisted, but Marina could hear the heartbreak in her voice. "You won't have to think about us."

"There must be another way. You must promise to stay here." Peter touched Desi's cheek. "You love your parents. I don't want to imagine you in a strange place, trying to cope with a baby alone."

Marina excused herself to the powder room to give Desi and Peter some time alone. When she returned, Desi had dried her eyes, and she and Peter sat on the sofa together.

"I promise I'll take care of Desi," Marina assured him. "We're good friends."

Peter rested his hand on Desi's stomach. His mouth trembled as he spoke.

"When I return, I'll tell your parents I'll do anything if they allow us to get married." He reached up and touched Desi's cheek. "I love you, and I love our baby; I promise we'll be together."

Desi took Peter's hand and pressed it deeper against her skin. He put his arms around her, and they embraced.

"I love you too," Desi whispered.

• • •

Marina and Desi were about to get back in the car when Marina recognized a familiar figure walking toward them. It was Gerhard.

"Marina, this is a surprise!" he greeted her. "I just picked up a pastry; I was walking to work. The German consulate is around the corner."

"This is my friend Desi," Marina introduced them. "It's such a pretty day. We decided to drive into Florence for some lunch and shopping."

"I'm lucky that I live so close to my office," Gerhard acknowledged. "There are many cafés nearby, and I almost never have to drive." He smiled at both of them. "Let me know next time you are in Florence and I'll invite you both for lunch."

"We'll make sure to take you up on that." Marina smiled back.

They chatted with Gerhard for a few more minutes and then said goodbye.

After lunch, Desi was quiet on the drive back to the villa. Marina tried to imagine what was going through her mind.

"I apologize again for not telling you my plan," Marina said.

Desi turned to her. "I'm glad you didn't. I've missed Peter." Her face crumpled. "It's just . . ."

Marina felt as if she could read Desi's thoughts. "Don't worry too much about Peter. He has you and the baby to live for. He'll survive the war."

"That doesn't count for anything. All soldiers have people to live for." Desi gulped as if she couldn't get enough air. "Donato loved his family more than anything. But what if I made it worse? What if Peter is so busy thinking of us, he becomes careless and gets killed? I'll never forgive myself."

Marina reached over and squeezed Desi's hand.

"You have to believe he'll be all right. There's no other way," she said. "And you have to tell your mother about the baby," she went on. "Perhaps she can talk to God, and she and God can come to some kind of agreement."

Desi sighed heavily. "You've never heard my mother talk to God. It would make you afraid to ever do anything wrong. But you're right, I don't want to go away. Perhaps I can convince her to let me stay and have the baby."

"We've done enough for one day. I promised you lunch and shopping. I intend to keep that promise. My father and I once ate at a restaurant on Via del Corso. We'll go there. I remember it had the creamiest cappuccinos."

After lunch, they browsed in the shops. Marina found a pretty shawl for Desi and a yellow sweater for the baby with a matching knitted cap.

Marina tried to make conversation on the drive home, but Desi sat silently staring out the window. Marina worried about her friend. Was Desi already missing Peter? Had she truly forgiven Marina for lying about the reason they drove to Florence? At least Desi had promised to talk to her mother. Surely Desi wouldn't have to go away.

Later that evening Marina was sitting in the living room when Belle came in, pulling off her gloves.

"It's so cold outside. I'm going to ask Anna to make something hot to eat and drink," Belle said. "Would you like something?"

Marina shook her head. "No, thank you. Desi and I ate at a restaurant in Florence. Guess who we ran into? Gerhard Wolf."

"Gerhard!" Belle exclaimed, sitting next to the fireplace. "I ran into someone too—Carlos. His parents have invited us to dinner tomorrow. It will just be a few neighbors." She smiled at Marina. "Carlos specifically asked that you come."

Marina wondered if he had already received new items for her to value. She kept her face completely blank.

"Of course, it sounds like a lovely evening."

CHAPTER NINE

Florence, December 1943

Marina opened the jewelry case on her dressing table. She had borrowed one of Belle's dresses to wear to dinner at the Adamos' villa: a glamorous floor-length silver gown with a low neckline. Now she just needed a piece of jewelry to go with it.

She used to love looking through her mother's jewelry when she was a child. After she died, her father put all her mother's jewels in a velvet case, which Marina kept in her dressing table. She had forgotten to pack it when she fled Rome. She would have to write to Paolo and ask him to send it to her.

Belle entered after a quick knock.

"That dress looks stunning on you." She studied Marina approvingly. "The silver brings out the sheen in your hair."

"Do you think so?" Marina turned around. "My neck feels so bare. I was just looking for a necklace. I don't have anything that would be suitable for a dinner party."

"Borrow something from me," Belle suggested. "My jewelry is in my dressing room. You're welcome to go through it."

"I couldn't do that," Marina objected. "I might choose something that's too valuable."

"Nonsense. It wouldn't be in my jewelry box if it wasn't meant to be worn." Belle glanced at Marina's reflection in the mirror and smiled. "And remember, you have youth; that's the best accessory of all."

Bernard and Belle shared a suite at Villa I Tatti. The bedroom was decorated with silk wallpaper. There was a canopied bed and a white rug that was as soft as a mink coat. The writing desk was in the style of Louis XVI, with inlaid wood and a narrow drawer. Bernard bought it at an auction in Paris as a present for Belle.

Marina wondered what it would be like to be Belle. To have had lovers and a rewarding career. Then she thought about what Belle didn't have: a husband and children. Her mind went to Desi, who was determined to raise her child even if she didn't have Peter. And Marina's own father, who only needed his family and the gallery to be happy.

For a moment, she felt a terrible emptiness. She didn't have any of those things. When would she have the money to open a gallery? And what if she could never trust a man again? Surely all men weren't like Nicolo.

She shook off her mood. She should be happy. She had friends, and that night she had a dinner party to attend.

Belle's jewelry was fanned out on the dressing table. Padded drawers were lined with necklaces. Satin cases held bracelets, and a music box contained a selection of rings.

Marina chose a topaz necklace. It would look perfect with the topaz earrings Belle had been wearing the day before, she decided. But she couldn't find them. She glanced around the room, thinking that perhaps Belle had left them on the bathroom counter or bedside table. But they were nowhere to be seen. That was odd. Belle was so organized. Marina selected a pair of gold earrings instead, then went back to her room to get her cape.

It was strange standing in the entry of the Adamos' villa as if she hadn't been there before. Marina was reminded of how grand it was. The sweeping staircase led to the second floor, and chandeliers dropped from the ceiling. There were plush carpets and gilt furniture and a marble bust by Lombardo. One room had crimson-colored silk drapes and large mirrors resting against the walls. Everywhere there were crystal vases and marble statues.

Desi was standing next to the fireplace in the living room. She wore an empire-style dress that hid her waist, and her hair was tied back. Marina noticed how young she looked. Almost like a child playing dress-up.

"You're frowning," Desi said when Marina joined her. "Is my lipstick too much?"

"I was thinking how young and pretty you look," Marina commented.

"Every day I'm getting bigger." Desi sighed, glancing at her dress. "This evening my mother was looking at me curiously. I felt like one of her cows."

Marina squeezed Desi's hand. "You look nothing like a cow, and I'm sure she can't tell."

"I know I have to tell her soon," Desi said. "It's becoming hard to hide. I hope staying is the right decision." She sighed again. "She'll be horribly disappointed. I'll have to go to confession every week."

"It will be worth it," Marina assured her.

Bernard and Belle joined them. Bernard looked distinguished in a gray suit, and Belle was unusually sedate in a full-length silk gown and ruby earrings. Only a men's watch with a gold face and leather band gave away her unique style.

"Marina, you look lovely this evening," Bernard greeted her. "It's nice to see you away from the library. I'm afraid I've given you too much to do."

"I'm moving too slowly," she said with a smile. "Every piece in the collection is fascinating; I don't want to leave anything behind."

Bernard chuckled. "That's been my problem for the last thirty years."

Carlos's parents appeared, and Marina understood why Belle wasn't wearing one of her more outrageous outfits. Carlos's mother, Alba, was the picture of reserved elegance. She was slender, and her chestnut-brown hair was cut in the latest style. She wore a navy evening gown that crossed at the waist and a diamond brooch. Carlos's father, Matteo, seemed the opposite of Carlos. He was very serious and stood silently while his wife entertained the guests.

Marina excused herself and went to find the powder room. On the way back she passed a study with a distinctive bronze statue near the window. She stepped inside the room to examine it.

"Yes, that's an authentic Ghiberti," a voice said behind her.

Lorenzo Ghiberti was one of the most renowned of the Renaissance sculptors. His bronze doors of the Florence Baptistery were so magnificent Michelangelo himself deemed them "the Gates of Paradise."

Marina turned to see Carlos standing before her in a dinner jacket. His hair was slicked back from his forehead, and the signet ring on his left hand was gleaming.

"What a handsome ring," she commented. "My father wore a signet ring; he almost never took it off."

"I'm the same way." Carlos held it up. His

147

initials were engraved on the ring in sloping cursive. "I feel naked when it's not on my finger."

Marina examined the ring admiringly, then returned her attention to the statue.

"We studied Ghiberti sculptures at university. I've never seen one outside of a museum. And I noticed a Lombardo in the living room."

"My mother doesn't have her own taste, so she pays others to have it for her." Carlos's tone was biting. "There's a Della Robbia in my parents' bedroom. Personally, I wouldn't want to sleep next to a statue with three heads."

"You shouldn't talk badly about your mother," Marina admonished him. "There's nothing wrong with paying other people to choose one's artwork. Many of the clients at the gallery trusted my father and me to choose their pieces."

"You're right," Carlos agreed. "I'm sorry. I always get flustered at my parents' dinner parties. Whatever I say comes out wrong. I didn't mean it in a derogatory way."

Marina smiled at Carlos. She wasn't used to seeing him nervous.

"Parents always seem difficult to their children. I'm sure yours are lovely."

Carlos walked to the bar and poured two glasses of Scotch.

"You might want one of these before dinner," he said, offering her one. "If my mother was passionate about something, she would be easier to talk to. And my father is worse. He doesn't even try to engage me. Except when it comes to lumber. I tried, I really did, but I don't care about pine trees." He sipped his drink. "I suppose that's also why I joined the partisans. To my parents, I'm a failure. My father wants a son who'll take over the business, and my mother wants someone to tell her she resembles Hedy Lamarr."

Marina tried to imagine not sharing her father's love of art. What would they have talked about over dinner? Where would they have gone on the weekends if not to museums?

"I don't believe you," she tried again. "I'm sure your parents are proud of you."

"For what? Delivering wood?" Carlos said sharply. "Let me show you something."

Marina followed him down the hallway. At the end there was a rectangular-shaped room. Children's books lined the bookshelf, and there was a box of dominoes and a backgammon set on a small table in the corner.

A row of pictures leaned against the wall. They were landscapes: A village surrounded by a circle of fir trees. A forest in the autumn, the tops of the trees tinged with gold.

"This used to be the playroom, but I use it for painting now. When I was eighteen, I started painting landscapes. I attended art school, and Sara's husband, Benito, was one of my teachers. He said I was talented," Carlos explained. "I thought my parents would be pleased. Instead my father gave me a lecture, informing me that art was something you put on your wall. 'A successful man owns forests, he doesn't paint them,' he said." Carlos grimaced. "It was the longest conversation we'd ever had."

"Oh, Carlos, I'm sorry. They're wonderful," said Marina, studying them closely.

"Thank you, but no one is going to see them except the housekeeper." He shrugged. "I shouldn't feel sorry for myself. An entire ghetto of Jews could fit into this house, and we have more than enough food and firewood and clothing. Perhaps in a way I'm lucky there's a war." He jiggled the drink in his glass. "I'm not the only one giving up my dreams."

On the other wall, there were a few excellent copies of the great masters. Marina spotted Raphael's *Three Graces* and a painting she recognized as a copy of Titian's *Venus of Urbino*.

"What are these?" she asked.

"I tried copying a few paintings," Carlos explained.

"They're incredible, but why would you do that?" she asked curiously.

"The Nazis are pillaging paintings from museums. They say they're transporting them to Germany for safekeeping in case of Allied bombings." His face darkened. "But what if they're never returned to Italy? It would be better if the museums had copies, and the real paintings were already in hiding."

Marina thought of the priceless artwork at the Uffizi in Florence, at Villa Borghese in Rome and the Doge's Palace in Venice. The thought of losing them to the Germans made her stomach turn.

Carlos interrupted her thoughts. "We've looked at enough of my art for one night. We better go to dinner or I'll never hear the end of it."

Marina sat at the long table, eating a spoonful of pappa al pomodoro. She had eaten the traditional Tuscan soup made with bread, tomatoes, and olive oil when she and her father visited Bernard years ago, and it had been one of her favorite dishes. But that night, she could barely taste the rich flavors. It was impossible to enjoy her food when the discussion was all about war.

"In September, the Germans made a raid on Bari, on the coast," Bernard was saying. "The attack only lasted an hour, but one thousand servicemen and more than one thousand civilians died. There's a rumor that the Germans used mustard gas in their bombs. The Allies haven't confirmed it. They don't want word to get out and others to follow their lead."

The conversation moved to Hitler's attacks in Greece. The massacre in Kefalonia had left hundreds of women and children dead.

Marina was relieved when Alba changed the subject.

Alba picked up her wineglass and turned to Marina. "Belle said you were at university in Rome."

"I studied art history and worked in a gallery with my father," Marina answered. "After the war, I'm going to open my own gallery."

Alba pursed her lips.

"A woman can't run a gallery," she said, perplexed. "She has to get married."

"Why can't I do both?" Marina asked. "Since the war began, many women work."

"But that's because the men are fighting," Alba argued. "When they return, they'll want wives and children. A woman belongs in the home with her family."

Marina was about to answer when Belle interrupted.

"Not all women," she insisted. "I've managed to avoid having a family for twenty years. Bernard hasn't thrown me out yet." Belle smiled provocatively around the table. "I predict after the war women will find a new freedom. Perhaps one day all world leaders will be women who solve their problems sensibly instead of behaving like boys playing with toy soldiers."

The table was quiet. Marina sent Belle a silent thank-you.

After dinner, Alba suggested a game of

charades, and everyone moved to the living room.

"Dinner was wonderful, but I'm afraid Belle and I have to leave." Bernard took Belle's arm. "I have a phone call with a client."

"I'll go with you." Marina went to get her cape.

"You should stay," Belle insisted. "Carlos can bring you home."

"It will be my pleasure," Carlos agreed. "Now, let's plan our first charade. I refuse to lose to Desi. She always beat me at charades when we were children."

Later, after Desi and her mother had soundly beaten them all at charades, Marina sat in the front seat of Carlos's truck. When Carlos pulled up in front of Villa I Tatti, the lights were dimmed. Bernard and Belle had gone to bed.

"Thank you for bringing me home," Marina said.

"Oh, I'll take any excuse to leave the house after a dinner party. My parents always end up arguing."

"What do they argue about?"

"My mother wants reassurance that she did a fabulous job. She gets upset if my father doesn't give it to her." He shrugged. "So then she turns to me. I didn't want to spend the next hour complimenting her on the way the cook prepared the chicken."

"Your mother isn't that bad," Marina said. "She's used to entertaining. The war interrupted all that. It must be hard to live in a beautiful villa and not be able to have dinner parties other than with a few neighbors."

"How can you offer sympathy when innocent people are being killed all over Europe?" His eyes flashed. "Just because soldiers haven't stormed the villa and pointed a gun at her head, she thinks the war is something that exists only on the other side of a radio."

"Don't talk like that; she's your mother," Marina said. "And you're working with the partisans. You could be putting your parents in danger too."

Carlos turned to her. His voice was hard. "That's what makes it so difficult to stomach. I can't sit around playing charades when people are dying. I have to make a difference."

"You are," Marina reminded him. "Because of you, Jews and prisoners of war are reaching the border and being given the hope of a new life."

Carlos leaned back against the car seat.

"I don't like the things my mother said to you. How does she know what you want to do with your life?"

"Most women her age are the same. My mother put my father and me before her art. Belle is unique."

Carlos was silent. Even in the low light of the truck, she could see his brooding expression.

"I'm glad you came tonight," he confessed. "I wanted to get to know you better."

"What do you mean?" Marina asked, frowning.

"You have so many sides: the young woman who's focused on a career, the friend who'd do anything for Desi. Yet there's a part of you that's closed off. I thought if for one night everyone dressed up and drank wine, you might let your guard down."

Marina was flattered.

"There's nothing intriguing that you don't already know about me," she assured him. "I'm like you. I hate the war and want to do whatever I can to help."

He didn't answer. Instead he leaned forward and kissed her. It was only a brief kiss, but his lips were warm, and it left her feeling oddly breathless.

"What was that for?" she asked, trying to hide her surprise.

"You're kind to my mother even when she's rude. And you had the courage to leave Rome and start a whole new life. You're better than I could ever hope to be."

A light went on upstairs. Belle must be checking that she was home.

Marina opened the door and stepped out of the truck, then turned back to Carlos.

"None of us see exactly who we are when we look in the mirror," she told him.

CHAPTER TEN

Florence, December 1943

A couple of days after the dinner party, Marina woke to snow blanketing the valley. The trees were white, and the ancient stone walls of the villages were dusted with snow. Marina stood on the balcony admiring the scene. It was as beautiful as any painting.

Carlos was away again on partisan business so there were no new items for Marina to value. She decided to borrow Desi's car and run some errands in Florence. She wanted to buy a small gift for Desi to cheer her up before she told her mother about the baby.

She edged into a parking space on Via de' Tornabuoni, the most exclusive shopping district in Florence, and went looking for a jewelry store.

"Can I help you?" A man glanced up from the counter when she entered.

The jewelry shop was no bigger than a woman's dressing room. It had dark green carpet and gold wallpaper. Diamond necklaces sat in a glass case, next to a display of emerald and ruby bracelets. Sets of pearls were looped around a wooden block, a section for watches beside them.

"I've never seen so many wonderful things in

one shop," Marina exclaimed. "I was looking for a gift. Something pretty but not too expensive."

"I have many fine pieces." The man waved at the glass. "I've owned the shop for twenty years. Before the war, the showroom was always filled with wealthy Americans. The goldsmiths of Florence have been renowned for centuries." He shrugged. "But since the war began, I sell almost nothing."

"The tourists will come back when the war ends," Marina said hopefully.

"Who knows when that will be, and how any of us will survive until then?"

Marina wished she could afford one of the more expensive pieces: a honeycomb-cut gold pendant with diamonds or a gold ring engraved with delicate flowers.

Finally she settled on a silver charm bracelet. She was about to leave when a pair of earrings caught her eye. They looked exactly like Belle's topaz earrings.

"Could I see those earrings?" she said, pointing to them.

He took them out of the case and handed them to Marina.

"They're from Brazil," he commented. His smile returned and he was more friendly. "You have excellent taste."

They were Belle's earrings. Marina was sure of it.

"Where did you get these?" she asked.

"A customer brought them in." He reached into the jewelry case and took out a bracelet. "She brought this too. The bracelet is entirely made of rubies."

Marina wondered why Belle was selling her jewelry. Villa I Tatti and its contents must be worth a fortune. And Belle had her own money, surely.

"How much are the earrings?" Marina asked.

"The earrings are five thousand lire," he said.

At least the jeweler was asking a good price. But she still didn't understand.

"They're lovely, but I can't afford them." Marina handed them back to the jeweler.

"That's a pity." He shrugged, returning them to the case. "Who knows how much lire will be worth by the time the Germans leave? Jewelry will always keep its value."

Marina drove back to Villa I Tatti. The door to Bernard and Belle's suite was closed when Marina went upstairs. She wanted to ask Belle why she was selling her earrings—perhaps Belle was in trouble. But she didn't want to intrude in case Belle wanted to keep the sale private. Marina would find a way to bring it up in conversation later. For now, she put the charm bracelet in her bedside drawer and walked out to the library.

She had been working for a few hours when the library door opened. It was Bernard.

"Marina, I didn't know you were here. I can come back if I'm disturbing you."

She closed the book she had been studying and smiled. "Then you'll have to wait for ages. I seem to live here these days."

"It's wonderful, isn't it? All this history." Bernard waved at the bookshelves. "It makes me remember that nothing lasts forever. One day the war will end. Hitler will be gone, and the world will be sane again." He smiled wanly. "In America we believe the good guy always wins. Americans think life is a Hollywood movie."

"My friends and I used to go to the cinema on the weekends before the war. We were in love with Gary Cooper," Marina reflected. "I can't imagine ever having fun like that again."

Bernard rubbed his beard.

"Things are getting worse all the time. I went to a villa near Arezzo today. My client had an original Correggio he wanted valued. When I arrived, the villa was empty. German soldiers had showed up earlier and forced the family out. All their valuables were gone."

"Where did the family go?" Marina asked, horrified.

"To a deportation center nearby," he said. "The rugs had been rolled up, and there were hooks on the walls where paintings used to be. The family was Jewish. From the deportation centers, they'll be put on trains. There are rumors about

159

concentration camps. When the prisoners arrive, they are gassed to death. Mothers and children are separated first, then sent to the gas chambers to die."

Marina recalled Carlos talking about the deportation centers, but this was the first she had heard of concentration camps. Her skin crawled, and she fought the urge to throw up. What Bernard was saying couldn't be true. It was impossible to imagine anyone doing such a thing, especially to children.

"How did the soldiers know a Jewish family lived there?" She looked at Bernard with wide eyes.

"Have you heard of Villa Triste?"

Marina shook her head.

"It's the SS headquarters on Via Bolognese in Florence. They take partisans there after they've been captured. They're tortured so badly that sometimes they become informants.

"The cells are made to hold no more than six, but lately there are as many as thirty prisoners at a time. They sleep on the floor and on top of one another. There are no blankets, and disease is so rife that many die in their sleep. Once they enter Villa Triste, most prisoners never leave. The Germans can keep them as long as they want."

"What do you mean?" Marina asked, trying to keep the anxiety out of her voice. She fought back an image of Carlos imprisoned in the conditions Bernard described.

"The partisans are part of the Italian underground, so there's no record of them," Bernard replied. "They simply disappear."

The book in Marina's hands fell to the floor. When she picked it up, her hands were shaking. She wanted to ask Bernard more questions, but she was afraid the tremor in her voice might give her away.

"Are you all right?" Bernard asked. "You're very pale. I'm sorry, I didn't mean to upset you. But those are the realities of what's happening around us. It's better that you know the truth."

"You're right." Marina nodded. "I know some of the things that are happening. I saw my father murdered. It doesn't make it easier to hear. To picture women and children being killed that way . . ." Her voice trailed off.

"We've talked about the war enough for one day. You should go inside the villa and warm up," Bernard suggested. "Carlos delivered some wood and there's a fire in the living room."

"Carlos?" she repeated. Perhaps he had a new piece for her.

He nodded. "I just saw him."

"I think I will go inside. I've been out here so long; my fingers are stiff from going through the collection."

As Marina walked to the door, Bernard called after her.

"I didn't mean to upset you. You don't have to

worry about partisans here." He smiled warmly. "Belle and I only surround ourselves with people we trust. You're perfectly safe."

Belle was seated on the sofa in the living room. Her bright smile was missing, and her forehead was creased. Across from her sat a man in an SS uniform.

"Marina, I was going to come and get you," Belle greeted her. "It's too cold to be anywhere besides in front of a fire."

She folded her hands in her lap. "May I introduce Captain Siegfried Bonner? He recently arrived from Berlin."

Captain Bonner had closely cropped brown hair, piercing green eyes, and an aquiline nose. He wore the Gestapo red armband on his sleeve, and his pointed cap lay beside him.

Belle's whole manner seemed different; Marina sensed something was off. There was none of the warmth heard in her tone when she spoke to Ludwig or the respect she showed for Gerhard. Instead Belle resembled a lion tamer circling a new animal.

"It's a pleasure to meet you, Fräulein." Captain Bonner stood up. "I've been in Florence for only a few weeks, but I'm eager to discover everything it has to offer. This is my first time in Italy; it's more pleasant than I'd hoped. Being in the birthplace of the greatest artists has its

162

own pleasures. I pride myself on being a bit of a collector." He turned to Belle. "Nothing like Bernard, of course—I'm just starting out. I'm merely an amateur who appreciates beauty."

"Captain Bonner is doing a little tour of Tuscany," Belle said before Marina could respond. "I told him there's not much to see in winter. He should come back in the spring, when the fields are in bloom and the air smells of cherry blossoms."

"I'm sure I'll return before then," Captain Bonner said. "But it's the museums and galleries in Florence that excite me. Even the führer appreciates art from all over Europe. I'm told his collection at Berchtesgaden is becoming quite impressive."

Marina tried not to show the alarm she felt at his words. The thought of Italy's great art pieces being housed at the Eagle's Nest, Hitler's private chalet in the Bavarian Alps, was almost too much to bear.

Captain Bonner left, and Belle returned to the living room.

"He's as pleasant as a cobra," Belle said, pouring a cup of coffee.

"Why was he here?" Marina asked shakily.

"He said it was a courtesy call. But I don't believe him." She pursed her lips. "Don't worry. I'll have a word with Gerhard. Gerhard has been here a lot longer."

"You said Gerhard doesn't have any influence over the SS in Florence."

"He can still make Captain Bonner's life difficult." Belle stood up. She seemed distracted. "This room feels stuffy. I'll ask Anna to air it out and we can move upstairs. I want your opinion on a sweater I bought Bernard for Christmas."

That afternoon, Marina strode through the villa's gardens on her way to give Desi the charm bracelet. She remembered when she first arrived at Villa I Tatti how taken she had been with the gardens' beauty: the terraced lawns, the hanging trellises and marble fountains. Villa I Tatti in winter had its own majesty: the mist settling over the hills, the stark trees waiting for new buds. But crossing the grounds now, worrying about Captain Bonner and Desi, the winter landscape felt dangerous and forbidding.

Desi was in the kitchen when Marina arrived, eating a bowl of soup and some bread.

"I was just having lunch," Desi greeted Marina. "Would you like some? I made ribollita—it's a Tuscan soup with bread and every vegetable in our garden. I thought I'd distract myself by cooking. I was going to tell my mother about the baby this morning, but the priest, Father Garboni, had a small stroke. My mother went to be with him."

"It smells delicious, but I'm not hungry,"

Marina said, sitting opposite her at the table. "I hope Father Garboni will be all right."

"The doctor said he's likely to recover, but you never know," Desi fretted. "Father Garboni has known me since I was a child. He's the only one who could convince my mother it's okay for me to have a baby. If Father Garboni is replaced, the new priest might not have any sympathy for my situation."

"You can't worry about everything. It isn't good for you, and it isn't good for the baby." Marina handed her a small box. "I brought you this. It's a little gift to cheer you up."

Desi opened it and smiled. She took out the charm bracelet and fastened it around her wrist. "Thank you. It's lovely. I appreciate the thought, and I wish it could make my fears go away." A tear glimmered in her eye. "For years, I've dreamed of being married with a baby. I'd give birth here at home, and my husband would be waiting anxiously with my father in the living room. The midwife and my mother would be beside me, and when the baby was born—a sweet little girl with tufts of dark hair or a handsome boy with the bluest eyes—my mother would call out over the staircase. My husband and father would rush upstairs, and we'd all be so happy."

"One day you'll have all those things," Marina promised her, with more conviction than she felt.

Marina thought about all her new friends.

Bernard was transporting hidden art pieces across the border to Switzerland, and Belle had sold her jewelry. Carlos was gone again, involved in partisan work. She felt an overwhelming sadness at how the war had consumed their little community. They each carried their own burdens and fears; they were impossible to escape.

She tried to reassure herself that things couldn't go on like that; at some point life would surely change.

She hugged Desi. "The war is like the snow on the hills during winter—it can't last forever. Spring will come, and soon everything will be green again, you'll see."

A few days passed, and Marina didn't hear from Carlos. He had warned her that partisan business often took him away unexpectedly, but she couldn't help but wonder when he would return.

Desi was preoccupied and on edge. She still hadn't told her mother about the baby, and she was anxious about Peter. Marina didn't want to disturb her with her own worries, but she felt lonely.

Toward the end of the week, Marina finally received a message from Carlos. He asked her to meet him in the garden shed on the grounds of Villa I Tatti. The shed was used to store gardening tools; hardly anyone came out there. It was early evening, so Marina dressed warmly in a long skirt and wool sweater, boots, and her thickest gloves.

She stepped inside, her eyes adjusting to the half-light. The shed looked different from when she'd last poked her head inside. The bare floor had been covered by a rug, which was scattered with cushions. There was a small table covered with a tablecloth.

Carlos stood near the window holding two shopping bags.

"Why did you ask me to meet you here?" she asked, motioning around the space. "And what's all this? None of this belongs here."

"Don't worry, no one will see it. I'll remove everything after we finish." He pointed to the different objects. "The rug is from my bedroom. The cushions are from our old playroom, and I carted the table down from the attic."

"I don't understand."

"I wanted to do something special to thank you for valuing the art pieces. It's already made a huge difference. I brought a special dinner. Bread and olives and cheese." He smiled. "And a Sangiovese, of course. Desi gave me a bottle from her parents' cellar. And Desi also made a cheesecake from her mother's recipe."

"You did all this for me?" Marina's eyes were wide. "It's the nicest thing anyone has ever done."

"I can think of nicer things. Pretty dresses,

perfume for that lovely neck. But there's a war, and it's the best I could do."

Carlos cut thick slices of bread and poured two glasses of wine. They sat cross-legged on the cushions and ate.

"The bread and provolone are delicious," Marina said. They were on their second glass of wine, and she felt warm and happy.

"I love putting together a meal, creating dishes from a handful of ingredients," Carlos said. "But it isn't the same as painting. The happiest I've been was when I attended art school."

"Were you really an artist's model?" she asked teasingly.

He shrugged. "My parents wouldn't pay my art school fees. I was a terrible model though. I couldn't sit still, and the dust in the studio made me sneeze."

"So how did you pay the fees?" she asked.

Carlos's eyes darkened.

"I didn't. I quit school. I crawled home like a dog with my tail between my legs, took my old room back, and started working in the lumber business."

"I'm sorry." Marina wished she hadn't brought it up. "That must have been hard."

"It was going to be temporary, just until I'd saved enough money to return to art school. But then the war began. If I'd stopped working for my father, I would have had to fight in the army.

That's why I joined the partisans—so I wouldn't be a failure and a coward."

"You're not a failure or a coward," Marina argued. "Look at what you're doing for Sara and her children. And you're a good friend to Desi."

Carlos put down his wineglass. He drew Marina close and kissed her.

For a moment, she thought of holding back. How would this affect their working together? But the kiss was long and sweet, and she didn't want it to end.

"What are you thinking?" he asked when they parted.

"Only that it feels strange to kiss when there's a war going on. Who knows what will happen tomorrow?"

He traced her mouth with his fingers.

"That's why kissing is important." He kissed her again. "It's like the food and the wine but even better. We have to create a little bit of happiness while we can."

CHAPTER ELEVEN

Florence, January 1944

Marina had been dreading the Christmas season without her father. Before the war, they had celebrated so many Christmas traditions.

Every year in December, they visited the outdoor markets in Rome to see the nativity scene and listen to children dressed as shepherds play the zampognari. On Christmas Eve, they ate in the dining room, just the two of them. It was an Italian tradition not to eat meat the night before Christmas, so instead her father prepared pezzetti: artichoke, broccoli, and zucchini fried together. Afterward they attended mass led by the pope at the Vatican.

Marina's favorite part of the season was Christmas Day, when Paolo, along with any artists who had no place to go, joined them for the Big Dinner. All day, the kitchen smelled of pasta and simmering meat dishes. It was Marina's job to go to the bakery and buy the biggest panettone she could find. At night, they attended a Christmas concert and admired the lights in Piazza Navona.

Bernard and Belle made Christmas at Villa I Tatti special. They included American traditions that made Marina smile: Stockings hung on the fireplace, filled with oranges and chocolates and sweet-smelling soaps. Turkey with stuffing at dinner, and then an exchange of gifts, instead of waiting until January 6, when La Befana, the Christmas witch, left presents for Italian children.

Every time Marina began missing her father, Carlos seemed to appear. He brought new items for her to value, including a locket that seemed ordinary but contained a miniature by the eighteenth-century French artist François Boucher.

When they weren't working, they spent time enjoying each other's company. They ice-skated on the frozen lake and went snowshoeing in the forest. Marina had never worn snowshoes before and was afraid she would slip and fall. But she soon got used to it, and the forest was so peaceful. The winter sun glinted on fresh snow; the occasional squirrel crossed their path. Marina relaxed and allowed herself to be happy.

That night, Carlos's parents were going out and Carlos had invited Marina and Desi over for dinner.

That morning, Desi was in her bedroom when Marina arrived at her parents' villa. She wanted to talk to Desi alone before they joined Carlos. There were things she wanted to ask her. A pile of handkerchiefs sat on the bedside table.

"Your mother let me in. She said you weren't feeling well."

"I have a terrible cold." Desi picked up a handkerchief. "I can hardly breathe."

"You can't have a cold. We're going to dinner at Carlos's," Marina reminded her.

"You'll have to go alone," Desi groaned, blowing her nose. "The only thing I want for dinner is hot tea and chicken broth."

"You have to come," Marina insisted. "I don't want to dine with Carlos by myself."

She had dined with Carlos at his house the night he had showed her the items in the chest. But things were different now. She couldn't ignore her attraction to him. What if she did something she'd later regret?

"Why not? You've been alone with him every day. How many times has he kissed you?"

Marina had confessed to Desi about their kiss in the garden shed. Since then, they had kissed several times, and each time the kiss had become deeper and longer. But they hadn't done anything more. She wasn't ready, and Carlos didn't push her.

"Just a few times," Marina said. "It's been only a couple of weeks, and only kissing, I'm not ready for anything else."

"Peter and I waited to make love, but we both knew it was going to happen," Desi reflected. Her mind seemed far away. "I'd never felt that way before. It was as if I had known Peter forever, but at the same time everything about him was new and exciting."

Marina couldn't deny the way Carlos made her feel physically. When he kissed her, she wanted the kisses to last forever. But how would she know when the time was right?

"What was it like?" Marina asked.

"You mean sex? The first time, it was uncomfortable and too fast. By the time I was ready it was over." She flushed. "Neither of us were experienced, but we learned together. You can't imagine how it feels to have your body searching for something. Then when it happens, you never want it to stop. The second time we made love, I cried. Peter thought I was upset. But I was crying because I was afraid I'd never experience anything so wonderful again. I probably should have worried about getting pregnant." Desi looked at Marina pensively, then took an envelope from the dressing table. "I received a letter from Peter—it's even worse than I thought." Her voice broke and tears glimmered in her eyes.

"What did he say?"

Desi handed it to Marina.

"You can read it."

Dearest Desi,

I don't know how long this letter will take to arrive; I'm writing it before Christmas. Though I'd never know it was Christmas if not for the calendar one of the men keeps in his pocket. There are no Christmas lights at the Eastern Front.

I dread writing these words to you, I can imagine how you will receive them. But I don't want you to worry. The men are resourceful. Before we arrived, we traded cigarettes for bottles of vodka. The vodka keeps us warm, and it pushes away the fear. It's hard to be afraid when everyone is singing. That's what we do at night, we learned it from the Russian soldiers. They sing all the time, even when they're loading their tanks with ammunition.

The only time I'm frightened is during the day. I'm not afraid of Russian soldiers. They are even younger than the German soldiers fighting beside me. I'm afraid of the miles of whiteness that stretch on forever. Sometimes when I wake in the morning, the fields are scattered with dead horses who succumbed to the cold. A few times, I've discovered their soldiers lying next to them.

I tell myself I am luckier than most. My mother sent the thickest sweaters to wear under my uniform. My socks don't have holes, and I have leather gloves. Mostly, I'm lucky because I have you. My darling Desi, how can I complain about the conditions and the freezing temperature, when thinking of you and our baby warms my heart?

I promise that I will come back to you. When I do, we'll drink hot cocoa in front of a roaring fire. Because even if I don't return until next summer, being with you again will feel like Christmas.

Stay safe for both of us. And take care of our precious baby.

All my love, Peter

Marina was afraid to look at Desi. The newspapers and radio reports were full of news of conditions on the Eastern Front. After two years of fighting, the German army was still ill prepared for the harsh Russian winters. The men huddled in their foxholes at night, and in the morning their horses were often dead beside them. Their jeeps and tanks didn't start; their guns froze and wouldn't fire.

The Eastern Front was the scene of the deadliest battles in the war. At the Battle of Kursk in July, hundreds of thousands of soldiers had been killed on each side. German prisoners of war were sent to Siberia to work in the coal mines. Many died of frostbite when they arrived. The Russians had thousands more soldiers than the Germans, and Stalin proclaimed they would fight until the last man. Hitler was no match for him; the

German troops were cows being sent to the slaughter.

Marina took Desi into her arms and held her while she sobbed. The bright-eyed girl blossoming with impending motherhood had transformed into a young woman expecting certain death.

"Peter wouldn't have written if he were in danger," Marina reasoned. "He's going to be all right."

"How can you say that?" Desi pulled away. "None of us are special. When we were young, Donato and Carlos and I would sleep in the vineyards during the summer. I'd gaze up at the stars and think we were blessed. Now Donato is dead and Peter is away fighting. He may never come back."

"It's still the Christmas season." Marina hugged her again. "Miracles happen all the time. You just have to keep believing."

Marina knocked on the door to Belle's suite. Bernard and Belle had always been together during the holidays. Now Bernard was on another trip to Switzerland, and Belle was alone.

"Marina, please come in." Belle wore a pink silk robe, her hair twisted into a towel. "I just got out of the bath. I love Bernard, but there's a great luxury in being alone and doing whatever I please. I'm going to lie in bed all afternoon, reading novels. Remember that when you fall in love. Having time away from each other is the secret to staying happy."

"I can come back later," Marina offered.

"No, please sit, we haven't had a chance to talk." Belle pointed to an armchair. "I hope Christmas without your father wasn't too difficult."

"I enjoyed it," Marina said, smiling. "From now on, I'll serve fruitcake at Christmas dinner and hang stockings on the fireplace."

"It's silly that Bernard and I keep American traditions when we've lived in Italy for years," Belle reflected. "We never had children, and so I fall back on the traditions of my childhood. Christmas was the one time of year that my mother splurged. There were always presents under the Christmas tree, and she made a huge meal, with turkey and stuffing and pecan pie," she said pensively. "When I started making my own money, nothing made me happier than buying presents for my mother. One year, I bought her a pearl necklace and matching earrings. She never took them off."

This was a good time to ask Belle about the topaz earrings.

"I wanted to ask you something," Marina began. "You don't have to answer. But I was curious, and I can't get it off my mind."

Marina told her about seeing the earrings at

the jewelry store. About the jeweler showing her other pieces that had belonged to Belle.

"If keeping me here is a burden, I could write to Paolo and ask him to sell more of my father's belongings," she offered. "Or I could get a proper job to contribute to the household."

"Don't even consider doing anything like that! I'll tell you why I sold the earrings, but you can't say anything to Bernard," Belle said. "Usually, Bernard sells a client's art collection and earns a commission. Now that he's taking the pieces to Switzerland for safekeeping, he isn't earning anything at all. Villa I Tatti and its contents are worth a lot, but it doesn't pay the bills. None of it is cash.

"My own money is in an American bank, and I can't bring it to Italy," Belle continued. "So I've been selling my jewelry. Bernard doesn't know. He leaves the running of the household to me."

"Surely Bernard suspects you can't afford to pay for everything without his income?" Marina asked, perplexed.

"I told him I had enough stashed away to last awhile," Belle admitted guiltily. "I couldn't let him worry, he has so much on his mind."

"You have such gorgeous pieces," Marina said. "It must be terrible to part with them."

"I do miss them, but they're the ones I can bear to part with," Belle replied. "Thank you for the offer to contribute, but there's no need. You're our guest, and you'll need money when the war is over." She patted Marina's hand. "We'll manage; we always have. Sometimes the greatest rewards come from fighting for things. You appreciate what you have. Bernard is risking his life to help others. The least I can do is sell a few trinkets to make things easier at home. That reminds me. Ludwig, Bernard, and I were discussing something. You should know what it's about.

"This new man, Captain Bonner, wants to move most of the collection at the institute to Germany," Belle continued. "Ludwig is afraid if the Nazis get their hands on it, the collection will never be returned. He's asked if some of the more valuable books could be kept in Bernard's library. I wanted you to know, in case you wonder where the books came from."

A chill ran down Marina's spine.

"But Bernard is already worried his own collection isn't safe," Marina said. "He told me that's why he's going to send some of it to Harvard."

"For now, the institute's pieces are safer here," Belle said slowly. "No one besides the four of us will know. There isn't a better option right now. The idea of losing some of the greatest critical works about Renaissance art is unthinkable."

"I understand. I'm glad you and Bernard are able to help."

Belle leaned back in her chair and smiled. "Let's not talk about the war anymore," she suggested. "I'm going to ask Lucia to make an omelet with lots of garlic for lunch. Then I'm going to curl up with the most frivolous novel on my bookshelf."

Carlos answered the door to the villa himself. He was dressed casually, and for a moment he almost appeared carefree: an art student who wore his hair a bit long, instead of a partisan risking his life.

"Come inside—it's too cold to be standing out here." He took her arm before she could speak.

"I can't stay. Desi has a bad cold; I only came to tell you."

"You have to stay," Carlos replied, smiling. "I've been slaving in the kitchen for hours. I even baked a cake. I had to sit there the whole time to make sure it didn't fall."

"You can take the cake to Desi's," Marina suggested. "It will cheer her up."

"I baked the sponge cake for you; it's my best recipe. And I found some of my parents' records and made a space where we can dance."

He led her into the living room. The sofas had been pushed to the side. A phonograph stood in the corner. On the coffee table there was a bottle of brandy and some glasses.

"I'm sorry, I really can't stay," Marina said again. But she felt herself wavering.

Carlos had gone to so much trouble, and she

loved to dance. But what if she gave in to her growing desire and regretted it later? It was easier if she left.

"I should take Desi some soup."

Carlos glanced at her curiously. She was wearing a new dress and the lipstick that Belle gave her for Christmas.

"Her mother can give her soup. And you're all dressed up. If you weren't going to stay, why are you wearing a pretty dress and lipstick?"

Marina flushed and smoothed her skirt anxiously.

"The dress was a present; I felt like wearing it."

Carlos crossed his arms. "You want to stay, but you're nervous."

"What do you mean nervous?"

"My parents aren't home, and there are four empty bedrooms upstairs." He pointed to the staircase. "We've been alone before and you weren't nervous. But now it's different. You're frightened you'll give in to your desires and we'll make love."

"You're imagining things. There's nothing about sex that is frightening."

Carlos looked at her levelly.

"Unless you've never had it before."

Her cheeks turned hot, and she glanced down at her hands. "Carlos, we've kissed, and I enjoyed it as much as you do. It's just . . ."

She hesitated, not sure how to explain how she

felt. She wanted Carlos to make love to her, but she still wasn't certain it was the right time. What if she regretted it afterward or things changed between them? And what would her father say if he were alive? Marina had always been a good girl. But times had changed.

"We enjoy each other's company, and we work so well together," she finished. "Perhaps that's enough for now."

Carlos touched her cheek. His voice was soft.

"It's not enough for me. You're so lovely that when I look at you, I want to take you in my arms. And when I kiss you, the kiss is sweeter than milk with honey."

Marina's legs trembled, and there was a lump in her throat.

"We haven't even had dinner yet. And what if your parents come home early? They would be shocked to find us dining alone."

The cheeky smile returned to Carlos's face. He took Marina's arm and propelled her toward the dining room.

"If that's all that's worrying you, you have to stay. My parents' dinner party is in Pisa; they won't be home for hours. Come see how I set the dining room table. I used my parents' wedding china, and the wineglasses are Murano glass."

The table was set with gold-and-white china and deep wine goblets. Pink roses stood in a vase, and there were flickering candles.

"The roses are from my mother's hothouse. The color is so pretty in the candlelight."

"It looks beautiful. All right, I give in—I'll stay for dinner."

The meal was delicious. Carlos brought out dish after dish. In between courses, he refilled their wineglasses and served little bowls of gelato.

"Where did this all come from?" she asked when they were eating the sponge cake, which was as delicious as Carlos had promised. "There's a food shortage."

"The vegetables are from the hothouse. I drove to three different villages to find ingredients for the pasta sauce," he said merrily. "I've been hoarding sugar for days for the cake. My mother wondered why I wasn't drinking sugar in my coffee." He grinned. "I told her I was watching my weight."

After dinner, they cleared the dishes and moved to the living room. Carlos put a record on the phonograph and held out his hand.

"Why don't we dance?"

Marina took his hand, and they spun around the room. The music slowed, and they stood in the middle of the rug, rocking back and forth.

"I want you," he whispered into her hair. "I've never wanted anyone more."

He wrapped his arms around her and kissed her. She kissed him back, their bodies entangled together.

Suddenly everything felt right. Marina couldn't think of a reason to wait. They might not get another chance to be alone together. It was better to make love now, in a warm bed with wood crackling in the fireplace, than later, in the back of Carlos's truck or on the hard floor of the garden shed.

"I want you too," she breathed.

Carlos took her hand and they climbed the staircase. He led her down the hall to a room facing the garden.

"It's a guest bedroom," he said, ushering her inside. "I thought it would be more romantic than my childhood bedroom."

Marina took it all in: the king-size bed and blue bedspread, the gold tassels on the pillows, and bedside tables set with porcelain jugs. Firewood was stacked in the fireplace, and the windows were covered with pretty lace curtains. Two armchairs were arranged around a little table.

For a moment she felt shy and uncertain. Was she supposed to undress, or would Carlos insist on taking off her clothes? Then he turned her toward him and kissed her slowly, running his hands down her back.

A surge of desire shot through her, and she returned his kiss fervently.

Carlos unbuttoned his shirt, then unzipped his pants and folded them over a chair. He slowly took off Marina's dress, stopping to kiss her shoulders. His fingers caressed her breasts, and then he pulled her down onto the bed.

Marina recalled Desi saying her first time was too fast. But Carlos went slowly. He kissed her endlessly, running his hands over her body. She felt safe yet dizzy with longing at the same time. When he finally entered her, his chest hovering above her, his hands stroking her hair, she didn't want him to stop.

Afterward, when he got up to get a glass of water, she arranged the sheets to cover her nakedness.

"It's a little late to be shy now," he said, smiling. "I've seen your breasts. I could gaze at them all day."

"You probably say that to all the women you bring here," she blurted out.

She was suddenly anxious about what they had done. What if Carlos looked at her differently?

Carlos sat on the bed and put his hand on her chin.

"I've never brought a woman here." He kissed her shoulders. "It was worth the wait."

Marina let the last of her inhibitions melt away.

She smiled mischievously and removed the sheet. "I've heard there's so much to learn about making love. Why don't we do it again?"

Marina crept up the stairs to her bedroom a little after midnight. Belle's door was closed, and

Marina was glad. Even if Belle approved of sex, her night with Carlos was private. Marina wanted to keep it to herself.

She stood in front of the mirror and unzipped her dress. Her reflection stared back at her. She somehow looked different: her mouth was fuller, and the nipples on her breasts were dark.

She was a woman now, with all the pleasures of being a woman before her.

CHAPTER TWELVE

Florence, February 1944

Marina stepped back from the bookcase. Outside the library window, the trees were bare and a light snow covered the ground. The rest of January had been colder than she'd ever experienced in Rome, but Marina didn't mind. She spent her mornings in the library and her afternoons sitting by the fire at Villa I Tatti or visiting Desi.

Father Garboni was still recovering from his stroke, and Desi's mother visited him daily. Desi vowed to tell her mother about the baby every day, and every day she put it off. Soon she wouldn't have a choice; Marina could see the bump under Desi's dresses. Marina assured her it would be all right. Catarina was a mother, after all. How could she be upset about a baby?

Marina discovered a newfound confidence. She worked through Bernard's papers more efficiently. When she drove into Florence on an errand, she wasn't disturbed by the German soldiers she saw patrolling the streets. Even at night, when she was alone in her bedroom, instead of fretting about Desi, about Belle and Bernard and Captain Bonner, her heart beat with a new kind of thrill.

The change in her was because of Carlos. Sometimes he brought her something hot to drink while she worked in the library. He never stayed long; she wouldn't let him interrupt her work. But she enjoyed watching him stride up the path, his face bright with desire.

A few afternoons, she helped him deliver wood. In the evenings, they sat in the living room with Bernard and Belle and discussed the war. Then Bernard and Belle would excuse themselves to go upstairs, and Carlos would move close to Marina on the sofa. It took all her willpower to only kiss; she always wanted more.

After the first time they made love, they decided they needed a permanent place to meet in private. Carlos had taken her hand and led her through the gardens of Villa I Tatti. He stopped at the garden shed and pulled Marina inside. She couldn't believe her eyes. The hard floor had been replaced by a thick carpet; there was a daybed and a little washbasin. A heater had been installed, and the window had proper curtains.

No one used the garden shed; it was the perfect place for their rendezvous. Carlos had transformed the shed by himself. She pictured the time they spent there: the slow, careful lovemaking, the hours afterward when they talked about everything. She almost felt guilty that she could experience such happiness during the war.

It was now the middle of February. Outside the library, Marina spotted Ludwig walking up the path and went out to greet him. His fair hair was covered by a hat, and he wore a red scarf.

"Ludwig. This is a nice surprise. What are you doing here?"

"I came to see you." He followed her inside.

"Of course, let me take your coat."

Ludwig glanced up, surveying the room.

"I sometimes forget how beautiful Bernard's library is," he said, admiring the stained glass windows. "Like a cathedral with bookshelves instead of pews."

"My father would have loved it," Marina mused. "He appreciated beauty. He bought flowers every week for the table in our entryway. And he loved to buy me a pretty dress for my birthday." She smiled at the memory. "Then he'd insist we get dressed up and eat at some fancy restaurant. I wasn't interested in clothes or expensive dinners, but I'm glad we went." She sighed. "I'll always have my memories of those nights together."

Ludwig's brow creased, and he stuffed his hands in his pockets.

"Did I say something wrong?" Marina asked.

"It's not what you said, it's the war." Ludwig sat down. "Belle told you that Captain Bonner is transporting the works in the institute to Germany. Since the occupation, the Nazis act

189

as if everything in Florence belongs to them. The other morning, Captain Bonner packed up a book of sketches by Correggio. I discovered the sketches last year on a trip to Palma Campania. I wish I had left them there." He gritted his teeth. "They'll end up in the basement of some Berlin office building, lost once again."

"You're saving the important pieces," Marina reminded him. "Like the diary you showed me that Titian kept of his time in the court of the Duke of Ferrara."

Bernard had allowed her to flip through that the day before.

Ludwig's eyes lit up. "That's one of my most treasured possessions. I would have pulled a gun on Bonner if he tried to take it." He stopped. "I shouldn't say things like that. I'll end up on the wrong end of a German rifle."

"Everything will stay safe here," Marina assured him. "The library is locked; German soldiers haven't come to the villa in months."

"It's not just Bonner I'm worried about," Ludwig said soberly. "It's the Allies too."

"What do you mean?"

"The Allies landed at Anzio last month, and they're fighting their way north, taking back cities occupied by the Nazis."

"That's what we want," she said, perplexed. "Unless, that's not how you feel because . . ." She stopped uncomfortably.

"Because I'm German?" He finished her sentence. "You know how I feel about the war. But if the Allies are successful, the Nazis will retreat, and they won't leave the cities intact. First, they'll plunder the remaining artwork: Michelangelo's *David* will disappear in the middle of the night. Then they'll blow up the roads that lead into Rome, the bridges in Florence and Venice."

Marina felt as if she had been punched in the stomach. Ponte Vecchio, Ponte a Santa Trinità, demolished. She imagined returning to Rome and finding the roads that led into the city a heap of rubble.

"I never thought about that," she said.

"I want the war to end, but I don't want Italy's great art and architecture to be lost in the process," Ludwig said.

"There must be something we can do," Marina urged.

Ludwig's shoulders sagged.

"Gerhard offered to go to Berlin and discuss it with Hitler. Hitler has always seen himself as an art lover," he said ruefully. "But I fear that will only make the plundering worse. Hitler has seized many pieces for his private collection at the Eagle's Nest. If he worries that art and books will be taken by the Allies, he'll send for them now. None of the books would ever be returned to Italy."

Ludwig stood up and paced around the library.

"Bernard can only hide so many books here. I've decided to transport more of the books in the institute's collection to Milan. There's a monastery outside the city. I know the monks there; they're willing to help."

Marina frowned. "That sounds dangerous. What if the Nazis discover that some books are missing?"

"I've thought about it for so long, I've worn out the rug in my room from pacing." Ludwig smiled thinly. "I've devoted my entire career to building that collection. I have to save what I can, I can't let all of it disappear. The institute and all its works belong to Italy. The Nazis can't be allowed to take from it for their personal benefit."

His voice lowered, and he looked at her searchingly.

"I probably won't leave for a while, there's still a lot to do to get ready. But if I go to the monastery, I might not see you again," he said. "I wanted you to know that I'll always value our friendship."

"Of course we'll see each other again." Marina tried to smile. "After the war, I'll need someone to frequent the museums with. My father and I used to visit the Palatine Gallery at the Pitti Palace when we came to Florence. I can't think of anyone I'd rather stroll through it again with than you."

Marina entered Desi's parents' villa through the back door. A sweet smell came from the kitchen.

"Marina, I'm glad you're here." Desi stood at the counter. She looked more composed than Marina had seen her in weeks. "My mother and I baked a cheesecake."

Desi had been avoiding her mother since Father Garboni had his stroke. She spent all day in her bedroom or in the morning room with a shawl draped over her to hide her stomach.

"You and your mother were baking together?" Marina frowned.

"She knows so many recipes. Milk and cheese are important when you're pregnant," Desi went on. "That's how the baby builds healthy bones."

Marina realized what was different about Desi. The fear and uncertainty were gone from her face.

"Your mother knows about the baby!" Marina exclaimed.

"Father Garboni has completely recovered; he won't be replaced by another priest," Desi announced happily. "I told my mother about the baby this morning at breakfast. At first, she was furious. I was afraid she'd make me pack my bags and leave. Then we went to see Father Garboni together. He told her that God is more forgiving during wartime. He said the baby was God's way of bringing some happiness to our family after losing Donato, which made her cry."

"What did you tell her about the baby's father?" Marina asked, sitting at the kitchen table.

"I pretended I got swept up in some romance while grieving Donato's death." Desi sat opposite her. "I hated to use Donato as an excuse, but it worked. She understood."

"I said your mother would surprise you," Marina said happily.

"She's in the chapel right now, thanking God for giving her a grandchild. She believes if she prays enough, God will deliver another miracle and end the war."

"I hope God is listening," Marina sighed.

Desi wiped her hands on her apron. She hugged Marina.

"Even after I told my mother, I was still anxious about having the baby," Desi reflected. "But last night, while the baby was kicking, I decided something. Peter said he was lucky because he has me and the baby. Well, then I'm luckier than anyone. I have a home and parents and good friends. There's no point in worrying. Instead I'm going to do everything I can to make others happy.

"I'm going to take this cake to my father in his study and tell him about the baby." She determinedly cut two slices of cake. "And then I'm going to talk to him about the management of the vineyards. Donato was going to take them over eventually, but now I want to help run the family business. I can't sit around knitting baby booties forever. There's so much I'll be able to do when it's springtime."

Marina smiled across the table at Desi. She had never looked so beautiful. Her cheeks were rosy and her eyes were large and brown.

"You'll have a baby and the vineyards," Marina agreed. "And your parents will have their first grandchild."

Marina gazed out the living room window, waiting for Carlos. He was taking her to a restaurant in Montelopio for dinner.

The truck pulled in front of the villa, and Carlos bounded up the steps. She opened the door before he could knock.

"I thought we could have a drink before we go. It's warm and cozy here in front of the fireplace," Marina suggested. Carlos had told her to dress warmly, so she wore a wool skirt and sweater.

Carlos shook his head. "We don't have time. We have an important reservation."

"Where?"

He leaned forward and kissed her.

"It's a surprise—you'll see when we get there."

They drove toward the village of Montelopio, where he had rescued her when her bike had a flat tire. But instead of following the road, Carlos turned onto a dirt path.

"Where are we going?" She peered out the window, thinking the passing scenery looked familiar.

"You'll see," he said gaily. He squeezed her hand. "I promise the pasta will be better than anything you've had in Tuscany."

He stopped in front of a farmhouse, and Marina realized where they were: at the barn where Sara and her children were hiding.

"Is Sara joining us for dinner?"

He jumped out and opened Marina's door.

"Not exactly; we're joining her."

This time, when Carlos knocked, the barn door opened immediately. Sara's son, Eli, greeted them. He was taller than Marina remembered. He wore a white shirt and trousers that fit him perfectly for once.

"The beautiful Roman signorina has returned." Eli took Marina's hand. "Carlos said you would. At first I didn't believe him. Then he insisted I wear the clothes he bought me for Christmas." He pointed at his shirt. "I've never received Christmas presents before. My mother said it was all right, God wouldn't mind."

"You look very smart," Marina said, smiling. "And you're so tall. Next time I see you, you'll be as tall as Carlos."

A table with four chairs was set up in the corner. A bread basket and glasses sat atop a lace tablecloth.

196

"I'm getting muscles." Eli began to roll up his sleeves. "Would you like to see?"

"Not now," Carlos stopped him. "I promised Marina dinner."

"Wait until you taste the dessert." Eli kissed his fingertips. "I begged Carlos for a bit, but he said it's not polite to serve a cake with a slice missing."

Sara climbed down the ladder, carrying the baby. Francesca had also grown since Marina had seen her in December. She was eight months old and even prettier than Marina remembered. Her dark hair curled around her ears, and her blue eyes had long thick lashes.

"Marina, it's good to see you," Sara greeted her. "Carlos and Eli have been preparing the food all day."

Marina turned to Carlos.

"You made dinner?" She glanced around the barn. "I thought there wasn't anywhere to cook."

"There isn't." Carlos took off his coat. "I had to make everything at home and bring it in my truck. Eli and I heated it on the burner. Eli cut the bread; he's very good with a knife." He looked at Marina. "I know I promised you a special dinner, but I thought you'd want to help celebrate." He beamed at Sara. "Sara and the children will be leaving the barn soon."

"Where are you going?" Marina asked, turning to Sara.

"The children and I are going to Switzerland. Carlos arranged everything." Sara's cheeks shone, and Marina's heart was warmed by the joy she saw in her face. "A Swiss family in Lugano has agreed to take us in. Eli can go to school; he doesn't even have to learn a new language."

"I didn't do it all by myself." Carlos squeezed Marina's hand meaningfully, and Marina understood why he had brought her there. The items she'd valued had bought their passage.

"Of course I want to celebrate." Marina nodded. "I'm honored to be invited."

"Carlos promised you would sit next to me," Eli said, leading her to the table.

Carlos ladled vegetable lasagna onto the plates. Eli finished his portion before Marina had even managed a few bites.

"I'm not that hungry, Eli can have the rest of my lasagna too," Marina said, pushing her plate toward him. Eli needed the food more than she did. "I'd rather hold the baby."

Marina held Francesca while the others ate. Her breath smelled of mother's milk, and her skin was silky against Marina's cheek.

"The best part is we don't have to go somewhere far away to be safe," Sara said as they were eating dessert. "When Benito returns from the labor camp, it will be easy for him to join us."

Carlos's brow furrowed, but Sara was so excited she didn't notice. Marina wondered if he knew something about Benito that she didn't.

"I'm so glad." Marina nodded.

"You don't know what it's been like, alone in the loft with the children." Sara's voice was anguished. "Francesca has never been able to play outside. Every time Eli looks out the window, I'm frightened someone will see him." Her eyes brimmed with tears. "Because of Carlos, my children will have a future."

"The only bright spot in this war is being able to help others," Marina said slowly. "I'm sure Carlos is happy to be able to do something."

After dinner, Sara and Marina cleared the table while Carlos held Francesca. Finally, it was time to leave.

"Carlos promised he would visit us in Switzerland," Eli said as he walked with them to the door. "You must come with him. All the boys at my school will be jealous that I know a beautiful Roman lady."

"I promise I'll try." Marina leaned forward and kissed Eli on the cheek.

Eli held his palm to his cheek.

"A kiss from the beautiful Roman signorina." He sighed theatrically. "I won't wash this cheek until I see you again."

Carlos ruffled Eli's hair and grinned. "You'd better or you won't be allowed at school in the first place. Go help your mother with Francesca. I have to take Marina home."

．．．

Marina sat silently in Carlos's truck. The sky was black, the forest only a faint outline.

"You're very quiet," Carlos said, reaching for her hand.

"It was a wonderful evening," Marina began. "Eli has so much energy. And Francesca is growing to be a beauty."

"I'm glad you enjoyed it," Carlos said. "Sometimes it helps to see how much good you're doing. There are many Jewish families like Sara and her children. Thanks to the help of people like you, we're able to outfit them in warm clothes and put food on the table."

"I love what I'm doing," Marina said. "And I admire Sara so much. I can't imagine being as brave as she is. Caring for two children without her husband, and now taking them across the border to Switzerland alone."

The truck pulled up in front of Villa I Tatti. Carlos turned off the engine.

"That's one of the reasons I wanted you to come tonight," Carlos began. "Sara's papers haven't arrived. There's been a delay. I have to go sort it out, and I may be gone for a few weeks." He ran his hands over the steering wheel. "When I'm not here, I wonder if you'd check on Sara and the children. Make sure they're warm and have enough to eat."

"But Sara thinks everything is taken care of,"

Marina objected. "What will she say if you're gone and she and the children are still here?"

"She's so thrilled about going to Switzerland, and I only found out about the issue a few days ago," Carlos replied. "I know I can take care of it; I've always managed before. There isn't any need to worry her."

Marina couldn't help feeling concerned. Carlos had promised Sara, and Eli was so excited. How would they feel if they had to stay in the barn for another month?

"Sara and the children are very important to me," Carlos said, as if he were reading her thoughts. "I won't let them down."

Marina had to trust that Carlos knew what he was doing.

"Of course, I'll keep an eye on them," she promised.

CHAPTER THIRTEEN

Florence, February 1944

Marina pulled her scarf around her shoulders and strode through the courtyard of the Uffizi Gallery. She had driven into Florence to run errands and couldn't resist stopping at the Uffizi. Even though many of its masterpieces, like *Annunciation* by Leonardo da Vinci and *Primavera* by Botticelli had been spirited to a villa outside Florence until after the war, it was still one of Marina's favorite museums.

She and her father had visited the summer after Marina's mother died. Until then, Marina had believed that museums were drab places to be explored on school trips. But the Uffizi reminded her of a medieval castle with its endless maze of rooms, its mysterious corridors, its spectacular gardens arranged around a stone sundial. Her father had laughed at her description and said Marina was right, the building had been constructed as a castle. The Uffizi was commissioned in the sixteenth century by the Duke of Florence to house the administrative and legal offices of the city. The gardens connected it to the Pitti Palace, the duke's personal residence. It was only later, in the eighteenth century, that it became a museum open to the public.

Marina remembered feeling the history of the museum settle over her like some magical cape. She was walking through corridors that had been used for centuries. After that, every museum she visited—the Doge's Palace in Venice, the Villa Borghese in Rome—wasn't just about the art on the walls. Marina drew pleasure from the buildings themselves.

Footsteps sounded behind her. She turned and noticed a man in an SS uniform. Her heart raced and she walked faster.

"Fräulein, please wait," the man called.

Marina wanted to keep walking, but she couldn't ignore the command of an SS officer.

She stopped and waited for him to reach her, and her eyes widened when she realized it was Captain Bonner.

"Marina, I thought that was you." He held out his hand. "It's Siegfried, Siegfried Bonner. It's nice to see you again."

"Good afternoon, Captain Bonner." Marina ignored his use of his first name. "What are you doing here?"

"I could ask you the same question." Captain Bonner cocked his head, and his tone was friendly. "I was visiting Gerhard at his office around the corner in Piazza della Signoria. Gerhard is lucky—the SS has nothing so fancy.

Our headquarters at Villa Triste have leaky plumbing and no heating. There's a rumor it was once a house of debauchery."

Marina raised her eyebrows in shock.

"Forgive me, I shouldn't talk like that in front of a woman." Captain Bonner stopped himself. "I've been living the solitary life of a bachelor for too long. It's one of the hazards of the war."

"Apology accepted." Marina tried to stay calm. The last person she wanted to talk to was Captain Bonner, but it was better to remain polite. "It was nice to see you. Please excuse me, I have to go."

"Don't leave yet." Captain Bonner put his hand on her arm. "Gerhard speaks so highly of you. I would love a little company. Perhaps we can take a stroll together through the museum's courtyard?"

"It's too cold to be walking outside," Marina answered.

Captain Bonner eyed her coat and wool scarf.

"A short walk," he suggested. His eyes glinted. "I've never been to the Uffizi before. I've heard it's a must for art lovers."

Marina couldn't refuse. It would only make Captain Bonner more determined to have his way.

"All right," she relented. "But I must warn you, I'm a fast walker. It's the only way to keep warm."

"I grew up in Berlin, and even as a child I

enjoyed visiting museums," Captain Bonner said, walking beside her. "The Kaiser-Friedrich Museum has a wonderful collection of Byzantine art. Sadly, it's suffered a great deal of bombing since the war started."

"I'm sorry to hear that," Marina said stiffly.

"It's not until recently that I took a real interest in art myself," Bonner continued. "I happened to visit the Rijksmuseum in Amsterdam before the war. It's impossible not to be moved by Vermeer's *The Milkmaid* or Rembrandt's *The Night Watch*."

Marina had never been to Amsterdam, and she refused to be drawn into conversation about art with a German officer.

"I'm sure that was educational," she said noncommittally.

"There are many great painters of every nationality, but nothing compares to the Italian Renaissance artists," he continued. "If I want to become a serious collector, I have to become more educated. It's hard for a beginner like me to get an understanding of how much paintings are worth."

She turned to him. "Why do you want to know how much paintings are worth?"

"I find it so intriguing. Everything has a price, even art." He shrugged. "I've heard of auctions where a simple sketch can be worth thousands of lire while a painting done in watercolor fetches half of that." He pulled at his gloves. "Art is so subjective; I'm trying to get a deeper knowledge of how the art world works."

A cold wind whipped through the courtyard. Marina drew her scarf around her neck.

"I don't have the time or money to attend art auctions," she said.

Bonner looked at her strangely.

"I was told you're quite an expert on Renaissance art. Perhaps we can discuss it over dinner tomorrow evening. The dining room at the Hotel Savoy is open. I'd love to hear your views and ask you some questions. Nothing too technical, just an overview."

"I can't. I don't have a car," Marina replied. "I borrowed Belle's to run some errands."

Captain Bonner took a card out of his wallet and handed it to her.

"I'd be happy to pick you up. Here's my card." He smiled. "I've enjoyed our walk. It's refreshing to discover that Florence has such knowledgeable companions."

Marina paced around Bernard's library. Since returning from Florence, she had tried to work on the collection, but she couldn't concentrate. Everything about Captain Bonner—his heavy boots, the black swastika on his armband— reminded her of her father's death.

She jumped as the door to the library opened.

Carlos entered, holding two cups. "I brought you hot coffee. There's something I have to tell you." He glanced around the empty library. "It couldn't wait, and I wanted to make sure no one was listening."

"I have something to tell you first."

She told him about running into Captain Bonner, and his dinner invitation.

Carlos sipped his coffee. "You must have dinner with him."

"What? You want me to go to dinner with Captain Bonner?"

"Rumor has it that Bonner is forming his own art collection. He keeps a painting or two for himself and smuggles them to a safe-deposit box in Switzerland."

"You think he wants my opinion on which pieces he should steal?" she gasped.

"I can't think why else he would invite you," Carlos said. "Apparently, he's one of the few Nazi officers who doesn't fraternize with local women; he's faithful to his wife in Berlin. You must have made quite an impression.

"This might be our only chance to stop him. Think about it, Marina," he urged. "If Captain Bonner is able to keep paintings for himself, the pieces may never be seen again. The Raphaels and Leonardos he takes will eventually be sold to private collectors in other countries. They'll disappear from Italy forever."

The thought of any of her beloved paintings ending up in Captain Bonner's hands filled Marina with horror. Carlos was right. Here was her opportunity to protect some of the artwork she loved and cherished.

"But how would I be able to stop him?" she asked.

"He said he wanted your opinion on what was valuable," Carlos said. "Perhaps he's planning to steal something and wants to ask you about it first. If we know what it is, we can get to it before he does." He paused. "We would keep it hidden until after the war, and then return it to its rightful owner."

"All right, I'll do it." Marina remembered that Carlos wanted to tell her something. "You had something to say when you entered. What was it?"

"Last night there was a raid on a safe house in San Gimignano, not far from here. German soldiers stormed the house, seizing the radio and guns and ammunition." He paused. "Then they shot everyone inside, including three small children hiding in the pantry."

She gasped. "How do you know?"

"A neighbor discovered them," he said. "One of the partisans was still alive then but died a few hours later."

Marina imagined the children cowering in the pantry. Soldiers flinging open the door and riddling the space with bullets.

"I can't imagine anything so terrible. But what does it have to do with us?"

"That was the safe house where Sara and the children were going to go on their way to Switzerland," Carlos replied. "Now I have to find another route as well as getting them false papers. I want to make sure you're safe if you visit Sara and the children. I might have to be gone for longer than I expected. But I want to get you a gun to protect yourself."

Marina remembered the pistol Ludwig gave her. She walked over to the drawer.

"I already have a pistol." She took it out and showed it to Carlos.

Carlos turned it over in his hand. He glanced up at Marina.

"A German pistol! Where did you get this?"

She explained that Ludwig and Bernard had arranged it, concerned about her working in the library alone.

"I'm glad you have this, but you need to find a safer hiding place. A thief would go straight for the drawer. In that case, it wouldn't do you any good at all."

He walked over to the bookshelf and took out a book to put the gun behind. As he did, another book fell to the floor. It was larger than the others on the shelf.

"What's this?" he asked, picking it up and opening it carefully.

Marina glanced at the cover. It was one of Ludwig's books.

"It's Titian's diary from his time at the court of the Duke of Ferrara. It's part of a collection of books that Bernard and Belle agreed to store for Ludwig."

"I see." Carlos digested the information. His mind seemed elsewhere. "If they're really valuable, perhaps move them to a higher hiding place. Somewhere that would be harder for a thief."

"That's a good idea," Marina agreed, pleased that Carlos had thought of it.

Together they climbed the staircase and hid Ludwig's books behind a row of books on the third floor.

When they were finished, they descended the circular staircase together.

Carlos kissed her briefly and walked to the door.

"Thank you." She nodded. "I feel better that the books are well hidden."

"Don't think about anything right now except your dinner with Captain Bonner," Carlos urged.

Marina went back to her work. Captain Bonner's card sat on the library desk. When she finished, she would call him and accept his invitation.

Belle poked her head in.

"I saw that the car was back, I thought I'd come out and join you," she said, entering the library.

"Carlos was just here, he brought me coffee," Marina greeted her. "It helps me work."

Belle pulled down one of her own boxes. She started sifting through her letters.

"I've been drinking hot things all day. I find it impossible to keep warm." Belle sighed. "February is so dreary, and there's nothing to look forward to. In fact, I had an idea today, and I wanted your opinion. I need to do something to break the monotony, so I've decided to throw a little costume party. Just our close circle. We could all use some cheering up."

"That's a good idea," Marina said absently.

"Bernard and I will be Antony and Cleopatra; I've always been fascinated by their love affair. Did you know that Antony married someone else while Cleopatra was pregnant? They reunited three years later as if they'd never been apart. Their lives certainly weren't boring." Her eyes danced. "I always admired Cleopatra; she was so strong. She ruled ancient Egypt for two decades." Belle paused. "You and Carlos could go as Tristan and Isolde. Carlos would make a perfect Tristan. I've always imagined Tristan to be terribly handsome, with dark hair and smoldering eyes."

"I read it years ago in school," Marina said.

Belle glanced at Marina curiously. "Is everything all right?" she asked. "You seem distracted."

Marina tried to focus. It was impossible to discuss a costume ball when all she could think about was the children who had been shot while hiding in the pantry, and Sara, Eli, and Francesca's difficulty in reaching the Swiss border.

"It's nothing." Marina forced herself to smile. "You're right, a party is just what we need."

"Good, I'm glad you agree. I'll work on the invitations this evening." She smiled slyly. "I'll invite Desi, of course. She can come as Piero della Francesca's pregnant Madonna. It's one of my favorite paintings."

Belle's words sunk in.

"You know Desi is pregnant?" Marina's eyes widened. "Nobody knows. Desi only told her mother recently."

"I guessed weeks ago. I could tell by the way she carried herself." Belle's eyes twinkled. "I'd never say anything. I'm good at keeping secrets."

They worked together for the rest of the afternoon, and then Marina went upstairs to her room. She picked up the phone and dialed the number on Captain Bonner's card.

"Captain Bonner? This is Marina Tozzi."

"Marina, how lovely to hear from you," Captain Bonner replied. "Did you consider my invitation?"

"I did." She gripped the phone and sat up straight. "I would love to join you for dinner tomorrow night."

CHAPTER FOURTEEN

Florence, February 1944

Marina stood outside the Hotel Savoy and searched for Captain Bonner. She had driven Belle's car to the hotel so she could arrive separately to him. Even if Captain Bonner wasn't interested in her romantically, she wanted to make sure he knew it wasn't a date. The hotel was near Piazza della Repubblica, only a couple of streets away from the Duomo. Long black cars with swastika flags pulled up in front, and she wondered whether all the guests were German.

A bellboy opened the door to the lobby. For a moment, she set aside her nervousness, focusing instead on admiring the black-and-white marble floors, the gilt mirrors lining the walls, the chandeliers, seemingly as heavy as the roof of the Duomo itself. A glass table with a huge vase of flowers stood in the middle of the room, surrounded by sofas upholstered in burgundy velvet.

She was reminded of an evening the summer before, when her father had taken her to dinner at the Hassler Hotel in Rome after Marina had made her first sale at the gallery. Ever since she was a girl, Marina had longed to dine at the famous hotel at the top of the Spanish Steps, the destination of movie stars and celebrities. The dining terrace had breathtaking views, and the food was supposed to be the best in Rome.

But when the maître d' led them to the table, Marina had suddenly felt uncomfortable. A meal there would cost a fortune; they couldn't possibly afford it.

Her father had ordered scallops and champagne for them both and said that good work needed to be rewarded. The next time a customer entered the gallery, Marina would remember the taste of the champagne, the elegance of the dining room, and make an even bigger sale.

"Marina, I'm glad you were able to meet me after all." Captain Bonner's arrival interrupted her thoughts. "I apologize for being late. I had some business at the office."

"I've been here only a few minutes," she replied. She wore the silver dress she'd borrowed for the Adamos' dinner party with a pair of low heels.

Captain Bonner took her arm. The maître d' escorted them directly to a table with an ease that suggested Captain Bonner had visited before. She waited until they had their wine, then she looked at him pleasantly.

"It's a beautiful hotel. Do you come here often?"

"I've been here a few times." He shrugged. "Some people think a German officer's life is filled with social functions, but it's lonely being away from my wife and children in Berlin. The Hotel Savoy is always lively. Did you know it was built on the site of the Jewish ghetto? The ghetto was demolished a hundred years ago."

"The Jewish ghetto?"

"I've been doing some reading on the city since I arrived. Don't you think it's interesting that there were no Jewish artists in Italy during the Renaissance? The Jews were more like Shylock, the money lender in Shakespeare's *The Merchant of Venice*. They were only interested in lining their pockets with money. Hitler knows what he's doing. Even six hundred years ago, Europe would have been better off without them."

Marina felt sick. She gripped her wineglass to keep her hand from shaking.

"*The Merchant of Venice* is not real life, it's a play," Marina said stiffly. "I'm sure you'd think that about any of Shakespeare's villains."

"I disagree. I found Shakespeare's description of Shylock to be accurate."

Marina set her glass on the table.

"There were only a handful of wealthy Jews during the Renaissance, and they worked very hard. Most of the Jews during that period didn't have the luxury of becoming artists. They had to earn a living to survive."

Captain Bonner sipped his wine. "I disagree. The truly great artists, the Michelangelos and Donatellos, had wealthy benefactors. If there had been talented Jewish artists, they would have found patrons, too."

Marina's mind went to Enrico. Her father had sponsored many talented Jewish artists. Who knew how many of them would return after the war?

She tried to keep the distaste out of her expression.

"You wanted to have dinner so you could ask my opinion on what makes a painting valuable," she reminded him.

Captain Bonner put down his glass. "You're right, I apologize. Italy has so many important paintings, I can't keep the names of all the artists in my head. Tell me, if you came across a Verrocchio, only a very small one, would that be something of value?"

Marina glanced down at the tablecloth so Captain Bonner wouldn't see her jaw drop. Verrocchio was one of the most influential Renaissance artists. He'd had his own workshop with apprentices that included Botticelli and Leonardo da Vinci. But only one signed piece by him had survived, an altarpiece in the Pistoia Cathedral. Any painting signed by Verrocchio, no matter how small, would be worth a fortune.

"It could be." She kept her voice even. "It would have to be signed and authenticated to make sure it was not painted by one of his apprentices."

Captain Bonner studied her carefully as if deciding if he could trust her.

"I happen to have one in my quarters," he replied. "We could go there after dinner."

Marina pretended to be shocked.

"That wouldn't be proper," she declared.

"I appreciate your concern, but I'm a happily married man." He smiled, dismissing her objection. "Don't get me wrong, any man in his right mind would be attracted to you, Fräulein. But I love my wife very much. I'm only interested in your opinion about art."

Marina smiled back. She was tempted by the chance to get a glimpse of the rare Verrocchio.

"In that case, I'd be happy to take a look. But first, I haven't eaten at such a fine restaurant since before the war. What do you suggest from the menu?"

They ate dishes that Marina hadn't dreamed of tasting again since rationing began: bistecca alla Fiorentina—Tuscan steak from a special breed of cow cooked very rare with roasted potatoes and beans—and for dessert, cantucci, small almond cookies with Vin Santo for dipping. Marina wondered where the Hotel Savoy found such luxuries and how the other diners afforded it.

"Here it is," Captain Bonner said, standing in his parlor.

Captain Bonner's quarters were three rooms

in an apartment building near the Duomo. They passed through an entry with a small closet. There was a galley-style kitchen and a little balcony with a chair.

Marina picked up the painting. It was of an angel wearing a loose-fitting white gown and a halo. The angel stood in a field with a palm tree far in the background. A small prayer book was open in the angel's hands. Marina remembered seeing the same painting in a textbook she studied at university. There was no signature. Without one, the painting could be attributed to any of the artists from Verrocchio's workshop.

Captain Bonner gingerly pried off the gold frame. He pointed to the spidery writing in the bottom corner. "Could that be Verrocchio's signature?"

Marina examined it closely. A thrill of excitement ran down her spine.

"It could be," she replied. "I can't believe no one has discovered it before. Where did you get this painting?"

"I found it in a storeroom at the Uffizi." He shrugged. "It was under many other paintings, and the frame was loose. Perhaps this is the kind of piece Hitler might want for his own private collection at the Eagle's Nest?" Captain Bonner asked eagerly. His eyes gleamed with excitement. If Carlos was right about Bonner's personal collection, he had no intention of presenting the painting to Hitler. It would end up in Captain Bonner's safe-deposit box in Switzerland.

Marina's mind went to the Nazi officers who killed her father and Enrico. She couldn't let Captain Bonner profit from art, and she couldn't let a signed Verrocchio leave Italy.

"There's always a chance it could be fake," she said.

"But then why would the Uffizi have it?" Captain Bonner argued. "It's more likely that it's an original. Somehow it got buried under the other paintings and no one knew it was there."

The smug smile on Captain Bonner's face confirmed her fears. He was going to keep the painting for himself. She needed to talk to Carlos. They hadn't discussed how she was going to stop Captain Bonner.

"Even paintings by Verrocchio's workshop are coveted by museums. It would be hasty to jump to conclusions." Marina tried to sound authoritative.

Captain Bonner studied her appreciatively. He seemed to make up his mind.

"You mustn't be so modest, Fräulein. You came highly regarded for your expertise," Captain Bonner said firmly. "Your opinion is good enough for me."

When Marina returned to Villa I Tatti, an unfamiliar car stood in the driveway. Voices came from the living room. She had been hoping to go upstairs without seeing anyone.

"Marina!" Bernard called. "Please, come join us."

Bernard and Belle sat on the sofa; Gerhard Wolf across from them. Bernard and Gerhard wore black dinner jackets and Belle was beautifully dressed in a pleated evening skirt and a brocade jacket.

"Gerhard took us to *Rigoletto* at the opera," Bernard told Marina. "I was going to invite you, but Belle said you had other plans."

"It was great fun," Belle piped in. "The best part was watching the faces of the German officers sitting near us. They couldn't follow the story because they don't speak Italian." She smiled coquettishly at Gerhard. "Except for Gerhard, of course. He converses in Italian like a native."

"Carlos and I went to dinner in Florence," Marina explained hastily.

She felt terrible for lying, but she couldn't admit that she had been out with Captain Bonner.

"I'm glad you're getting out and enjoying yourself." Bernard smiled. "You're so often working in the library."

"I enjoy it very much," Marina said earnestly. "Especially reading your scholarly works. Harvard will be lucky to have them."

"Gerhard has been telling us about recent

developments in the war," Bernard said, pouring a glass of sherry and handing it to Marina. "The Allies have landed at Anzio and are trying to cross the Gustav Line, the German defensive line that stretches from the Tyrrhenian Sea to the Adriatic Sea. But the German army is holding firm. Who knows how long it will be until the Allies reach Florence?"

Gerhard nodded. "Bernard is correct, and I'm afraid rationing is going to get worse. Hitler has ordered all the supply routes cut off. He doesn't want anything helping the Allies. Even here in Tuscany, there won't be enough flour to make bread. And this new officer, Captain Bonner, is not making life pleasant. He's intent on removing all the valuable pieces from the museums.

"Hitler says it's to keep them safe from bombing, but there's no way to tell." Gerhard sighed. "Hitler's private collection already rivals those of the greatest museums in Europe. Many of the pieces were taken from the homes of Jews. The Eagle's Nest houses quite a few paintings formerly owned by the Rothschilds."

"Just having Captain Bonner here for coffee made me uncomfortable." Belle shivered. "It's like inviting a snake in from the garden."

"I wish I could have him transferred, but I've already used my influence for other favors," Gerhard lamented. "I was able to have my nephew, Peter, stay with me for a while.

Unfortunately, even with my position I couldn't keep him safe from the war forever. Recently he was forced to return to Berlin. He's fighting on the Eastern Front. My sister is frantic with worry."

Marina almost spilled her sherry.

"I'm sorry, did you say your nephew?"

"Yes," Gerhard confirmed, brightening. "Peter is about your age, actually. I have a picture of him right here." He took out his wallet and handed her a photo of a young man with blond hair and a dimple on his chin. "When he was a boy, he used to rescue wounded animals and nurse them back to health. He's the last person who should be carrying a rifle."

Marina's mind reeled. The young man in the photo was Desi's great love and the father of her baby.

So that's how Peter was able to avoid the German army for so long. She wondered if Desi knew of the connection. Marina doubted it. Desi had met Gerhard only once, outside Peter's apartment. And she would have said something.

"That's what I hate about this war," Gerhard said. "Young men should be attending university, starting careers. Instead they have to fight in a war they might not believe in."

Belle noticed Marina's troubled expression and changed the subject to her costume party, scheduled for the first week in March.

After Gerhard left and Belle and Bernard had retired, Marina opened her handbag and took out Captain Bonner's card once again. She had to hatch a plan with Carlos to somehow retrieve the Verrocchio.

CHAPTER FIFTEEN

Florence, February 1944

The next day, Marina woke to rain falling outside her window. The sky was gray and the valley was shrouded in mist. She got up and hurriedly washed her face. She had to tell Carlos about her dinner with Captain Bonner and the signed Verrocchio. Then she would go and see Desi. She wanted to find out if Desi knew Peter was Gerhard's nephew.

Marina hurried up the steps of the Adamo villa and knocked.

"I made breakfast," Carlos announced when he opened the door. He kissed her briefly. "Come and join me."

The kitchen was warm and inviting. A pot of porridge simmered on the stove. There was a pitcher of milk and a pot of honey too.

She took off her jacket and sat at the table. "I'm not hungry."

He ladled porridge into a bowl and sat down. "I'm the opposite. When I'm upset, I eat. This is my second bowl, and I'm still hungry."

Marina glanced at Carlos across the table. There were circles under his eyes and his cheeks were haggard.

Her mind went to Sara and the children. "Did something happen?" she asked anxiously.

Carlos gripped his spoon.

"There was another raid last night. On a house in Montelopio. The partisans were storing ammunition and guns under the floorboards. Everyone inside was shot or captured." He paused. "Including a neighbor of the farmer who is hiding Sara and the children."

Marina stared at Carlos in horror. The farmer was probably being held at Villa Triste. What if he knew about Sara, Eli, and Francesca? If he was tortured, Sara, her children, and Carlos could all be at risk.

"Are Sara and the children okay?" Marina gasped.

"They're safe, but the neighbor is dead." Carlos's voice was thick. "It's all getting too close. Who knows where the next raid will be?"

"How soon will you be able to move Sara and the children to Switzerland?" Marina asked.

"I still haven't found a new route, and it's getting risky. Two safe houses have been discovered in a matter of days. I think it may be too late to evacuate them."

"But Sara is counting on reaching Switzerland," Marina insisted. "Eli is going to start a new school. Sara's husband will meet them there when he is released from the labor camp."

"Benito wasn't sent to a labor camp," Carlos

admitted, and Marina suddenly understood the expression on his face when Sara had mentioned it. He hung his head. "Benito was a partisan like me. He was arrested last year and deported. I haven't heard from him since."

"I promised Benito I would watch out for them," Carlos went on. "But it's not just Sara. It's hundreds of others. The partisan network is a game of dominoes. Remove one piece, and the whole thing tumbles down."

"And Sara doesn't know what really happened to Benito?"

"When he was arrested, he made me promise not to tell her," Carlos replied. "They can't stay in the barn much longer, but there are so few other options. I don't know what to do."

They both sat lost in their thoughts. She reached across the table and squeezed Carlos's hand.

"I'm sorry I'm so preoccupied." He sighed. "I haven't asked about your dinner with Captain Bonner."

She told him about her dinner and the painting Captain Bonner had shown her.

"Are you certain it's a Verrocchio?" Carlos asked.

Marina nodded. "As certain as I can be. What will we do now? How will we get it out of Captain Bonner's quarters without him noticing? He'll suspect me if it goes missing."

Carlos's green eyes sparkled, and the man

she knew, confident and determined, seemed to return.

"Unless he thinks it's there all along."

Marina didn't understand. The painting couldn't be in two places at once.

"What do you mean?" she demanded.

"I could paint a copy, and we can switch them when he's not there," Carlos suggested. "The fake will end up in Switzerland, while the original stays safely in Italy."

It was brilliant.

"That's a wonderful idea!" Marina exclaimed.

"I once saw a photograph of the same painting in a book," Marina said to Carlos. "Perhaps I can find the same textbook in Florence. You'll need to match the painting exactly. How long would it take you to make the fake?"

"If you bring me the book, I can do it," Carlos said confidently. "Hopefully, it won't take more than a week. Then it will have to dry." He frowned. "But how will we exchange the paintings?"

"I'll find some excuse to visit him and switch them myself," Marina said eagerly.

Carlos frowned. "That could be dangerous. What if he catches you?"

"I'll think of something." Marina shrugged. She was getting excited. Plus, how else were they supposed to execute their plan?

"I'll borrow Desi's car and go into Florence tomorrow to find the textbook."

"There's something I want to show you before you go." Carlos led her down the hallway to the old playroom.

"What am I looking at?" she asked.

"My painting—I've been working on it for days." He pointed to his easel in the corner.

She studied the painting of a young woman standing in a forest. Tree branches were dusted with snow and the sun shone through her hair.

"I finished it last night while you were at dinner. I was going to put it in the garden shed, but it was raining."

"You painted me?" she said, turning to face him.

"I always wanted to try my hand at portraiture, but I never had the right subject. Benito said that for a portrait to be good, the subject has to become part of the artist."

Marina had discovered the same thing at university. The *Mona Lisa* was originally commissioned by the model's husband, Francesco del Giocondo. All Leonardo da Vinci had to do was paint an attractive woman dressed in the Renaissance fashion, but instead he spent years on the project. The woman in the final painting isn't conventionally pretty. Her lips are too thin and her eyes are set close together. But if the viewer sees her with Leonardo's eyes, she's the most beautiful woman in the world.

Marina stepped closer to the canvas. Carlos

had captured the color of her eyes and the shape of her mouth. There was something else too, a brightness she hadn't seen before. It was the look of someone who was determined to get everything out of life.

Marina reached up and kissed him.

"It's perfect."

"Marina! Come inside," Desi said, kissing her on both cheeks when she arrived at the Pirellis' villa. She peered outside. "I've been so busy; I didn't notice it was raining. I've always enjoyed the rain. Donato and I used to love rainy days as teenagers. Carlos would come over to play cards and charades. Carlos and Donato were so competitive, and they both loved to win."

They walked down the hall to the morning room. Books were piled on tables and spread out on the floor.

"What are all these books doing here?" Marina asked.

"They're for my new project." Desi knelt on the floor. "I talked to my father about getting involved in the family business, and I have an idea. I'm not just going to design the wine bottles, I want to study winemaking. I'd planned to, but then the war started. At our vineyard here, we grow only one type of grape: Sangiovese, the most popular in Tuscany. But if we add Merlot grapes as well, we can create a whole new blend and offer something unique that no one else has."

"That sounds exciting." Marina knelt beside her.

"The midwife said when women are close to giving birth, they find a new energy," Desi continued. "I'm going to create a wonderful future for our new little family."

"Speaking of which, I have some news about Peter," Marina said. She told her about Gerhard's visit. "Perhaps Gerhard can get your letters to Peter."

Desi didn't look convinced. "But I couldn't tell Gerhard about Peter and me. He would find out about the baby. And besides, I'm not ready to tell my parents about Peter. It's better to wait until after the baby is born."

"I suppose you're right," Marina agreed grudgingly.

"I decided it doesn't matter if the letters sit here for months," Desi said. Her eyes sparkled with determination. "Peter can read them when the war is over.

"In the meantime, I found a book on vineyards in the Rhine Valley in Germany. I'm going to read it to the baby so he knows where his father comes from. If neither of our families accept us after the war, we'll start our own vineyard."

"How do you know it's a boy?" Marina asked, puzzled.

"I don't know, I can just feel it," Desi declared.

"It's the way he kicks me. He's going to be a great soccer player."

"I'm sure you're correct," Marina agreed, laughing. She smiled at her friend. "And Peter's parents would be crazy not to accept you. You'll be the best wife and mother, and you're becoming the smartest businesswoman too."

"In the meantime, I'll go to confession and ask Father Garboni to put in a word with God to keep Peter safe. I've already lost Donato. Perhaps God will take pity."

Marina sat at the desk in Bernard's library, an album of old photographs open beside her. One photo was sepia-colored with age, and the writing on the back read: *The East Room, J. P. Morgan's library, New York.* It was the most magnificent library Marina had ever seen. The walls were draped with tapestries, and Persian rugs covered the floor. Three stories of books climbed the walls, protected by an exquisitely ornate iron grille.

The album belonged to Belle. There were photos of Belle wearing a turban with an ostrich feather, Belle dressed head to toe in black, except for a purple cape and matching boots, Belle in her early thirties sporting wide culottes and a patterned vest. All the photos had inscriptions below: Belle in Bombay, in Sweden accepting an award, in Africa about to meet an archbishop.

231

And then photographs with Bernard appeared. Bernard and Belle sitting in a Ford roadster, Belle in the passenger seat wearing a wide-brimmed hat and jaunty scarf. Bernard and Belle on a train, snow-covered peaks and a ravine visible in a window behind them.

What would it have been like to lead Belle's life? What would it be like to have a brilliant career, to visit so many places and meet fascinating people? Marina tried to imagine it for herself. To travel the world, buying paintings for her gallery. To have lovers and friends.

But truthfully, Marina felt more like Desi. She wanted her career, but she also wanted a proper family with a husband and children.

After the war, Marina would open an art gallery and support unknown artists. Perhaps she and her husband would buy a villa outside Florence. On Sundays, they'd invite Desi and Peter for lunch, and their children would play together.

All they had to do was survive the war.

CHAPTER SIXTEEN

Florence, February 1944

It took Carlos a few days to make the copy.

Marina had spent two days searching every bookstore in Florence for the textbook. She finally found it in a used bookstore in the Piazza Santo Spirito. Marina practically hugged the bookseller when he dug it out from a pile in the back room.

The caption under the photo said the painting was presumed to be from Verrocchio's workshop. But without his signature it couldn't be attributed to Verrocchio himself.

Now Marina hurried up the steps of the Adamos' villa to see Carlos's handiwork. He led her down the hallway to his studio.

"You have to tell me exactly what you think," he insisted, when they stood in front of the painting. "If I got anything wrong, even the size of the brushstrokes, Captain Bonner might notice."

Marina studied the canvas in astonishment. Carlos had matched the original remarkably well. Even smaller details, the angel's halo and robes, were the same.

"I can't tell them apart!" she exclaimed. She kissed him.

"Are you sure?" Carlos asked, and for a moment she saw him as the art student hoping desperately for approval. "The copy has to be perfect."

Marina held up Carlos's painting next to the photo in the textbook. Then she switched hands and studied them again.

"I'm sure. Now I just need to swap the paintings. It might take me a little time to get the original out of its frame and slip this one inside," Marina pondered. There was no way she'd be able to get an identical frame. "I'll think of something to get Captain Bonner out of the room: ask him for a drink or something."

"What excuse will you give for going to his apartment in the first place?" Carlos rubbed his forehead. "You're a beautiful young woman. You can't just appear at his door."

Carlos's canvases were stacked against the wall. There were landscapes of Tuscan villages and a painting of the sun setting over the Arno. Suddenly Marina had an idea.

"I know just the thing," she said excitedly.

Marina put her satchel with the copy of the painting in it on her bed. She picked up the phone and dialed Captain Bonner.

"Captain Bonner, this is Marina Tozzi."

"Fräulein Tozzi. What a pleasant surprise to hear from you so soon."

"I wanted to thank you for dinner," Marina said.

"I should be thanking you for offering me your expertise. You did me a great favor."

Marina gripped the phone more tightly.

"I'm glad. In fact, I have something that might interest you. It concerns another piece of art," she said. "I wonder if we could meet."

"Intriguing. I have dinner engagements all this week, unfortunately. How about next Monday?"

The Verrocchio might be in Switzerland by next week. It had to be today.

"Oh, it doesn't need to be over dinner. My information is time sensitive," she added. "Why don't I drop by your rooms later tonight?"

Captain Bonner waited a moment before he answered.

"You have certainly piqued my interest, Fräulein Tozzi. How about we meet at my quarters at nine o'clock?"

Marina dressed carefully in a cashmere sweater and pleated skirt, a silk scarf knotted around her neck. She wanted to appear confident and professional, even at an officer's apartment late at night.

She climbed the steps to Captain Bonner's rooms and knocked on the door.

"Fräulein Tozzi, please come in," Captain Bonner said, waving her inside. He still wore his

SS outfit, although he'd taken off his cap. "Please forgive my uniform. I've just come from dinner."

"Please, call me Marina," she said, following him into the living room.

She quickly surveyed the room. She was afraid that the Verrocchio had been spirited away or hidden elsewhere in the apartment for safekeeping, but she spotted it on the little table, just where she'd seen it on her last visit, next to a book and a pair of reading glasses. Either Captain Bonner had been admiring it or he didn't want something so valuable to be out of his sight.

"Please sit down. Can I offer you something to drink?"

Marina shook her head. The drink would come later, when she needed to get him out of the room.

"No, thank you."

She unwrapped the canvas that she had been carrying.

"I wanted to show you this piece," she said, propping it on the coffee table.

It was a landscape of Florence with Ponte a Santa Trinità in the foreground. The Duomo rose in the distance, Giotto's Bell Tower instantly recognizable.

Captain Bonner leaned forward to examine it.

"I don't recognize it. Is it by an old master?"

"It's something even better." She pointed at the bridge. "The Ponte a Santa Trinità is one of

236

the oldest bridges in Florence. It was built in the fifteenth century. See the four arches with the marble statues? Each one represents a season." She looked up at Captain Bonner, whose brows were furrowed. "As you've said, the Allies are threatening to bomb Florence. If they do, all of this, Florence's six bridges, the Duomo, Giotto's Bell Tower might be destroyed. A painting like this—with beloved landmarks of Florence that no longer exist—could be quite valuable."

Captain Bonner studied it more closely. The furrow in his brow relaxed, and she could see he was getting excited.

"Who's the artist?"

"The artist is not famous yet. His name is Dario Rossi," Marina said. That was the name she had told Carlos to use to sign the painting. "I discovered it in a local gallery. The gallery owner didn't realize its potential significance, so I paid only a few hundred lire for it. My father had an incredible eye for talent—that's why his gallery was so successful. He always said that I inherited that skill. In a few years, a Dario Rossi might be worth a good deal of money."

Marina waited for Captain Bonner's reaction. He leaned forward and examined the painting carefully.

"I see what you're saying." He nodded slowly. "The brushwork is exquisite, and the attention to detail on the bridge is quite extraordinary."

"Captain Bonner, you learn fast." She looked admiringly at him, aiming to flatter him. "In fact, I want you to have the painting for your collection."

"I can't allow that." He shook his head. "I'll be happy to pay for it."

"I don't want your money," she insisted. "For someone like my father or myself, art is not always about the painting itself; it's about the joy of sharing important pieces with others. My father couldn't keep all the paintings he admired, and neither can I. It will make me so happy to know that it has ended up in good hands, with someone who can truly appreciate it." She paused to give her words full effect. "Just think, if some of the great landmarks of Florence disappear, you will own something that keeps their memory alive forever."

Captain Bonner leaned back in his chair and looked at Marina appreciatively.

"I'm very grateful, Fräulein Tozzi." He stood up and walked to the sideboard. "We must have something to drink to celebrate."

Marina's heart pounded. She hadn't considered this possibility. He couldn't simply pour her a brandy right there. She had to get him out of the room—and fast.

She yawned loudly, forcing him to turn around.

"I'm so tired, I don't feel like a brandy. What I would really love is some hot chocolate. I have heard that it's one of the luxuries you German officers enjoy; surely you have some?"

This would give her enough time to switch the paintings.

He laughed. "You know all our secrets. As it happens, I do have my own stash—it's a weakness of mine." He stood up and walked to the kitchen. "I'll be just a few minutes."

Marina waited until he was in the kitchen, then took the copy out of her purse and tiptoed to the little table. The frame on the original didn't come off right away. She jiggled it carefully, guiding the painting out and slipping it into the satchel. She hastily inserted the copy, returning to the sofa with only a moment to spare as Captain Bonner's footsteps sounded in the hallway.

"Here you are," he said, handing her a cup.

Marina accepted the hot chocolate, working to slow her breathing.

"It's delicious, thank you. I always forget how cold Florence is at night. It will be good to have something to warm me up before I drive home."

"I really don't know how to thank you," he said.

Marina smiled. "Nothing makes me happier than sharing my love of art with others. My father taught me that."

Driving home through the winding streets of Florence, Marina reflected on the evening. She was relieved that it had gone according to plan. Captain Bonner seemed to believe everything she'd said. But when the Ponte a Santa Trinità stretched in front of her, her stomach turned. What if everything she had said came true? What if all the treasures of Florence—the Boboli Gardens, the Palazzo Vecchio, the Pitti Palace— were destroyed by bombs?

She forced the thought from her mind. The original Verrocchio sat in her bag. For tonight, that was enough.

CHAPTER SEVENTEEN

Florence, March 1944

Preparations for Belle's costume party had been in full swing for days, and delicious aromas wafted from the kitchen. Belle joked that there wouldn't be an egg left in Tuscany or a cow left to be milked after the occasion.

The entire villa hummed with activity. A red carpet had been placed in the entry and vases of daisies were everywhere. The fireplaces had been stocked with wood, and champagne was chilling in the fridge.

"I do love a party," Belle admitted to Marina. "It takes your mind off everything."

They were in the ballroom, arranging place cards on the long dining tables.

Marina had never been in the ballroom before. It was in the back of the villa, with French doors leading onto the terrace. There was a dance floor and a small stage for an orchestra.

"We haven't used this room in years. It's not really Bernard's style," Belle confided, smoothing a tablecloth. "He prefers a small group gathered around a dinner table, everyone talking over one another." She stepped back, admiring the table. "Usually I agree, but sometimes you need a party with music and dancing. The news of the war is so grim that some days I can barely drag myself out of bed."

"Has something happened?" Marina asked, thinking about the raids on the safe houses nearby. Belle seemed very eager for this party.

"It's just all so bleak," Belle explained. "Italian workers are going on strike; they're sick of producing things for the Germans. The trains will stop running soon. Bernard worries he won't be able to get to Switzerland anymore." She sighed. "I'm not going to think about it today; I have to finish my costume. It will take all night to put the last touches on Cleopatra's headdress." She glanced at Marina. "I haven't seen Carlos lately. Is everything all right?"

Marina flushed and busied herself with the place cards.

"Everything is wonderful. We've both been busy," she answered. "I'm going to go and see him when we finish here."

"You're both so beautiful with your youth and your energy." Belle sighed and gave the tablecloth a final pat. "It makes me happy to see you together."

Marina hadn't seen much of Carlos since she switched the Verrocchios two weeks prior.

The morning after she took the painting from Captain Bonner's apartment, Carlos had come to

Bernard's library to see it. Marina had hidden it inside the cover of Titian's diary. It was the safest place she could think of until they could return it to the Uffizi.

They had celebrated with a romantic dinner in the garden shed, then afterward, they made love. Marina had never felt so happy.

But since then, there wasn't much time to be together. The raids meant new safe houses had to be found. Sara's false papers never materialized—the forger had gone into hiding.

Carlos had disappeared for several days over the past few weeks. Marina knew better than to ask questions. She longed for the early days of their courtship when they had the time to tell each other their thoughts and dreams. Now even their lovemaking was rushed—afterward, Carlos would kiss the top of her head and apologize for having to leave.

"Marina—I thought I wouldn't see you until tomorrow," Carlos said when she arrived at his parents' villa, carrying a garment bag.

"I brought you a costume," she announced, holding up the bag.

Carlos was going dressed as a French artist, like the ones who filled the Left Bank in Paris. Marina planned to be a French peasant girl, the kind an artist might paint. She had borrowed a red blouse from Desi, which she would pair with a skirt she'd had since university. Belle had found a scarf for Marina's hair and a woven basket for her to carry.

"I'm glad you came." Carlos took her hand and led her down the hallway. "I have something for you too."

They entered the old playroom, and Marina spotted the book she had lent him on Botticelli's portraits sitting open on the table.

"What are you smiling about?" Carlos asked.

"You're reading the book I suggested." Marina had given him the book so that Carlos could learn about portraiture during the Renaissance.

He smiled. "You were right. Botticelli is the greatest portrait artist of his generation. I'm learning a lot. When the war is over, perhaps I might paint something worthwhile."

"Any gallery will be proud to carry Carlos Adamo portraits." It felt good to talk about a time after the war. "You'll be so popular, there'll be a waiting list as long as my arm for your paintings."

Who knew, perhaps Captain Bonner's Dario Rossi painting would go on to be very valuable after all. Carlos leaned forward and kissed her.

"I'm lucky to have someone who believes in me." He stroked her hair, and she felt a glimmer of happiness, the first in several days.

The recent news had all been terrible. The Vatican had been bombed days earlier, killing a workman and damaging the Palace of the

Holy Office. In Salerno, four hundred fleeing citizens on a freight train bound for the southern Apennine Mountains died from carbon monoxide poisoning. The incident on the train was merely an accident, but the number of casualties was still shocking. Marina was beginning to despair that the suffering would never end.

Carlos went to a little desk and took a box from the drawer.

"I was going to give this to you tomorrow before the party. But my plans have changed, and now I can't go."

"What do you mean you can't go?" she asked sharply. She had been looking forward to this night for weeks. They all needed some fun to break the gloom of the war.

"I discovered a possible new route for Sara and the children. We don't think it will be safe for long though, and I have to investigate. I might be gone for a week or more."

Marina tried to conceal her disappointment. She wanted Sara and the children to be safe too. But she had been looking forward to one night of fun.

Trying to distract herself, Marina focused on the box Carlos had given her. She opened it and gasped at the cameo ring inside.

"It's beautiful. Where is it from?"

"It was my great-grandmother's." He reached over and lifted the ring from the box. "My great-grandfather was a sea merchant. He gave it to her before he left on a voyage to the West Indies. He was only nineteen. He wanted to give her a diamond engagement ring, but he was afraid the ship might sink." Carlos paused and looked at Marina. "He promised to exchange it for an engagement ring when he came back, but he never did."

Marina's breath caught as she understood his meaning. "And now you're giving it to me?"

"I want to give you everything," Carlos said urgently. "A villa, your own art gallery, dresses and shoes. A warm coat so you're never cold again, and juicy steaks so you won't be hungry."

Marina looked at Carlos. A strange feeling came over her, as if she had just discovered something that had been in front of her all along. This didn't feel like a simple wartime romance that would end when the Germans left Florence and real life resumed. She and Carlos had developed true feelings for each other.

"You mean after the war?" she asked softly.

Carlos took her hand. He nodded.

"Lately, I can't think about anything else. I don't want to let you go, war or not."

"I don't either." Her words came out in a whisper.

Carlos kissed her, pressing her against him as he caressed her breast. He locked the door, pulled her down onto the rug, and entered her gently, cradling her head in his hands. She feared it would end too quickly, but he kept her on the edge, his eyes locked on hers, his hands traveling over her body until she urged him to go faster.

Afterward, Carlos fell asleep. Marina sat up and slipped on the cameo ring. It was old-fashioned and heavy, but she loved the way it looked on her finger. She lay down again beside Carlos, nestling against him.

For a moment she allowed herself a glimmer of hope that one day the war would end, and they would be happy and safe.

Belle's party was in full swing. Duke Ellington played on the phonograph, Anna passed platters of hors d'oeuvres, and Bernard tended bar. He mixed traditional Negronis, and Campari with orange, and an American cocktail called a southside, which was tart but delicious.

Marina was pleased to see that everyone had come in costume. Belle was as glamorous as a queen in her gold headdress and long black eyelashes. Ludwig wore velvet pantaloons and a broad black hat, a paintbrush in hand. Gerhard claimed to be Rodolfo, from the opera *La Bohème*, a book of French poetry tucked under his arm. Desi's mother, Catarina, came as a Swiss milkmaid with an apron tied around her waist and her hair in braids.

Marina couldn't help but smile at Carlos's

parents. Alba was Scarlett O'Hara from the American movie *Gone with the Wind*. Carlos's father was Ashley Wilkes from the same movie, in a waistcoat and broad hat, like a Southern gentleman attending a picnic.

Desi wore a gown with a velvet bodice and voluminous skirts. Her hair was covered by the kind of blond wig worn by royalty in the eighteenth century.

"Where's Carlos?" Desi asked. "I can't wait to see him in the beret."

Marina's face fell.

"He's not coming. He had to go away on business."

"He's missing the costume party? You would have looked so charming together. A French artist and a peasant girl."

Marina shrugged. "He'll be back in a week. You look stunning, but why is there a mole painted on your cheek?"

"I'm Marie Antoinette. I borrowed the wig from Belle. She saves all her old costumes," Desi explained.

"It suits you; you look like a queen." Marina grinned.

"I feel like a small whale," Desi groaned. "I'm afraid I got the dates wrong. I thought the baby was due in May. But the midwife said it will be the beginning of April."

"That's in less than a month! Are you sure?"

"Quite sure. I'm relieved—it's getting hard to move. He's kicking so much, I keep expecting my stomach to have bruises."

"Gerhard is here, you could talk to him," Marina suggested. "Perhaps he has information about Peter."

"I can't risk telling Gerhard, he and Belle and Bernard are good friends. My parents might find out that Peter and I were lovers. They wouldn't approve of Peter being German." Desi sighed and rubbed her stomach. "Marie Antoinette understood. Sometimes you have to accept your fate and make the best of it." She touched her curls, the laughter returning to her eyes.

As Desi moved away toward the food, Marina surveyed the party. She twirled the cameo ring on her finger. Why had Carlos given it to her now? He was often away on partisan business. Was it because this time he was afraid he might not return?

Her thoughts were interrupted by Ludwig making his way toward her.

"You shouldn't be standing alone," Ludwig greeted her.

"I'm not alone now that you're here. You look dashing," Marina said, glad to have company. "Let me guess, you're Leonardo da Vinci."

"How could I choose to be anyone else?" Ludwig said, smiling. "Leonardo is my favorite artist."

"It's a wonderful costume," Marina said happily. Ludwig always made her feel relaxed. "Bernard and Belle are so pleased everyone came."

"I never thought I'd see Bernard in a Roman toga." Ludwig chuckled. "And without his beard. I almost didn't recognize him."

"He's wearing pants underneath," Marina assured him. She looked over at Bernard, who was laughing at something Belle said. "They're a striking couple. I wasn't sure if I'd see you here. . . ."

"Ah, I haven't gone yet," Ludwig explained. "I'm leaving next week for the monastery. I was going to come later this week to say goodbye, if that's all right?"

"Yes, of course. Are you sure it's still necessary for you to go?"

"More than ever. I fear for Florence. Hitler knows he's losing, and worried leaders act impulsively. Nothing in Italy is safe."

"I'm sad to see you go. If it wasn't for you, I may not have made it to Villa I Tatti. My life is so full now." She looked over at Desi, who was happily eating a slice of cake, and at Bernard and Belle. "You've become a big part of it."

"You're an important part of my life too," Ludwig said. "Good friends last forever. Hopefully one day, when the war is over, we can live close to each other again."

Their conversation was interrupted by Bernard

tapping his glass, and everyone in the room turned in his direction.

"I know everyone is surprised to see me like this," Bernard began, waving at his toga. "No one knew I had such good legs."

There was a ripple of laughter, and he paused until it dissipated.

"To be honest, I don't like standing in front of groups; that's why I never became a professor. But I wanted to take this moment to thank a few people for making this awful time brighter. Ludwig for his intelligence and thirst for knowledge, and Gerhard for his friendship and excellent bottles of brandy." Bernard glanced fondly at Marina. "We're very blessed to have welcomed Marina into our little fold, and she has become like a daughter." He paused. "Mostly I want to thank Belle. Being with Belle, I never worry about dying. She keeps me much too busy." He raised his glass. "Let's all toast to my beloved Belle."

Everyone clapped loudly, and Marina was surprised to find her eyes were filled with tears.

Belle joined Bernard next to the fireplace.

"I doubt I can add anything to that, but that certainly won't stop me from trying," Belle began. "Tonight is very special to me. For one thing, Bernard shaved his beard." Everyone chuckled. "The bearded academic look is sexy, but there's something about a clean-shaven face that is quite appealing." Her tone grew serious. "Some people might say this is the worst time to hold a party. There's strict rationing; next month we might run out of coal. But I believe it's moments like this when we need to find a little joy. It reminds me too much of the last war in Europe. Hatred is everywhere, and human life has as much value as a pair of boots has to a soldier who has lost his leg.

"One thing we all have in common is that we love art. Art is about contrast in periods. The bleak ignorance of the Middle Ages gave way to the brilliance of the Renaissance. Much later came the Impressionists and now, God help us, the Modernists." She gave a small shudder. "This period of war and oppression will end; something bright and good will flourish in its place." Her eyes swept around the room. "Bernard wouldn't be a historian and I wouldn't be a librarian if we didn't believe that truth and beauty win in the end." She raised her glass. "I'm so glad we have good friends to help us through the moments in between."

CHAPTER EIGHTEEN

Florence, March 1944

Two weeks after the costume party, Carlos still hadn't returned. For the first week Marina tried to squelch her concern. He had warned her that he might be gone for a longer stretch this time. In the afternoons she worked in Bernard's library and pictured Carlos striding through the door. He would give her flowers or a pretty shawl. They'd make love in the garden shed and she'd feel silly for worrying.

But by the start of the second week, she couldn't shake the uneasy feeling that had settled over her. For the first time, she wished Carlos wasn't a partisan. She missed his coy smile that always came with a joke. She missed his confidence and his little kindnesses. There was no one to take her hand when she was cold, to make big plates of spaghetti when she had worked all day and forgotten to eat lunch.

The door to the library opened.

"Marina, is it all right if I come in?" Ludwig asked.

"Yes, of course."

"I came to say goodbye." He took off his jacket. "I'm sorry it's been a while. It took longer than I thought to select and pack the books."

Marina had been so preoccupied worrying about Carlos, she'd forgotten that Ludwig was going to the monastery. He looked older, Marina thought. His shoulders were hunched, and there were new lines around his mouth.

"Are you sure it's safe? What will happen when it's discovered that the books from the institute are missing?"

"I'm leaving most of the collection behind," Ludwig replied, sitting down. "I can hardly fit three hundred and sixty thousand books in my car." He rubbed his forehead. "The Nazis have arranged for two freight trains to cart everything to Germany. They won't miss one trunkful of books and paintings."

"I'm sure the institute will miss you."

"I've been packing for days," Ludwig told her. "There are so many priceless documents I have to bring, including maps of Florence from the thirteenth century. Did you know that Florence was once a small town where merchants came to exchange goods? I found the first architectural drawings of the Duomo, when Giotto's Bell Tower and Vasari's frescoes were merely visions in the artists' minds," he continued, as if he was talking about parting with old friends. "I will miss the beautiful buildings of Florence. But mostly I will miss the people I meet because of the collection, the visiting scholars: Experts on the Medici family, on Pope Julius II. A professor from Milan who devoted his entire career to examining Da Vinci's *The Last Supper*."

"What will you do at the monastery?" Marina hated hearing the anguish in Ludwig's tone. "Who will you talk to?"

"I suppose it's true, the monks aren't good conversationalists," Ludwig said wryly. "But I'm writing a new book. It will keep me busy until the war ends."

"Do you think it will end soon?" Marina asked.

Ludwig shrugged. "I've had no news from Berlin, but I think the tide is turning in Italy. The Allies are getting closer by the day; I predict the Germans will retreat by summer." He looked at Marina, and for the first time he smiled. "Perhaps you can go back to Rome."

Marina wondered if that was why Carlos had been away for so long, if he were somewhere in the hills, waiting to guide the Allies into Florence. She thought of her father's house and the gallery in Rome. Did she want to return to her old life, or did she want to stay near Belle and Bernard and Desi in Florence?

"I just want everyone to be safe," Marina said. Tears formed in her eyes. The thought of bombs falling, the museums being destroyed, was too much to bear.

"Are you all right?" Ludwig leaned forward in his chair.

"I'm fine." She pushed away the tears. "I've

grown so attached to Villa I Tatti and everyone here. I don't want anyone to get hurt."

"Do you still have the pistol?" Ludwig asked.

"Yes, of course." Marina pointed to the bookshelf. "It's hidden, and your books are safe."

"I do worry about you," Ludwig lamented. "Today on the street I was offered a gold watch by someone selling it on the black market. Thieves are growing bolder all the time. I'd never forgive myself if anything happened to you."

Ludwig was so kind to her, even though they'd known each other only a short time. He was almost like an older brother and they had so much in common.

"It won't, I promise," she assured him. She smoothed her skirt. "We're in a much better position than most. Few people get to sit out a war in a villa in Tuscany."

"Don't forget that you have Gerhard," Ludwig offered. "He's already said . . ."

"Said what?" Marina's head shot up.

"It doesn't matter." Ludwig stood and smiled warmly. "Just know that you can ask him for help."

Marina didn't want their conversation to end on a melancholy note. She didn't know when she would see Ludwig again.

"When I arrived at the Santa Maria Novella train station, I was cold and alone. It was the hardest night of my life." She twisted her hands.

"Then you showed up, and you were so kind." She gave a small laugh. "Though I don't know what you thought of me. I barely said a word in the car because you were German."

"I understood completely." Ludwig returned her smile. "I'm glad you gave me a chance to show you that not all Germans are Nazis. Everyone is guided by something: for me, it has always been art and beauty."

Impulsively Marina stood up and hugged him.

Ludwig hugged her back. When he left, Marina felt a small tug at her heart. The war had taken someone else from her.

She went to the bookshelf to check on the pistol. But when she felt for it behind the row of books where Carlos had hidden it, it wasn't there. She reached her hand further along the shelf, but there was nothing. She hastily removed the tomes, hoping it had just fallen behind one. The shelf was empty.

Her heart hammered.

No one but Carlos had known the pistol's new hiding spot.

She raced up the staircase to the third floor where she had hidden Ludwig's collection. The illuminated manuscripts, books on early Renaissance art and architecture, they were all there. The rush of relief changed to a pounding in her ears as she tried to account for everything. A book of sketches signed by Raphael was missing.

As was Titian's diary—which meant that the Verrocchio was gone too.

It had been Carlos's suggestion to move the valuable items to the third floor where it would be harder for a thief to find them.

Perhaps Carlos knew he was in danger, so he took the pistol from the library. But why would he have taken the books?

That evening, Marina was sitting in the living room at Villa I Tatti, trying to read but struggling to concentrate. Bernard entered in a smoking jacket and velvet slippers.

"Marina, I didn't know you were here." He carried a newspaper and some letters. "I came down for a glass of brandy. Would you join me?"

"I'd love to." Marina nodded, putting down her book.

Bernard poured two glasses of brandy and handed one to her.

"I've been reading the American newspapers. Eisenhower is all gung ho about the war. American troops are bombing everything in their path; everyone at home thinks we're winning. They don't see the destruction caused by the bombs or what Hitler is doing to the Jews." He frowned. "For many American women, the biggest inconvenience is living without a new vacuum cleaner. If they only knew what the rationing is like, that women and children are starving."

"At least they're trying to help."

"You're right." Bernard sat opposite her. "But it's getting worse in Florence all the time. I heard that two dozen prisoners are being held at Villa Triste and the guards don't even know why they're there. I doubt they have enough food and water."

"At Villa Triste?" Marina's heart pounded.

Carlos could be there. But Gerhard would have known. He would have told her.

"Are you all right?" Bernard asked. "You've gone very pale, and your hands are shaking."

Marina glanced down. Bernard was right—her hands were trembling.

"I'm fine. I just hate imagining innocent people in prison."

Bernard studied her expression. He sipped his drink.

"Is there anything else troubling you?" he asked. "We haven't seen Carlos since the week of the costume party. Is everything all right with you two?"

Marina stiffened. She put down her glass.

"Carlos is away on business for his parents. He'll be back soon."

"I saw something curious in Florence a few weeks ago." Bernard ran his fingers over the rim of his glass. "Carlos was standing in the Piazza della Signoria, talking to Captain Bonner. I didn't know they knew each other."

That did sound odd. A few weeks ago would have been before she had switched the paintings. Before Carlos encouraged her to accept Bonner's dinner invitation.

"Carlos must have met Captain Bonner when he was here at Villa I Tatti," Marina said.

But as soon as she said it, she had doubts. She had been alone with Belle when Captain Bonner visited. But perhaps he and Carlos had met while he was there. It was possible.

"Perhaps." Bernard set his glass on the coffee table. "How about a game of backgammon? I haven't played in years."

Marina tried to behave normally, even though her thoughts were racing. She needed to occupy her mind.

"I'd like that. My father taught me to play. He was a champion." She smiled at the memory. "Every now and then he let me win though, or he wouldn't have had anyone to play with."

When Bernard finally went to bed, Marina remained in the living room. She knew she wouldn't be able to sleep. Too many questions occupied her mind.

What possible business could Carlos have had with Captain Bonner? They certainly didn't socialize in the same circles. In fact, if Captain

Bonner knew what Carlos really did when he wasn't delivering firewood, he would have him arrested on the spot.

She hadn't heard from Captain Bonner since the night she switched the Verrocchio. Perhaps he had been called back to Berlin. She would have to ask Gerhard if he had heard anything.

Carlos's disappearance had nothing to do with Captain Bonner, she told herself.

She let her mind wander as the fire crackled in the hearth. The most obvious reason she hadn't heard from Carlos was that he was dead. But somehow, she thought she would know—her heart would know it. There was nothing to do but believe that Carlos was still alive. But where was he?

CHAPTER NINETEEN

Florence, March 1944

Several more days passed with no news. Every day, the possibility that Carlos was dead weighed on Marina like the rain that fell heavily on the fields. On the first sunny day of spring, she went to visit Desi.

Villa I Tatti's gardens were as green as they had been when she arrived last autumn. Rosebushes held new buds and early poppies dotted the landscape. Marina had always loved springtime in Rome, when the colors were more vibrant than at any other time of year. The Roman Forum shone white under a blue sky and the Colosseum turned golden at sunset.

If only Carlos were here. They would have a picnic on the velvety lawn. Carlos could paint a landscape, and Marina could make daisy chains, the way she did as a child.

Desi was in the morning room when Marina arrived. She sat on a love seat facing the window. Marina's gaze immediately went to her stomach, which was huge.

"Don't look at me," Desi groaned. "I resemble a hippopotamus. My skin feels like leather, and my whole body is all fat."

Marina smiled and sat opposite her.

"Nothing about you is fat besides your stomach," Marina replied. "I'm looking at you because the baby has grown since the party. I'm a terrible friend. I've only seen you once in the last two weeks."

"You haven't missed anything." Desi shrugged. "My mother doesn't want me to help in the barn anymore. She says I'll strain my back, but I think she's really afraid I'll scare the cows. Then they won't have any milk. Have you heard from Carlos?"

"He's still away on business. There is a war. Maybe he's been stranded somewhere."

Desi took a long time answering. "Carlos is a partisan," she announced.

"How do you know that?" Marina snapped. He had been so careful to keep it from Desi.

Desi shrugged. "He didn't tell me; I just know," she said. "Carlos was always good at keeping secrets. When we were teenagers, he bought a motorbike without telling anyone. He was afraid his parents would think it was too dangerous. They only found out when it broke down and he had to walk it home. But I could always tell when he was lying. He grew overconfident, as if he could distract you with his smile.

"He was so miserable when the war began. He refused to join the Italian army, and he hated all the killing. After Donato died, he became even worse. One day, he seemed his old self: cocky and joking, like an electrical cord that had been plugged in. A few months ago, I noticed him carrying something bulky under his coat, so I watched him. He loaded a radio into his truck and covered it carefully with a blanket. That's when I knew for sure."

Marina wanted to confide in Desi. To tell her about the missing books and the pistol. To confess her worst fears about Carlos. It would be a relief not to have to keep everything to herself. But she couldn't risk it.

"You're imagining things," Marina said. Carlos would hate for her to admit his secret to Desi. She was like his younger sister; he wanted to protect her.

"I'll never tell anyone," Desi continued, as if Marina hadn't spoken. "But I hope he confessed to you. Couples shouldn't keep secrets from each other."

Desi was so confident in her assumption, it seemed pointless to keep arguing.

"He did," she admitted. "I know Carlos is a partisan. But you mustn't tell him I told."

For a moment, Desi's eyes sparkled. Then she leaned forward and touched Marina's hand.

"Carlos is very capable of taking care of himself. I know you're worried, but everything will be all right."

Marina removed the small box containing the cameo ring from her pocket. She often took it with her, afraid to let it go.

"Carlos gave me this the night before the party," she said, showing Desi the ring. "I can't bring myself to wear it. Every time I put it on, I wonder if he gave it to me because he thought he might not come back." Her voice caught. "He knew he was in danger. It's been weeks. He could be captured, or dead."

Desi examined the ring.

"Did he say anything?" she urged. "About where he was going or when he'd return?"

Marina couldn't confide in Desi completely. She couldn't admit what Bernard had said about seeing Carlos with Captain Bonner, about the missing books and the Verrocchio, about her own role in valuing artwork for Carlos. But perhaps she could mention Sara and the children. She trusted Desi; Desi would never say anything.

"There is one place I can think of."

She told Desi about the barn. That Carlos had promised to help Sara and her children reach Switzerland.

"Perhaps he is there," Marina said. "Perhaps he's injured and there's no way to get help."

It was possible. She wondered why she hadn't thought of it before. There would be no way for Carlos to let her know without risking Sara, Eli, and Francesca's lives.

"You have to go," Desi declared. "You can take my car."

Marina hesitated. "I don't want to put Sara in danger."

"If Carlos is there, they're all in danger," Desi reasoned. "If he's not, she may know where he went."

Desi was right. And there were no other leads.

There was one other option though, she realized. Carlos had said the route wouldn't be safe for long. Maybe Sara was already in Switzerland with her family. If the barn was empty, she could take comfort in that. No new reports of German raids had reached her ears.

Marina nodded. "All right. I'll go this afternoon."

"We'll go now," Desi announced.

"You can't go anywhere!" Marina protested. "It's too risky."

"Having a baby while your lover is fighting in the German army is risky." Desi pushed herself up. "As long as I fit in the car, I'll be fine."

As Marina drove, she kept glancing over at Desi, hoping the bumpy road and sharp turns weren't too much for the baby. They pulled into the farm, and Marina led them to the barn.

She knocked on the door, reminding herself that the barn might be empty. In fact, she hoped it was.

But then came the sound of a bolt opening. A narrow face peered out.

"Beautiful signorina!" Eli called, opening the door wider. "I thought you were a German; you didn't knock twice. But I saw your face through a crack in the window."

"I'm sorry, I forgot," Marina replied. Her stomach dropped. She hadn't realized just how much she'd hoped they'd escaped.

"Come in." Eli waved them inside.

"This is my friend Desi," Marina introduced them. "Is your mother here?"

"Where else would she be?" Eli shrugged. "I keep telling her it's springtime. God wouldn't have created the fields and flowers if he didn't want us to go outside and enjoy them." He glowered. "She says it will be my last spring if I defy her."

Sara came down the ladder, Francesca attached to her hip. Marina almost didn't recognize Francesca. Her arms and legs were rounded, and her dark curls framed her face.

"Sara, this is Desi," Marina said.

Sara looked thinner than she had before. There were more lines around her mouth.

"What a beautiful baby!" Desi gushed.

"She's almost crawling." Sara stroked Francesca's cheek. "If I keep her in the loft, I'm afraid she'll fall down the ladder. When she's down in the barn, I worry that Eli will open the door and she'll get out."

"Can I hold her?" Desi stretched out her arms.

Sara gave the baby to Desi. Francesca curled her small fist around Desi's arm.

"Is Carlos with you?" Sara turned to Marina. "We haven't seen him in ages."

Marina's face fell. She had been hopeful that Carlos was here. She told Sara he had been gone for weeks.

"I wondered why he stopped coming." Sara twisted her wedding ring. "We were all set to leave, but he never brought our papers."

Marina could see the fear and uncertainty in Sara's eyes. Carlos must not have had time to tell her about the papers, or the escape route, or the neighbor.

"We're hoping he'll come back soon," Marina said firmly. "He was investigating a new route to Switzerland. He asked me to keep an eye on you while he was gone."

Marina felt guilty that she hadn't visited Sara and the children sooner. But the raids had made her reluctant to go; she didn't want to risk putting them in danger.

"I'm sorry, I should have come sooner. I'm sure he probably just got caught up."

"Nothing is certain during the war." Sara's brow furrowed. "It's springtime, and there are more people around, so I worry we'll be discovered if we stay here much longer."

Francesca made a small mewling sound. She buried her face in Desi's chest.

"Francesca is hungry," Sara announced. "We have a little extra to eat. Please join us."

Marina shook her head. "We don't want to take your food." They didn't have enough as it was.

Eli walked over to Marina.

"Please, signorina. There's plenty." He took Marina's arm and dragged her to the corner. A chest stood under the window, tins of meat atop it. There was a slab of cheese and a salami. A jar held crackers and there was even a chocolate bar.

"It's a magic chest, like in 'Jack and the Beanstalk,'" Eli said importantly.

"'Jack and the Beanstalk?'" Marina questioned.

"Carlos gave it to me to read to Francesca. In the story, Jack tosses a bean seed out the window, and it grows into a magical beanstalk. Jack climbs the beanstalk to a castle where a mean giant lives. He finds everything the giant stole from his family: geese and gold and precious jewels. He kills the giant and retrieves the stolen goods." Eli's face darkened. "It's just like what the Germans did to my family. If a German comes near the barn, I'll kill him with my bare hands."

"I don't know where the chest came from," Sara said. "It appeared outside the door, full of food."

It must have been Carlos. For a moment, relief

flooded through Marina. Carlos knew he would be gone for a long time and didn't want Sara and the children to starve. Yet surely he could have let Marina know something of his whereabouts or when he would be returning?

They ate at the makeshift table downstairs. It was early evening, and the sun fell behind the fields.

"We thought we'd be in Switzerland by now." Sara ate a bite of salami before pushing her plate to Eli.

Marina and Desi glanced at each other. Marina knew what Desi was thinking. Sara was right; the barn couldn't keep them for much longer.

"Why don't you and the children come with us?" Marina said. "We have a car."

Sara's fork clattered to the table.

"We can't do that," she protested. "We have nowhere to go. And anyone who helps us will be in danger."

It was true. But Marina couldn't leave them here.

"My family owns a vineyard," Desi suggested. "There are a few empty cottages on our land, so you can stay in one of those."

"But what would your family say?" Sara said. "And for how long? No one knows when the war will end."

Marina glanced at Desi, but Desi's mouth was set in a firm line.

"My parents don't have to know. And you can stay for as long as you need to." Desi placed her hand on Sara's. "Please let me do this. I'm going to be a mother too. Your children can't suffer because of this war."

"I visited a vineyard once," Eli said, swallowing his salami. "I can help to stomp on the grapes."

"I'm sure you could." Marina leaned over and ruffled Eli's hair. "But for now, you'll need to stay inside the cottage and help your mother with Francesca."

Sara glanced around the barn, the worry evident on her face. A cottage would be much more comfortable. And they would have people nearby to help.

"All right, we'll come," Sara decided. She looked between Desi and Marina. "I don't know how to thank you."

When they finished eating, Marina climbed into the loft to help Sara gather their belongings while Desi and Eli cleaned up.

Suddenly there was a popping sound. Marina thought it was a gun and hurried to the ladder. When she looked down, Desi was standing in a puddle of water.

"I don't know what happened," Desi called up to them. "I was just standing here and now the ground is all wet."

Sara peered over the railing.

"It's not a leak—your water broke."

"I'm not due for two weeks!" Desi exclaimed. "And I don't feel any pain."

But as soon as Desi said the words, her expression changed. A moan escaped her lips and she clutched her back.

"The signorina is having a baby!" Eli cried excitedly.

"Babies don't come that quickly." Sara climbed down the ladder. She placed her hand on Desi's stomach. "That felt like a contraction."

"I'm pretty sure it was," Desi said through gritted teeth. She grabbed the table to steady herself.

"I'll get the car," Marina said.

Marina hurried out the door. She ran up the hill and climbed into the driver's seat. But when she turned the key, there was nothing. She tried again. The car made a coughing sound and then was silent.

Marina's heart raced. She got out of the car and ran back to the barn.

"The car won't start!"

Desi was sprawled on a chair. Sara held her hand and balanced Francesca on her hip at the same time.

"There's nothing to worry about." Desi tried to sound confident. "The midwife says first babies can take a whole day to be born."

"Is there a bicycle?" Marina asked Sara. "I can go to the village for help."

Sara shook her head. "It's too far to the village. And how could we trust a stranger to come to the barn?"

"You're right, but I have to do something," Marina insisted. "Desi can't have the baby here."

"My aunt was a midwife. I know what to do," Sara replied. "Eli will bring down blankets to make a bed. There are some sheets in the loft. I'll boil water."

Sara was right. The closest village was Montelopio, but it would take Marina a while to bicycle there. And even if she found someone to help, it would be dangerous to bring a stranger to the barn. But if anything happened to Desi or the baby, Marina would never forgive herself.

"All right," Marina agreed. She turned to Desi. "But you have to tell us if the pain gets too bad."

Marina and Sara took turns holding Desi's hand. Sometimes the contractions were far apart, and they told stories to pass the time. Other times they were so fierce Marina couldn't bear to hear Desi's cries. Eli covered his ears and sang to drown out the sound.

Finally, around midnight, Sara pulled a stool between Desi's legs.

"It's time, the baby is coming," Sara said. "All you have to do is push."

Desi's hair was tangled, and her cheeks were shiny with sweat. "I can't. I'm too tired."

"You have to," Sara said matter-of-factly. "It's not hard, you've been through the worst."

Desi opened her mouth to protest but only a grunting sound came out.

"I'll sit with her," Marina suggested.

Marina sat next to her on the makeshift bed and took Desi's hand. Desi pressed down so hard that Marina was afraid her wrist would break. Desi pushed as hard as she could.

"I can't, I just can't," Desi moaned. Tears spilled down her cheeks. "There has to be another way."

"Of course you can." Marina stroked her hand. "You're Desi Pirelli. You're the strongest woman I know."

Desi gave a piercing cry, and then another almighty push. A small form slithered from her body. Sara caught the baby and rubbed its back but no sound came out. For a moment Marina was so frightened she couldn't breathe. Then Sara rubbed it again and the baby started crying.

"What's he like?" Desi gasped. "Does he have Peter's blond hair?"

Marina studied the baby in Sara's arms. She wiped the tears from Desi's cheeks and started laughing.

"The hair is blond," Marina said, giddy with relief. "But you were wrong about the sex. The baby is a girl."

A few hours later, Eli and Francesca were asleep in the loft. Sara had washed the baby in the little sink and wrapped her in a blanket.

"I didn't think I could do it," Desi admitted, stroking the baby's tufts of blond hair. "Then I closed my eyes and pictured Peter sitting in a foxhole on the Eastern Front. How could I be afraid when he's risking his life?"

Marina wondered if it would always be like this, if every joy or pain would be compared to something about the war.

"What will you name her?" Sara questioned.

Desi frowned. "At first, I thought Donatella, but that's too much of a mouthful."

Marina gazed out the window. Outside, the sky was black. There was a sheet of stars, like the notes in one of Bernard's musical scores.

"What about Luna?" Marina offered. "She was the Roman goddess of the moon. She rides on a chariot, and her hair is spun gold."

The baby's eyes were open. They were pale blue with silvery blond lashes.

"Luna is perfect," Desi announced.

The next day, Marina bicycled to Montelopio and convinced a shopkeeper to lend her his car. Then she drove Desi and Luna, Sara, and the children to Desi's parents' property.

It was all worth it when they arrived at the

cottage. It was bright and sunny and had a fireplace and a proper stove. Eli hugged the stove as if it were a long-lost friend. He was going to make spaghetti with red sauce, the way Carlos showed him. Sara almost burst into tears when she entered. The children had a bed and a rug to keep their feet warm. The window was covered with pretty curtains.

The next day, Marina would return to Montelopio and hire a mechanic to fix the car. But tonight, she was going to take a bath and ask Anna to bring up some soup and bread. Although the food would fill her belly, that night she felt a different kind of hunger. She yearned for Carlos: his lips on her mouth, his body pressed against hers. She didn't want to have to learn to live without him.

CHAPTER TWENTY

Florence, August 1944

It was a little over four months since the night Desi's baby was born. Marina couldn't remember such a hot summer. In Rome, the warm weather lasted only a month. When the temperature rose in August, Marina and her father would go out after dinner for gelato. Her father always stopped on the way home to chat with Paolo and other neighbors. His gelato would melt while he stood there, but he didn't mind. He enjoyed talking with friends even more than he loved the sweet dessert.

By September the evenings in Rome were cool with the promise of autumn. In Tuscany Marina felt the heat would go on forever. It was the beginning of August, and the sun beat down on Villa I Tatti's gardens. Even Bernard's library was hot and stifling. The only relief was in the kitchen. The walls were made of stone and the floor of blessedly cool tiles.

Marina sat at the kitchen table drinking a glass of lemonade. She had tried to stop counting the number of weeks Carlos had been gone. Every time she recalled the afternoon before the costume party—Carlos giving her the cameo ring, them making love in the old playroom—her stomach filled with a sense of foreboding.

With each passing day, it seemed less likely Marina would ever see Carlos again.

Over the past few months since Luna was born, Marina had spent most of her time with Desi, who had become a magnificent cross between a queen directing her subjects and a girl with a new doll. She ordered Marina around with a barrage of requests. The crib was too close to the window. Could Marina move it across the nursery? Luna's carriage wasn't padded enough. Could Marina get more blankets? When Marina did as Desi asked, Desi burst into tears and apologized for being bossy.

Luna was as sweet and round as a peach. Her eyes only became bluer over time, and her hair blonder. As she wrapped her fingers around Marina's hair, Marina could only imagine what Desi felt: being a mother must be the most thrilling, terrifying thing in the world.

Marina also spent time at the cottage with Sara. The cottage was in the middle of the vineyards, and so far, no one had noticed they were there. But Marina was sure Desi's mother had her suspicions. Even a new mother like Desi couldn't finish off a gallon of milk in a day. And the oranges in the fruit bowl disappeared the minute Catarina brought them in from the garden.

Marina suggested they should tell her mother,

but Desi said she had enough things to work out with God at the moment.

Eli and Francesca had grown so much that it became difficult to keep them in clothes. Eli was so tall that he had started to resemble the magic beanstalk in the fairy tale. By now, the cuffs on his new pants were too short, and the buttons popped off his shirt. Eli happily announced that one day he'd be so strong that he'd never have to worry about the Germans again.

Francesca loved to pull herself up on the furniture. She jiggled her legs and tipped her head as if she was dancing. Marina watched her and tried to imagine Francesca as a young woman with her dark curly hair and large blue eyes, dancing at a party, the war a long-ago and distant memory.

But it was impossible to truly enjoy her time with the children, or even give all her attention to Desi and the baby, when Marina kept picturing Carlos dead.

"Marina, here you are!" Belle entered the kitchen. "I was just in Florence seeing Gerhard. It's even hotter there than here in the countryside, even though it's only thirty minutes from Montelopio."

She poured a glass of lemonade and sat across from Marina.

"Gerhard looks terrible. He has dark circles under his eyes. His clothes are rumpled. He would never admit to it, but I think he's been sleeping at his office."

Marina's fingers curved around her glass. So much had happened in the previous months. At the beginning of June, the Allied forces landed in Normandy and invaded northern France. The same month, the Germans dropped the first doodlebugs—jet-powered bombs—on London and hundreds of civilians were killed. And in July, an attempt by senior Nazi officers to kill Hitler had failed.

"Did something happen?"

"The Allies are drawing closer." Belle sipped her lemonade. "The Germans are preparing to blow up the bridges any day. Gerhard has been on the phone with Rudolf Rahn, the German ambassador. There's nothing he can do."

Belle stirred her lemonade thoughtfully.

"We'll be safe here, but I worry about the people in Florence. The Germans have installed a curfew. If anyone is on the streets after dark, they could be shot.

"I've already told Bernard not to go into Florence. Perhaps you can warn Desi and her parents," Belle said worriedly. "How are Desi and the baby? I haven't seen them in weeks."

"They're fine. Desi is adjusting to being a new mother. Luna is the loveliest thing you've ever seen. All fair hair and porcelain skin like in a Dutch painting."

"I'm glad they're all right. The blond hair is curious, since Desi is so dark," Belle remarked. "But children are a mystery to me. I suppose that's why I never had them. Desi is lucky to have you; it's hard to raise a child without its father."

"Desi has her mother, but I'm glad to help," Marina acknowledged. "It keeps me busy so that I don't . . ."

She didn't want to think about Carlos.

"Still no word from Carlos?" Belle asked, as if reading her thoughts.

Marina shook her head.

"His parents think he joined Mussolini's army, but Carlos would never do that. He hates the fascists as much as he hates the Germans." Marina's voice grew urgent. "He could have found some way to communicate with me. A letter or a phone call. Instead, he's disappeared." She looked at Belle. "It's hard to maintain hope."

Belle walked to the counter and placed her glass in the sink.

"You have to have faith that Carlos is alive; there's nothing else you can do."

Marina parked in front of the German consulate. Belle had warned her to stay away from Florence, but she needed to ask Gerhard about Captain Bonner. Where was he? Perhaps Carlos's disappearance had something to do with him after all.

"Marina!" Gerhard exclaimed when his secretary escorted her into his office. "What a wonderful surprise."

Belle was right. Gerhard seemed to have changed almost overnight. His hair had gone white, and his forehead was lined. His clothes hung off him loosely.

His office was furnished with a desk and a low bookshelf. A fireplace took up one wall and there was an armchair draped with a blanket. A pile of newspapers was scattered on a side table next to a pitcher of water and an empty glass.

"I hope it's all right that I came," Marina said nervously. "Belle mentioned she'd seen you. I was running an errand in Florence and thought I'd say hello."

"She probably told you what bad shape I'm in." He waved his hands around the room. "Don't blame my secretary. I won't allow her to clean up. I just make it untidy again. It's better to leave it until . . ." He stopped. "Well, for the time being." He motioned for Marina to sit down. "To what do I owe this pleasure?"

"Belle told me that the Allies are advancing on Florence," she began. "That the Germans are going to start blowing up the bridges."

"All of Florence could end up in ruins." Gerhard rubbed his brow. "My superiors don't care; they'll do anything to stop the Allies." He studied Marina. "I probably shouldn't tell you this, but I'm working on a plan to keep the citizens safe."

"Safe how?"

"They'll leave their houses and go to the Pitti Palace." Gerhard pointed to a map on the desk. "It's the only structure in Florence that will hold enough people. It's shaded from the heat and it's architecturally sound." He sighed. "Those fifteenth-century builders did a fine job. And the courtyard of the portico stays cool."

Marina couldn't imagine it. The Pitti Palace had once been the home of the Medicis. Now the rooms made of gold, the museum that housed the works of Titian and Perugino, would be overrun by thousands of families fleeing the destruction.

"Is there somewhere outside the city they could go instead?" she asked.

"I'm afraid there isn't time to get everyone out of the city," Gerhard said gravely. "The Nazi military commander, Albert Kesselring, has been instructed to blow up the bridges tomorrow night. The command comes straight from Hitler."

Marina was silent. She didn't know what to say.

"You're safe at Villa I Tatti," Gerhard assured her. "Don't go anywhere until this is over."

"I have nowhere to go." Marina shrugged. She tried to sound casual. "It's been quiet near the villa lately. Captain Bonner's men haven't made any more searches of the countryside."

"Captain Bonner was called back to Berlin in June," Gerhard replied. "Most of his men are gone now too." He sighed. "Soon, I'll be the only one left.

"In 1939, I was going to resign." He paced around the room. "But the thought of leaving my adopted city, not strolling through Piazza della Signoria on my lunch hour or spending a Saturday in Palazzo Vecchio, was impossible to imagine. But this is worse. I promised the people of Florence to protect their city, and I failed them." His eyes misted over. "Ludwig and I used to argue over which statue of David, Donatello's or Michelangelo's, is of more artistic significance. Then we'd throw up our hands and laugh. What great good fortune to have two of the finest statues ever crafted in the same city. I can't bear to see it harmed."

"You have done the best you can," Marina said softly. "No one could have tried harder."

Gerhard's expression changed. He sat heavily in his chair.

"I shouldn't make this about me. The war is difficult for everyone. My sister's son has been injured. He's been transferred from the Eastern Front to a hospital in Germany."

Marina's pulse quickened.

"Your nephew?"

"Peter." Gerhard nodded. "He was hit by a grenade in a foxhole. Thank God, his injuries aren't too serious. He has some broken bones and a concussion."

"Where is the hospital?" she asked, trying to keep her voice steady.

"Near my sister's house in Baden," he said absently. "She's thrilled to have him home, and it could be much worse. But it will take a while for Peter to recover."

Marina stood up and walked to the door.

"I hope your nephew is all right," she said, suddenly getting misty-eyed. "And you mustn't blame yourself for anything. We're all lucky to have you as a friend."

Marina sped back to Villa I Tatti, eager to tell Desi about Peter. She thought about Captain Bonner. She was glad that he had left Florence without bothering her again. But his departure told her nothing new about Carlos. Carlos disappeared in March, and Captain Bonner didn't return to Berlin until months later. She was no closer to learning the reason for Carlos's disappearance.

Desi was in the nursery when Marina arrived. It was furnished completely in white. The crib was white, and a white rug had been thrown over the floor. Even the dresser and clock on the wall were white.

"I just finished Luna's feeding," Desi said, buttoning her blouse. "She's so busy; she hardly sits still to nurse. Another few months and she'll be at the kitchen table, demanding fruit and cereal."

"I was in Florence," Marina explained. "With Gerhard."

"Does he have any news about Carlos?" Desi asked.

"No, not about Carlos," Marina answered slowly. "He had news about Peter."

Desi's eyes darted up.

"I thought you hadn't mentioned Peter to Gerhard."

"I haven't. He has no idea that you and Peter were lovers," Marina assured her. "We were discussing the war, and he mentioned that Peter has been injured. He's at a hospital in Baden."

Desi put her hand on the windowsill to steady herself.

"How badly?"

"A grenade went off in his foxhole," Marina replied. "Gerhard says his injuries are not too severe—some broken bones and a concussion."

Desi crossed the room. She placed Luna in the crib and sat in the rocking chair, clutching her daughter's blanket. Her shoulders shook as she cried.

"You swear you're telling the truth? He's not terribly injured?" Desi hiccupped. "Peter is really safe?"

Marina moved her hand over her chest in the sign of the cross.

"You have my word," she said firmly.

Desi rubbed the tears from her eyes. She jumped up and walked to the little desk.

"Then you need to help me. We need to take these to the post office in Montelopio." She pulled out a stack of envelopes.

"What are those?" Marina asked.

"Letters to Peter," Desi replied. "I write to Peter while Luna is napping."

There were piles of envelopes. They spilled off the desk and onto the carpet.

"All of those are for Peter?" Marina asked incredulously.

Desi's chin clenched. She folded her arms over her chest.

"It's a good thing that Peter will be in the hospital for a while," she declared. "He'll have time to read every single one."

Later that evening Marina sat in her bedroom watching the sun set. She tried to imagine what it would be like to be in Florence. Did people know the Germans were preparing to set off mines to destroy the bridges? Could they sense it in the mood on the street?

There was a knock. Anna stood outside Marina's room, holding an envelope.

"This came for you." She handed it to her. "A driver delivered it."

Marina opened it and drew out a letter.

Dear Marina,

I wanted to thank you for visiting me today and to let you know that I'm leaving the consulate building here in Florence. I've been ordered to relocate to Fiesole. I'm glad I was able to see you. As I've said many times, I have great respect for youth. Sometimes the only thing one can learn from history is to ignore it. Every generation has its own beliefs; I pray that your generation is wiser and kinder than mine.

I haven't failed the people of Florence completely. I secured Kesselring's promise that Ponte Vecchio will remain standing. I hope that one day I will return and be able to cross it back to my beloved city.

Until then, yours, Gerhard Wolf

Marina placed the letter back in the envelope. Her heart ached for Gerhard, yet she felt a small stab of happiness at the same time. He had accomplished what he set out to do and saved the Ponte Vecchio. Perhaps there was hope for the future after all.

CHAPTER TWENTY-ONE

Florence, August 1944

The next morning was somehow even hotter than the day before. Marina got out of bed and walked to the window. Gerhard said they were going to start blowing up the bridges that night. She was grateful to be safe at Villa I Tatti.

Marina grabbed eggs and cheese from the kitchen and crossed the gardens to Desi's vineyards.

Sara was standing at the stove when Marina entered the cottage.

"Marina." Sara turned around. "I was just making breakfast for Francesca."

Marina sat at the small table.

The cottage was spotless, except for a pile of books that lay on the rug.

"Thank you for the books," Sara said, following her gaze. "Eli loves to read to Francesca." She chuckled. "Francesca pretends to be interested, but she'd rather eat the pages."

"It's my pleasure."

Francesca climbed into Marina's lap. Fourteen months old now, she wore a pinafore and smelled of soap.

"Francesca just had a bath. She puts her head

under the water and looks like she is swimming. Having a bathtub is the greatest luxury. Eli says we're living like the king of Italy.

"I'm so grateful to Desi for letting us have the cottage. We're going to stay as long as she'll allow," Sara said. "Francesca has grown so attached to Luna, and Eli seems happy. He loves the vineyards. He decided he wants to grow his own grapes when he's older."

Marina glanced around the one-room cottage.

"Where is Eli?"

"He left a note that he was going into Florence before I woke," Sara said anxiously. "He borrowed a motorbike from Desi's garage. He won't be gone long but I've been sick with worry. He's only fifteen, and he thinks he's so mature. What if something happens to him?"

"Into Florence?" Marina said in alarm. "You left the city almost a year ago. Why would he go back now?"

"It's my fault," Sara admitted. Her cheeks were pale, and her eyes filled with tears. "The other night, you and I were talking about the Germans blowing up the bridges. I thought Eli was asleep, but he heard us.

"He went back to get things from our apartment. He's afraid when the bridges are blown up, the buildings around them will fall down."

Marina hadn't mentioned exactly when the bridges would be blown up. If Sara knew it was that night she would be even more panicked. Marina had to keep it to herself.

"I'll go into Florence and find him." Marina stood up.

"You can't do that!" Sara exclaimed. "It's too dangerous. If anyone goes, it should be me. Perhaps you can stay and watch Francesca."

The bridges wouldn't be blown up until that night. If she hurried, Marina had time to find Eli and bring him back.

"Francesca would be upset without you," Marina reasoned. "Don't worry, I'll be fine. I'll borrow Desi's car; we'll be back soon. You know what teenage boys are like on motorbikes. They drive as if they own the road." She kept her voice light. "I'll feel better if we come back in my car."

In Florence, she first passed the Santa Maria Novella train station. Then she drove through the medieval streets in the city center, with their crooked sidewalks and haphazard houses. People were loading their possessions into small cars. Families carried suitcases down the sidewalks. Marina wondered where they were going.

Her search for Eli took on new urgency. Sara had given her the address for their apartment, but she seemed to be driving in circles. Three times she ended up at Piazza della Repubblica. When finally on track, she drove past the church of Santa Croce to San Niccolò and found the apartment. It was once an artisan's neighborhood and the streets were the narrowest in the city. People were tossing their belongings into parked cars, leaving little room to maneuver. One man carried a drawer, and Marina caught a flash of movement inside; it contained a baby not more than a week old.

There was no sign of Eli, and there was no place to park. She drove up and down, searching for a tall, skinny boy on a motorbike.

Suddenly, she saw Eli carrying a chest. He was coming out of the apartment building. She squeezed the car behind another stopped car and ran out.

"Eli, what do you think you're doing?" she demanded.

Eli's eyes lit up. He placed the chest on the ground.

"Beautiful Roman signorina!" He beamed. "What are you doing in this part of Florence? There aren't any museums or fancy shops."

"I came to find *you*." She placed her hands on her hips. "You worried your mother and me to death."

"There's nothing to worry about," he assured her. "The Germans have left already. I saw their trucks as I entered the city. Cowards!" He spat on the ground. "They're afraid of their own mines."

"You should be afraid of the German mines," Marina snapped. "We have to leave now. The roads will become congested and we won't be able to get out of Florence."

Eli crossed his arms. For a moment she saw the man he would become: proud and defiant.

"I can't leave without our belongings," he said stubbornly. "And what will I do with the motorbike?"

Marina glanced from the chest to the motorbike.

"We'll put the chest and boxes in the car," she decided. "Leave the bike here." She set her mouth firmly. "It will be our present to the Germans."

Eli ran up to the apartment. He came out with boxes and a basket.

"What's that?" Marina pointed to the basket.

"It's the basket Francesca came home in from the hospital when she was born," Eli explained. His eyes filled with emotion. "I know how much it means to my mother."

Marina sighed and began filling the car. Finally, the boxes were all loaded. The chest didn't fit, so Marina wedged it into the trunk and went to drive with the trunk open.

The car lurched into the street. In front of them, a truck stopped suddenly, and Marina stepped on the brake to avoid running into it.

"I can drive," Eli suggested.

"You're fifteen," Marina returned, narrowly missing a bicycle.

"I know how. I'm responsible enough."

"Responsible enough to come into a city where

the bridges are about to be blown up?" Marina reprimanded.

They drove silently through San Frediano. The streets were so thick with cars, it was difficult to see ahead.

Eli craned his neck out the window. He pointed in front of them.

"What are all those people doing in the Boboli Gardens?" he asked.

Marina looked in the direction he was pointing. The Pitti Palace stood in front of them. The huge brass doors were flung open, and people were camped on the steps. Children played in fountains and a woman cooked on a makeshift stove.

She almost laughed and cried at the same time. Gerhard had somehow pulled it off.

"They've left their homes and have nowhere to go," Marina said, slowing down.

"Can we stay here too?" Eli asked eagerly.

Marina shook her head. "You'll be safer at the cottage."

"It might be safe, but it won't be exciting." Eli slumped in his seat. "Think what stories I'd be able to tell my grandchildren if I spent the night in the house of the Medicis while the bridges into Florence were blown up."

Traffic eased as they left the city. Eli started singing, and Marina tried to relax. But she couldn't get the people in the Pitti Palace out of her mind. What if the explosions destroyed the neighborhoods around the bridges too?

When they finally reached the cottage, all her fears bubbled to the surface and she turned to Eli angrily. "You'll be lucky if your mother doesn't lock you in the cottage. And what if I hadn't come? You couldn't have carried everything on the motorbike. You would have frightened your mother for nothing, and you might have been killed."

Eli's eyes flashed with rage.

"Every day someone tells me what I can't do. I can't go to school, and I can't work in the vineyards. I can't even climb a tree or ask a pretty girl to go swimming like I did on holiday last summer. The worst part is I can't help my mother. I hear her at night. She sits at the table and cries for my father." His hands became fists. "If I can do one thing to make her smile, it will be worth it."

Eli jumped out of the car. He pulled the chest out of the trunk and dragged it inside.

Marina hurried after him.

"You're home!" Sara exclaimed. "I've been so worried. How could you take the motorbike? What if you had been trapped in the city? What if I'd lost you!"

"I brought you this," he said simply.

He showed her the chest.

Sara opened it. Inside was a white lace gown.

It had a gathered waist and the bodice was sewn with tiny pearls. She unfolded the gown and held it against her chest.

"You brought my wedding dress?" Sara gasped.

She put her arms around Eli and hugged him tightly. Sobs convulsed her body.

Marina's eyes filled with tears. She watched Eli's face when Sara released him.

"I couldn't leave it behind," Eli replied. "What would Francesca wear when she got married?"

Marina entered Villa I Tatti. She was hot and tired and wanted to take a bath.

A voice called to her from the living room. Bernard was seated in an armchair holding a glass of whiskey, a pile of books beside him on the coffee table.

"Will you join me?" he asked.

"Thank you." Marina nodded. "I can't think of anything I'd like better."

Bernard took a glass from the sideboard. He poured the whiskey and handed it to her.

"I have some news, and I don't know how to tell you."

The hairs on the back of Marina's neck stood on end. She glanced up sharply.

"What kind of news?"

Bernard stood up and paced around the room. He motioned at her drink.

"Finish that first."

Marina gulped her drink and placed the glass on the table.

"Now?" She turned her face to Bernard.

"There was a disturbance in Barga a few months ago. It was merely a street scuffle, but a German officer was shot and killed. The remaining officer followed orders from Berlin. For every German officer killed, four Italians must be shot. A group of men were sitting outside at a café. One of the men made a snide comment to the officer." He paused. "The men were lined up against a wall and shot."

Marina felt glued to her chair. She could barely breathe.

"They were executed in broad daylight, for the whole village to see. One of the men matched Carlos's description. He was wearing this on his hand."

After another sip of whiskey he took something out of his pocket and handed it to Marina.

"I thought you should have it."

It was Carlos's gold signet ring. His initials were engraved on the ring in sloping letters. The first time Marina had seen it was at the Adamos' dinner party. Carlos almost never took it off.

The room seemed to spin and she felt dizzy.

"How did the ring find its way here?" Marina said in shock.

"I don't know exactly." Bernard shrugged. "Another partisan must have taken it from

Carlos's finger before the Germans carted off the body. It was returned to his parents and they gave it to me." He looked at Marina. "They thought you should have it."

"But that happened a while ago," she continued in a rush. "We're only finding out now?"

"I'm sorry—news like that takes a while to travel."

What if someone else was wearing Carlos's ring? Anything was possible during the war.

"Are you sure it was him?" she demanded, pressing the ring against her palm.

"Not completely. The bodies were taken away by the Germans," Bernard said. His voice became gentle. "But there's no reason to doubt it."

All those months that Marina believed Carlos was still alive, and the whole time he was already dead.

What was Carlos doing in Barga? There were so many questions, and she would never know the answers.

Marina picked up her glass. She ran her fingers over the rim.

"I'm very sorry," Bernard said. "No one deserves to die that way. And you don't deserve to lose another person close to you."

Bernard and Belle had been so kind to her. She couldn't cry in front of Bernard when he had already given her so much. She didn't want to burden him with more of her grief.

"Don't worry about me. I have you and Belle, and Desi and the baby." She managed a half smile. "I'm luckier than most."

A few hours later Marina sat at the kitchen table. She had a headache, and her eyes stung from crying. Her heart felt like it was going to split open. She imagined Carlos sitting outside at a café, a scarf wrapped around his neck, the scuffle going on in front of him, and the German officer being shot. Had Carlos been thinking about Marina when he was lined up against the wall?

There was a loud popping sound, and she ran to the window. The night sky was bright with lights, like the Christmas tree on Piazza Navona in Rome. A bang followed and then more searing lights, as if a gash had opened up above Florence.

The Germans must have set off the mines. By this time tomorrow, she wondered if any of the bridges would still be standing.

But for once, she couldn't think about art or architecture or even other people's suffering. The wound in her own heart was too deep. Tears rolled down her cheeks and she didn't try to stop them.

She cried for her father, whom she adored and who would never see his daughter marry and start her own family. She cried for Carlos, who taught her how to love, and for Desi, who almost lost Peter forever. She cried for all the men and women who tried to make a difference during the war.

Eventually her sobs subsided, and she sat and listened in silence to the destruction of her beloved Florence.

CHAPTER TWENTY-TWO

Florence, July 1945
Eleven months later

The war had been over for two months. Sometimes, Marina couldn't believe it was true. Hitler and Mussolini were both dead, though not forgotten.

Gerhard's orders were followed, and the Ponte Vecchio survived, although a third of Florence remained in ruins, a casualty of a fire that had raged for days. More than two hundred citizens were killed. The only bright spot was that despite a collapsed fresco ceiling, Marina's beloved Uffizi Gallery remained standing.

But dwelling on the war wouldn't bring back her father or Carlos. And now, with the war behind her, she had decisions to make about her future. Paolo had written that the gallery had taken a direct hit nearly a year ago; the bomb had left nothing. Marina had no desire to go back and live in her father's house. It held too many memories.

Even though the war was over, Bernard was still cataloging the books he was going to donate to Harvard after his death. Marina could work on that, and she enjoyed helping Desi with Luna. But she couldn't do that forever.

Desi had gone to collect Peter from his parents' house in Baden in the spring after the Germans surrendered. The day they drove up, with Luna bouncing on Peter's knee and Desi beaming with love and pride, had been one of the happiest of Marina's life.

At first, Desi's parents were wary of Peter. But he brought bottles of wine for Desi's father and a huge rind of cheese for Catarina. They sat at the dining room table and ate plates of pasta and talked about wine and Italy and Germany.

Desi's parents were impressed with Peter's intelligence and ambition. Mostly they were taken by the loving way he gazed at Desi and Luna. He held Desi's hand and stroked Luna's round cheeks as if he couldn't believe they were his, as if he was the luckiest man on earth.

Desi had finally told her parents about Sara and the children staying in the cottage last August, after the Germans retreated. Her mother had been angry at first. Desi had put them all in danger. But the first time Catarina met the little family— Eli with his charming manners and Francesca with her dark curly hair and dimples—Catarina squeezed Desi's hand and whispered that she couldn't have done anything else.

Marina had made inquiries and discovered that Benito had been sent to a concentration camp and perished. She worried that Sara would be inconsolable when she learned the news. Sara let herself mourn for a week and then forced herself to be strong for the children.

Now Sara helped Catarina with the cows, and Eli was learning to work in the vineyards. Marina had never seen Eli so excited. Every week, he regaled Desi with plans about how they would become the biggest wine producers in Tuscany.

It was a beautiful summer day. Marina crossed the gardens to Desi's parents' villa and entered the morning room, which was flooded with sunlight. A wine bottle and some sketches stood on the table. Desi swept them aside and laid out a tiny white dress. It was satin with a pink bow.

"Do you like it?" Desi asked. "It's for Luna. I found it in the attic."

"It's very pretty, but where will she wear it?" Marina sat down.

"To the wedding," Desi answered. She brightened. "I found a dress for Francesca too. I'm going to ask Sara if Francesca will be a flower girl." She rolled her eyes. "Luna follows Francesca around like a puppy. They're both lovely. When they're older, every boy in Tuscany will be in trouble."

"What wedding?" Marina asked.

Desi's eyes danced. She held out her hand.

"I was waiting for you to notice." She pointed to the ring. "Peter officially proposed. We're getting married next month."

"He proposed!" Marina gushed, admiring the

square-cut diamond. "Tell me everything."

"I may have pushed him into it," Desi admitted. "He wanted to wait until his leg was properly healed and he could dance at the reception. But I don't care about a big wedding. I told him if he didn't ask me properly, he couldn't stay here anymore. How does it look to Luna, her parents living in the same house without being married?"

"Luna is sixteen months old; she doesn't notice." Marina laughed.

"She'd know when she was older," Desi replied. "It happened last night, out in the garden when the moon was full. It was so romantic. He'd hidden the ring in our dessert. It was Peter's grand-mother's ring; he had it with him the whole time."

"I'm glad." Marina hugged her. "You're the best couple I know."

"Will you be my maid of honor?" Her face clouded over. "That is, if . . ."

"If the wedding doesn't remind me of Carlos?" Marina finished her sentence.

"I'm sorry," Desi said. "You've been so brave, but it can't be easy."

"He's been dead for more than a year. I still can't believe it." Marina sighed. "Sometimes I expect him to show up in his truck, delivering firewood." She felt the familiar sting of tears. "He was so young and full of life. It seems impossible that he's dead."

Desi squeezed her hand.

"Carlos loved you. That's what memories are for," Desi offered. "So that our loved ones never die."

"I don't know what to do now," Marina reflected. "There's nothing for me in Rome, and I can't stay here forever. I suppose I could work in a gallery in Florence, but somehow it doesn't feel right. I want to do something important; I just don't know what."

"Something will come up, that's how life works," Desi assured her. "In the meantime, you can help me plan this wedding. I convinced Father Garboni to hold the ceremony here. We're supposed to be married at the church, but I promised him a big donation to make an exception. The church roof needs fixing and the pews haven't been redone since before the war."

"The villa is a perfect place for the wedding," Marina agreed.

Desi smoothed the tiny flower girl dress.

"Do you remember when we met in the garden?" Desi mused. "I felt so sick, and I missed Peter. I thought I'd never be happy again. Now I'm getting married and I have a baby and a best friend." She kissed Marina on both cheeks. "One day, you're going to have everything you want too."

Later that afternoon Marina was sitting at the desk in the library when Bernard appeared in the doorway. He wore a light summer suit and carried a sheaf of papers.

"Marina. I thought I'd find you here."

Marina looked up and smiled. "I haven't seen you in a few days. Belle said you were in Switzerland."

"I just returned." He pulled up a chair. "It was a successful trip. It feels good to return certain things to their owners."

Marina nodded. "I'm glad."

Bernard's trips made her think about Ludwig. She hadn't heard from him since he went to the monastery. She often wondered if he was safe and if the books the Nazis transported to Germany would one day be returned to the institute.

Bernard set the papers on the desk. "I have a proposition for you."

"What kind of proposition?"

"I know a man in Argentina, Luc Feron, the son of an old friend of mine who moved to Buenos Aires before the war. Luc is a private investigator. Lately he's been taking on work from an organization there that reunites art pieces with their rightful owners."

"What do you mean?" Marina asked curiously.

"Have you heard of ratlines? Nazis use them to travel secretly between Germany and Rome and Argentina. Germany and Argentina remained friendly during the war, and now the country is full of former officers. Although ratlines were first established a couple of years ago, they're used more frequently now. When the war ended, hundreds of Nazi war criminals managed to escape via these routes." He paused. "Many of them took paintings and jewelry with them. Some of the pieces are incredibly valuable, Van Goghs and Matisses hidden in secret compartments of luggage. Diamonds and rubies sewn into the hem of a fur coat. Of course, they're all stolen. Mostly from Jews."

"Go on," Marina prompted him.

"Jews who survived the concentration camps returned to discover their apartments stripped. Framed paintings gone from the walls, jewelry boxes empty. They want their valuables back and it's this organization's job to help them. Luc is getting so much work, he needs someone to assist him with the cases. He asked if I knew anyone who might be interested, and I thought you would be perfect."

Marina knew nothing about South America. She had never been on a ship.

"How do they locate the items if they're privately held?" she asked.

"Mostly they're sold to private parties, or they end up in galleries," Bernard said. "Those fleeing need the funds to start a new life. Luc has contacts in the art world. I know you want a career in art and to open your own gallery someday. He can get you access to the right people. He can't afford to pay much, but perhaps you could get a job in a gallery as well."

"In Argentina?" Marina asked doubtfully. She studied Bernard to see if there was something he wasn't telling her.

"Belle and I have been there. Buenos Aires is quite beautiful, and the people are very welcoming." He stroked his beard. "I thought you would appreciate being somewhere . . ." He paused as if he didn't know how to finish the sentence.

"Where there aren't any memories of Carlos and my father," Marina said.

Bernard nodded. He was quiet, letting her think about it.

There was still some money that Paolo had sent her, which she kept in an envelope in her drawer. Enough to fund her passage there.

Bernard handed her a business card.

"I told Luc about you," he said. "Take some time to think it over."

Argentina was thousands of miles away. There would be no anchovies at the outdoor markets to remind her of the night her father died, no plates of spaghetti to make her miss Carlos with an impossible ache. Marina was glad Bernard had suggested it. Although far from everything she'd known, it was also a fresh start. A place without memories. A place wholly hers.

Desi was getting married; she had her own life.

Bernard didn't really need her; he only kept her busy to be kind.

She slipped the card into her pocket.

"I don't need time to think about it. I'll call Luc right away," she declared. "It's a wonderful opportunity; thank you for thinking of me."

"I was hoping you'd say that." Bernard nodded, smiling. He studied Marina as if she were someone new. "There are many different kinds of people in the world. People who love art are the same. Art becomes their country; wherever there is art, they're at home."

Belle sat in the living room, holding an envelope. A tray rested on the coffee table.

"Marina, come join me," Belle greeted her. "I received some letters. The first one is from Gerhard. He's in Switzerland. His sister told him about Peter and Desi and the baby. He sends his best wishes." She turned to the next letter. "And here's one from Ludwig. He's in Germany trying to retrieve the books taken from the institute." She smiled at Marina. "He wanted to tell you that he used these months to finish work on his book on Leonardo da Vinci."

"Tell him I can't wait to read it." Marina smiled.

Belle put aside the envelopes and reached for a notepad.

"Bernard and I are planning a trip. Europe is

still so dismal. So many cities were destroyed by bombs. Munich and Rome and London are in ruins. We've decided to go to America. Bernard wants to see some people at Harvard, and I'm dying to go to New York." Her eyes danced. "I'm taking an empty steamer trunk for all the dresses I'll buy."

"Actually, I'm thinking of going away too," Marina said. She told her about Bernard's offer.

"I wouldn't leave until after Desi's wedding though. And I can stay at Villa I Tatti longer if you need me."

"No, I think it's a marvelous idea!" Belle exclaimed. "Bernard and I were in Buenos Aires before the war. The architecture is spectacular. The Basílica del Pilar is stunning. And you must see the frescoed domes of the Galerías Pacífico. Plus, the men are handsome and very cosmopolitan," she added coyly. "You never know who you'll meet."

"So you don't mind?" Marina asked.

Belle reached forward and squeezed her hand. "Not at all. I'll expect lots of letters, of course," she gushed. "And we'll have to give you a going-away party." Belle made notes on her pad. "The sun in Argentina can be brutal; you'll need light summer clothes and some hats. Cocktail dresses for nighttime, and a few evening bags. We'll have to go shopping. Buenos Aires society is quite elegant. You'll get tons of invitations."

Belle kept scribbling, and Marina laughed to herself. Bernard was right. People who loved art and beauty were the same. Marina had discovered a new family in Florence, and she was confident she would find it again.

For the first time in months, she looked forward to everything ahead of her.

CHAPTER TWENTY-THREE

Buenos Aires, October 1945

When Marina first arrived in Buenos Aires she had been determined not to succumb to its charms. The ratlines that transported Nazi war criminals to Argentina made her wary. Surely, she couldn't love a country that welcomed the monsters who had killed millions of Jews.

But from the first night, with the smell of sizzling meats drifting out from restaurants and people dancing the tango in the streets, she fell in love with the vibrant culture. And everyone was so friendly. Taxi drivers offered directions. The owners of roadside carritos explained how to eat a choripán—a chorizo sandwich—with freshly prepared and spicy chimichurri sauce.

The city reminded her of Florence. The Metropolitan Cathedral was grand and imposing; the Casa Rosada, the presidential palace, made her think of the Pitti Palace. Only here there were no signs of war. No Red Cross offices where people were desperately trying to locate their loved ones, no gaping holes where palazzi once stood, or families without homes. Only wide boulevards lined with palm trees, and bustling market stalls in San Telmo that resembled the outdoor market in San Lorenzo.

She had hated leaving Villa I Tatti and agonized on the journey to Argentina about whether she'd made the right decision. Desi and Peter's wedding had been one of the happiest days of Marina's life. Desi had worn a long, white dress with a lace train as she walked across the rose-strewn lawn to Peter, holding a bouquet of lilies. Francesca and Luna scampered down the aisle like fawns.

Peter's parents traveled over from Baden. Belle wore a striking chiffon dress with a feather hat that Marina worried would overshadow the bride. But then she saw the light in Desi's and Peter's eyes when they exchanged vows and knew that wasn't possible.

The only shadow on the day came during the speeches, when the family expressed their wish that Donato and Carlos could have been there to celebrate. Marina stifled a sob. She grieved for Desi and her parents but also for herself. She missed Carlos sitting beside her, imagined him whispering in her ear that it was their turn next.

After allowing herself a week to get to know the city, Marina turned onto Plaza San Martín to present herself at the address Bernard had given her. It was a small office above a dress shop, sandwiched between a bookstore and a café. A park engulfed by jacaranda trees sat across the street, a stone fountain in the center of the square.

"Can I help you?" a secretary at the front desk asked in accented English.

Belle had told her that most people in Buenos Aires spoke English, so Marina had practiced her English on the ship.

The woman wore a simple brown sheath dress, and Marina worried she hadn't dressed appropriately. She wore one of the outfits she and Belle bought in Florence: a floral dress with a cinched waist that she had matched with a chic little hat and short white gloves.

"My name is Marina Tozzi. I have an appointment with Señor Feron," Marina replied.

The woman smiled. "He's expecting you. I'll tell him you're here."

A man in his late twenties appeared. He was tall and quite handsome, with long legs and broad shoulders. His light brown hair was brushed to the side and his cheeks were tanned from the Argentinian sun. There was a dimple on his cheek and his teeth were very white. He wasn't at all what she had expected.

"Marina." He held out his hand. "I'm Luc. It's nice to meet you. Come into my office."

The office was simply furnished with a wood desk and two chairs. The only unusual thing was the number of file folders. They were everywhere: on the desk, propped against the windowsill, and strewn across the coffee table. Among the folders were empty cups.

Luc followed her gaze, his hazel eyes lively.

"As you can see, I have a lot of work. These are all open cases." He waved at the folders. "Thank God for Argentinian coffee. I practically live on it. I'm lucky my mother doesn't see me every day. She believes too much caffeine spoils one's chances of having children." He gave a small laugh. "That's her way of pushing me to settle down and give her grandchildren. But the world is still a mess; there will be time for that later."

Marina shifted nervously in her chair. She wasn't used to someone being so forthcoming. And it had been a long time since she had talked to an attractive man.

"I've been in Buenos Aires for a week and I'm eager to start working." Marina wanted to sound professional.

"What did Bernard tell you about the job?"

Marina recounted their conversation. When she finished, Luc leaned back in his chair.

"That's not all of it, of course. Most Jews never returned from the concentration camps. Their relatives ask our organization to retrieve their belongings: Torah scrolls, rare books, sculptures. And we assist various European governments." Luc rubbed his brow. "During the war, Hitler behaved as if the museums were his own personal department store. He plucked Rembrandts and Leonardo da Vincis right off museum walls.

"Much of the art smuggled out of Europe ended

up in South America." He waved at the files. "Sometimes it feels like the cases will never stop coming. I've been given so much work recently, these files could be piled to the ceiling and still there'd be more."

"And what will I do exactly?" she asked.

"Many of the pieces end up in private collections," he said. "I once attended a dinner party at the house of a wealthy Argentinian manufacturer. One of his guests was German. After the meal, the host and his guest slipped off to the study. I followed them. If anyone asked, I was going to pretend I got lost on the way to the bathroom. The German had a sketch by Rembrandt that had been taken from a Jewish couple's apartment in Berlin after they were sent to a concentration camp. I was able to establish its provenance before it changed hands and return it to the couple's surviving children."

"How were you able to retrieve it?" Marina asked.

"I cornered the guest and told him what I suspected, and he admitted it," Luc said, smiling. "You'd be surprised how often people blurt out the truth when they're taken by surprise."

"Do you always use underhand tactics?" Marina asked, amused.

"Let's just say I approach each situation differently," he offered with a grin. He looked even more handsome when he smiled.

"A friend of my mother's owns an art gallery. It's in Recoleta, one of the most elegant neighborhoods in Buenos Aires. The owner is Renata, and her clients are among the wealthiest in the city. She doesn't know exactly what we do, but working there will give you access to the auctions and collectors."

Marina missed working in a gallery. It would be wonderful to be around paintings.

"You want me to get a job there?" Marina asked.

Luc riffled through the folders and picked up a business card.

"I've already given you a recommendation." He handed the card to Marina. "You'll still have to impress her, but from what Bernard has told me, I'm sure you'll have little trouble. Renata is a very competent businesswoman, and the gallery is her whole life. She knows talent when she sees it." He paused. "You'll learn a lot from her too. I'm sure you'll enjoy it."

Marina was glad she had dressed formally. She slipped the card into her bag.

"I'll go right away."

Luc sat forward. His face took on a curious expression.

"I have just one question for you."

Marina wondered if he was going to ask about her professional experience. If she could identify a Raphael sketch or value a Caravaggio properly.

"I know you're perfectly qualified," he said. "But why would a beautiful young Italian woman come all the way to Argentina when the war is finally over?"

Marina stood up. She smoothed her skirt.

"It might be hard for you to understand, since you weren't in Europe during the war," she began. "There was so much loss. I decided it might be easier to start from nothing, rather than live among my memories of people and places that are gone." She paused, suddenly embarrassed at revealing so much. "That must sound silly."

Luc shook her hand. He smiled appreciatively. "It doesn't sound silly at all. I hope you count me as your first new friend in Argentina."

Marina walked back out into the sunshine. Renata's gallery was only a short distance away on the other side of the plaza, in a whitewashed building with gold lettering on the window.

Inside, the showroom was terribly elegant. There was plush white carpet and a small glass chandelier. Gold frames lined the walls and a sitting area held upholstered velvet chairs.

"Can I help you?" a woman asked.

"I'm Marina Tozzi," Marina replied. "Señor Feron sent me."

The woman was in her midforties. She had stylishly cut dark hair and wore an elegant navy dress.

"Renata Gallo." She held out her hand and studied Marina critically. "You look younger than Luc described."

"I'm twenty-two," Marina said. "I worked with my father at his art gallery in Rome." She paused. "He was killed during the war."

"I'm sorry about your father. But I need to make something clear before we go any further: This is a demanding position. Recoleta is the most expensive neighborhood in Buenos Aires. Our clients count on us to know which pieces belong in their homes."

Marina glanced around the space. Many of the pieces were by Latin American artists, but she recognized some familiar styles. She was quite sure the painting on the far wall was a Giacomo Favretto.

"Argentinian art lovers used to travel to Europe to purchase paintings," Marina explained. "That stopped during the war. I know almost everything about Italian artists." She pointed to the painting. "That Favretto, for instance. It would go well in the living room of an elegant mansion."

Renata's mouth dropped open. The lines on her forehead relaxed, and she smiled. She walked to the counter and tapped her long fingernails on the glass.

"The other thing you'll have to learn is how clients like their coffee," Renata said briskly. "There's a coffeehouse across the street. A lagrima is hot milk with a dash of espresso, while a cortado is an espresso with a splash of hot milk. Most clients prefer not one but two medialunas—sweet croissants. It isn't done to run out of pastry before finishing the coffee."

Marina exhaled. She squared her shoulders.

"That won't be a problem," Marina said confidently. "No one takes coffee more seriously than Italians."

"The pay is four pesos a week." Renata turned back to the counter. "You can start tomorrow."

On the street the springtime air smelled of cherry blossoms. It felt odd to Marina to be in the southern hemisphere, for the air to be so sweet and sultry. She was too excited to return to the pension where she was staying. She decided to go for a walk in the park.

A Frenchman named Jules Charles Thays had created the many parks in Buenos Aires. They were designed in the European style with rose gardens and wooden pergolas. Everywhere she looked were emerald-green lawns.

The park next to Plaza San Martín climbed high above the city. Marina sat on a knoll and gazed down at the art deco buildings, at the clock tower that reminded her of Giotto's Bell Tower in Florence. How wonderful it would have been to explore Buenos Aires with Carlos. They would have brought a picnic here after work. On the weekends, they would have visited the National Museum of Fine Arts. At night they would have made love. Afterward, they would have opened the window to listen to music playing in the street.

Marina had never felt so alone. She longed for everyone she left behind. Before she left, Eli had given her a bottle of perfume so that she would smell better than all the signorinas in Argentina. Sara hugged her so hard that Marina almost couldn't breathe. Bernard gave her a first-edition set of his scholarly works, and Belle hid her feelings by piling her with dresses and shoes. Marina said she didn't need a new wardrobe, but Belle counseled that a woman's self-confidence began when she looked in the mirror.

She wasn't going to think about Italy. She was in Buenos Aires for a reason. She had her job; that was enough for now.

Three weeks had passed since Marina started working at the gallery. The job was more enjoyable than she could have imagined. She adored the mornings when she arrived before Renata. When the cash register was sparkling clean and the cushions on the velvet chairs were newly plumped and the gallery smelled of lemon polish.

Marina made Renata's coffee just the way she liked it. She organized the book of client names and addresses and suggested holding a monthly show for local artists with wine and hors d'oeuvres. Gradually, Renata's reserve softened, and Marina learned a bit more about her. Her husband had died five years prior, and since they had no children, the gallery became her family.

That afternoon, Luc called to give her the first important assignment. She locked up the gallery at closing time and briskly walked the few blocks to his office.

"Marina, it's nice to see you." Luc wore a white shirt with the shirtsleeves rolled up. His tie was slightly askew, and his hair was brushed to the side. "You're probably hungry and tired after working all day; I promise this won't take long."

"I'm not hungry at all," Marina assured him, following him into his office. "One thing that Argentina and Italy have in common is that no one eats until late."

"Then I won't offer you any of my leftover lunch," he said, sitting down and waving at a crumpled paper bag with a sandwich. "I received an assignment that is perfect for you. The client's name is Saul Riggio, his family is from Venice. His parents were deported and died at Auschwitz. They left behind a portrait by Veronese."

Paolo Veronese was a Venetian artist from the sixteenth century known for his large paintings and bright colors. Marina's father once had a Veronese painting at the gallery. It took up an entire wall, and Marina had spent hours examining the vivid figures and bold colors before it sold a short time later.

"Paolo Veronese didn't paint many portraits," Marina cut in. "Most of his paintings were crowd scenes painted on huge canvases."

"You're right. I'm impressed; many people don't know that," Luc acknowledged. "I've managed to trace it to a gallery here. The gallery owner's name is Hans Becker; he's Austrian. He's having a private event there tonight. There will be quite a few people from local art circles. I want you to attend."

"How will I get an invitation?" Marina asked.

"You won't." Luc tugged at his tie. "You'll say your invitation got lost."

"And once I'm inside?" she asked, frowning.

"It will be your job to find out if Hans still has the portrait. Here's the address." Luc scribbled it on a piece of paper and handed it to her. "I'm sure you won't have any problem getting inside." He smiled. "Hans isn't likely to turn away a beautiful young art enthusiast."

The gallery, not far from Renata's gallery, was in a modern building with black awnings. Through the window, Marina could see men and women in elegant evening wear. They held cocktail glasses and examined the paintings on the walls.

A tall man of about thirty hovered inside the door.

"Could I please see your invitation?" the man asked.

Marina wore a tea-length dress that Belle had given her. She pretended to search her evening bag.

"I'm afraid I left the invitation at home."

The man shook his head.

"I'm sorry, this is a private event. You need an invitation to come inside."

Marina couldn't take no for an answer. She glanced at the window and noticed a painting of a farmer and his wagon in the middle of a farm. She was quite sure it was an Eduardo Sívori. Sívori practically founded the school of realism in Argentina. He had been dead for nearly thirty years, and it was becoming harder to find his work.

She smiled prettily at the young man and pointed at the painting.

"Perhaps the gallery owner will make an exception. Please tell him I'm interested in that painting."

The man disappeared and returned a few minutes later with a stocky man in his midfifties. He had thick blond hair and wore a navy suit.

"I'm Hans Becker. Can I help you?" he inquired.

Marina pointed through the window.

"I'm Marina Tozzi. I seem to have lost my invitation. I'm very interested in that Eduardo

Sívori, and I don't have time to come back during the day."

The man glanced at her with new interest.

"You recognize the Sívori?"

Marina nodded. "I'm a huge fan of his work."

"Perhaps I can make an exception for a signorina with excellent taste." He opened the door wider and ushered her inside. "Please come in."

Marina followed him into the gallery. She glanced at the paintings on the walls. The Veronese wasn't there.

She pretended to examine the Sívori.

"I'm also looking for something from the Italian Renaissance; it's my favorite period." Marina turned to Hans. "Do you have anything I might be interested in?"

Hans frowned. "Art from the Renaissance is very expensive."

Marina patted her hair.

"I'm able to afford it," she returned. "For the right painting, of course."

"In that case, come with me." Hans motioned to her. "I have just the piece."

Hans led her to a small room behind the main gallery. He unlocked a safe and took out a small frame.

"You're lucky. I received this recently." He turned it over. "As soon as I put it in the gallery, it will be gone."

It was a portrait of a young woman wearing

a velvet headdress, a cross around her neck.

"Could it be . . . Surely it isn't." Marina feigned surprise. She looked at Hans, her eyes wide. "It couldn't possibly be a Veronese. I've only seen them in a museum in Italy before the war."

"You're correct, it is a Veronese," Hans said. He was noticeably impressed.

"How on earth did it end up in Buenos Aires?"

He waved his hand evasively. "The war made things happen that never seemed possible before. The portrait will receive a lot of interest." He appraised Marina. "Unless some lucky collector scoops it up first."

Marina thought of the painting's owners who died at Auschwitz. It wasn't her place to say anything. Her job was just to confirm Hans had the portrait.

"How much?" Marina asked.

Hans eyed her sequined evening bag, her elegant high heels with black satin bows.

"For you, signorina, one hundred thousand pesos."

One hundred thousand pesos was the price of a small car.

"That's a lot of money," she said, pretending to be shocked.

"As you said yourself, it's worthy of a museum. If you are set on Italian Renaissance art, you won't find anything else of this caliber in Argentina."

"You're right. I need time to think it over." She gave him a small smile. "One can't rush into such an important purchase. Perhaps you could write down the name of the painting and the price on your card."

"Of course." He took a card from his pocket and wrote the details on the back. "I included my home number." He smiled. "Please call me anytime."

Marina browsed around the gallery and then said goodbye to Hans. It was after 9:00 p.m., and she was hungry.

The loneliness she'd felt a few weeks ago had disappeared. She had enjoyed putting on the little charade for Hans. And she knew Luc would be pleased with what she'd learned.

For the first time since she arrived, she wanted to write to Bernard, Belle, and Desi and describe everything. The young men on the streetcars who whistled, the fashionable women in their smart hats who walked their dogs on the boulevards, the blue and red buildings in La Boca, the children who crowded at the windows to wave to people passing by.

And she wanted to tell them about the gallery. The clientele was as snobbish as any of her father's clients in Rome, but they valued her opinion. Last week, a client brought her flowers to thank her for choosing the perfect gift for her husband.

Tonight, she was going to enjoy the mild weather and treat herself to a plate of locro—traditional Argentinian stew made with corn and beans and squash.

The restaurants were just beginning to fill up. They would stay crowded until midnight, when the young people piled into taxis and went on to nightclubs and parties.

She sat outdoors at a café and waved to the waiter.

"Are you waiting for someone, señorita?" he asked.

It wasn't common for women to eat alone in public, but she was tired of eating in her room at the pensione. She shook her head and smiled.

"I'm by myself tonight." She glanced at the menu. "But I know exactly what I want."

CHAPTER TWENTY-FOUR

Buenos Aires, November 1945

A week later, Marina stood in the pensione's kitchen, eating a slice of toast before work.

Elena, the owner of the pensione, poked her head in the door. She hardly ever interacted with Marina, who found herself missing Anna's pleasant chatter.

"There's a phone call for you," Elena announced. "It's a gentleman. He has a French accent."

"For me?" Marina repeated.

She went into the entryway and picked up the phone on the table.

"This is Marina," she said into the receiver.

"Marina, this is Luc," the man answered. "I wanted to thank you for the excellent work you did. I was able to reunite Saul with his family's painting. He's very grateful."

"I'm sure Hans wasn't happy about that," Marina said, laughing.

"Not happy at all," Luc agreed cheerfully. "But I received a new case. I'm busy all day, and I know you're working. Perhaps I can take you to dinner."

Dinner sounded like a date. Luc was handsome and fun, but she recalled what happened with

Nicolo. It was better not to get involved with a man she worked with.

"I have dinner plans," she told him, feeling a pang of guilt at the small white lie. "I could come by your office after work."

Luc paused before he answered. His voice was warm.

"How about drinks at the Alvear Palace Hotel instead?" he suggested. "You deserve more than a glass of water after a long day. I promise, you'll have plenty of time to get to your dinner."

"I suppose that would be all right."

"Six o'clock at the hotel bar?" He chuckled lightly. "Who knows, after a few drinks, you might even change your mind about having dinner with me."

"You have a high opinion of yourself," Marina said, laughing.

"It's not my opinion, it's my mother's," Luc responded. "And I wouldn't dream of disagreeing with her."

The Alvear Palace Hotel was on the corner of Alvear Avenue, in the heart of Recoleta. It was the most luxurious hotel in Buenos Aires. The lobby was furnished in the Louis XVI style with crystal chandeliers and rich damask sofas. The walls were covered with paintings by prominent artists and dotted with gold leaf. Marina wondered how Luc could afford drinks here.

Luc was sitting at a table in the corner, wearing a blue blazer and red-striped tie. He looked even more handsome than he did at the office.

Even though they had met a couple of times, she had forgotten how tall he was. Even in her heels, she hardly rose beyond his shoulder. His long, lean build belonged to a runner, or perhaps a swimmer.

"Thank you for coming." He motioned for her to sit. He noticed her gazing at his clothes. "I always dress up for the Palace Hotel. It's like cleaning my car before I have it washed. It's important to make a good impression."

"What did you want to talk about?" she asked Luc as she sat down.

Luc turned and signaled to the waiter.

"Why don't we order drinks first?" he suggested. "It's easier to discuss delicate subjects after a couple of the Palace's famous Gancia batidos."

Their drinks arrived swiftly.

"Gancia is Argentina's favorite liquor," Luc said when the waiter brought two glasses adorned with orange slices. "It's the way the bartender makes it that's special. He adds lemon and sugar and ice, and stirs it all in a cocktail shaker for a few seconds. Any longer, and it turns to mush."

Marina was growing anxious to know why he had invited her.

"I didn't come here to learn about Argentinian

cocktails," Marina teased, sipping hers. It was sour and sweet at the same time.

"Sorry, bad habit. I tended bar here when I was younger. I heard all sorts of conversations. In a way, it's what led me to become a private investigator." He fiddled with his straw.

"When Bernard first contacted me, it was for a reason," Luc continued. "He was looking for someone. Someone who disappeared during the war and might have used the ratlines to reach South America." He glanced at Marina. "Someone who was important to you."

"Someone important to me?" Marina repeated in surprise.

Bernard had never mentioned it.

"He didn't want to say anything unless I had any leads, and I didn't at the time." Luc took a slow sip of his drink. "I might now."

He took a photograph out of his pocket.

Luc showed her the photograph. It was of a man sitting at a café. His hair was cut short and his skin was tanned from the sun, but it looked exactly like Carlos. On the bottom of the photo was written *Federico Murano, Buenos Aires, Argentina.*

Marina's stomach lurched. She gripped the table and forced herself to breathe.

It was impossible. Carlos was dead.

"There must be a mistake," Marina said. She set the photograph on the table, shaking. "Carlos was killed more than a year ago. He was with a group of partisans who were executed by German soldiers."

"Are you sure he was one of them?" Luc asked.

Marina recalled everything from her conversation with Bernard.

"Completely sure." She nodded. "His signet ring was recovered from one of the bodies. Carlos almost never took it off."

Luc looked at her kindly.

"He could have sold it, or given it to someone for safekeeping," he offered. "Bernard sent me a photo of Carlos and asked me to keep an eye out, in case anything turned up. When I saw this, I couldn't ignore the resemblance; the hair is different, but they look like the same man."

Luc was right. But Marina couldn't wrap her mind around it. Agreeing with Luc meant admitting to herself that Carlos was alive and hadn't tried to contact her.

"Carlos and I were very close. He would never leave Italy without telling me," Marina insisted. She pressed her fingers against her glass. "Where did you get this photo?"

"It came in a recent batch of files." Luc shrugged.

"The war just ended. When was this taken?"

"I don't know exactly," Luc replied. He showed her another piece of paper, a copy of a passport. "Federico's immigration papers were stamped on January 22, 1945. His passport says he's from

Lugano, the Italian-speaking part of Switzerland, so that would explain his accent. He probably changed nationalities to throw off anyone who was looking for him."

"Why would anyone be looking for him?" she asked.

Marina examined the paperwork. The date was almost a year after Carlos had disappeared. If Federico was really Carlos, what had he been doing for a year? And why hadn't he sent her some kind of message?

But it was impossible to ignore. The photo couldn't have been anyone but Carlos.

For the past few weeks, Marina had been almost happy. But now it all came rushing back. The way Carlos had made her feel bright and alive. Her grief at his untimely death.

Trembling, she accidentally tipped over her glass, spilling her drink across the table.

"I'm terribly sorry." She mopped it up with a napkin.

"Don't worry about it," Luc said, helping her. "I'll order you another one."

Her brow furrowed. "Why do you have a copy of his passport?"

Carlos had never mentioned Argentina. And the war had been over for months. He would have let her know. Carlos loved her; he would want them to be together.

"I told you, the photo came in a new batch of

files. The client's name is Levi Balsamo. He's trying to retrieve items stolen from his relatives who were sent to a concentration camp. After I received the photo, I did some digging and discovered Carlos's passport."

"What kind of items is the client trying to retrieve?" she asked.

Luc took a notebook from his pocket.

"A sketchbook by Botticelli, some antiquated books."

Marina's throat constricted and she tried to swallow. It wasn't possible.

"Carlos would never steal from Jews. He helped a Jewish family hide in a barn for months."

"There was a war. People behaved differently. A lot of partisans felt as if they were modern-day Robin Hoods. They made up their own rules." Luc played with his glass. "Selling valuables on the black market became a way to survive."

Carlos's parents were wealthy. And Carlos was so generous. He never wanted anything for himself. But she recalled the items she valued for him, the ones he would sell on the black market. Had she ever asked where he'd gotten them? She couldn't remember.

And then she recalled Ludwig's pistol. The books missing from Bernard's library, the Verrocchio hidden inside Titian's diary.

"How did you know Carlos was a partisan?" she asked sharply.

Luc shrugged. "I've learned a little about him. He sold a few things on the black market when he arrived in Buenos Aires. Then he stopped. Either what he has left is difficult to sell, or he has to be careful. I can't prove anything unless I find the items. He lives right here in Recoleta, at Sixty-two Calle Herrera." He looked at Marina. "If this is too hard, I can handle it myself. But I thought you would want to know."

She knew the street, full of large, Italianate villas or Spanish-style mansions. What would Carlos be doing in a huge house by himself?

She didn't know if she wanted to see Carlos now. What could he possibly say to her? But perhaps there was an explanation. Maybe Carlos had had to leave Italy quickly and didn't want to put her in danger.

And there was the Verrocchio to consider. Carlos might still have it. She had taken it from Captain Bonner in order to return it to the Uffizi Gallery. But then it had disappeared.

"If Carlos does have stolen items in his house, he'd hide them before he invited me inside," she reasoned.

"I thought of that." Luc nodded. "I have an idea, but first I need to ask you something."

He smoothed his napkin and set the glass on the table.

"Bernard didn't exactly say what your relationship was with Carlos," he said slowly. "It's none of my business, and I don't mean to pry, but . . ."

Marina felt her cheeks flush. She smoothed her napkin.

"We were in love," she admitted. "We were going to be together after the war. I was going to open my own art gallery, and Carlos would paint."

Luc sighed. His face fell.

"I was afraid you'd say that. I was going to suggest that you get into the house by becoming friends with his wife."

Marina's napkin fluttered to the ground. The room seemed to spin and she felt dizzy.

"Let me get that for you," Luc said hastily. He picked up the napkin and then pointed at her glass. "Would you like another one, or perhaps something stronger? Nothing beats a straight vermouth for shock."

"I don't want anything, thank you," Marina said, trying to hide her embarrassment. "Carlos is married?"

"Recently so. Or at least, Federico Murano is," Luc said. "His wife's name is Valentina."

Valentina. Marina tried to imagine what she was like. A voluptuous Argentinian with lustrous hair and dark, flashing eyes. Her mind went to Nicolo all those years ago, and her chest tightened. But Carlos was different; he loved her. There had to be an explanation.

"How do you suggest I become friends with her?" Marina asked.

"You'll find something in common. Most young women love to shop." He wrote down the address and handed her the piece of paper, then glanced up and saw the hurt in Marina's face. "I'm really sorry, Marina. You'll find that one of the hardest parts of the job isn't locating stolen goods," he said somberly. "It's uncovering the faults in people. Not everyone is what they seem, especially during a war."

Desi's words from long ago came into her mind: *I'd never date anyone that good-looking. . . . Dating him is a recipe for a broken heart.*

"Call me at the office if you need anything," Luc volunteered. "I know how you must feel. I was born in Paris. My father died when I was eleven. My mother and I moved to Buenos Aires in 1935, when I was sixteen. We were lucky, our lives were untouched by the war. Our family and friends in Paris weren't so fortunate."

"My mother died when I was ten," Marina blurted out. "My father was killed by the Germans during the war."

Luc paused for a moment. He gulped the rest of his cocktail.

"I'm sorry." His voice was thick. "Losing one parent young is hard, losing two is unimaginable."

Marina left the bar and walked back to the pensione. It was good to stroll in the night air. There was so much to think about.

Why had Bernard suspected Carlos was alive, and why hadn't he confided in her? Perhaps he had learned something on his trips to Switzerland but was afraid to get her hopes up in case it led to nothing.

She had been hopeful that Carlos was alive for so many months. Then Bernard's revelation made it foolish to keep on hoping. How could Carlos's signet ring end up on the wrong man?

A pit formed in her stomach. *Married.* She couldn't believe Carlos was married. She didn't think she could sit across from his wife and pretend everything was normal.

Then she thought of the suffering caused by the war: the murder of her father and Enrico, Desi's bravery, Peter's injuries on the Eastern Front. She recalled the bridges being destroyed in Florence and the families cowering in the Pitti Palace.

Marina couldn't stop fighting. She had to find out if Carlos stole from the victims of the war, if he had betrayed her. And she had to return the Verrocchio to Italy.

That night, she'd go back to the pensione and try to sleep. The next morning, she would figure out a way to meet Carlos's new wife.

CHAPTER TWENTY-FIVE

Buenos Aires, November 1945

Calle Herrera reminded Marina of the Parioli neighborhood in Rome. Italianate mansions stood behind iron gates; willow trees shaded the sidewalk. A gleaming convertible stood in a driveway surrounded by palm trees and lush plants.

This was the third morning that Marina had spent in front of Carlos's house. Each day she took her lunch hour early and strolled up and down the sidewalk, concealing her face with a large hat and sunglasses. So far neither Carlos nor Valentina had come out the front door.

The house was even prettier than she imagined. A garden bloomed with plants and fragrant flowers in front of the pink building. Beside it was a garage; Marina wondered what kind of car Carlos had sitting inside it.

It was almost noon when the front door opened and a woman stepped out. It had to be Valentina.

Marina peered at her from behind her sunglasses. The woman looked too young to be married—she couldn't be more than twenty. And she was the opposite of what Marina had pictured. She was conservatively dressed in a pleated skirt and blouse. Her light brown hair fell to her shoulders and a string of pearls hung around her neck.

Valentina stopped to say something to the gardener, then she started along the sidewalk. Marina followed her. At the corner, Valentina turned and walked to Plaza San Martín. She bought a bunch of yellow lilies at a florist and browsed for a few minutes at the newsagent.

Then she entered a shop that sold baby clothes. There was a rack of pink and yellow dresses. Christening blankets were arranged on a table, and a rocking horse stood in the corner.

Marina pretended to be sifting through a pile of baby booties while the salesgirl attended to Valentina.

"Where would you like these items sent, Mrs. Murano?"

"To my home, please," Valentina replied, giving the girl her address. "I shouldn't be buying things so early. I'm only four months pregnant." She paused. "I've never designed a nursery. I want to get everything right."

Marina's heart thudded. Valentina looked so young to be pregnant. She had little time to dwell on it though. Here was her chance to make a connection.

"It's never too early to prepare for a baby," the salesgirl beamed. "I'm sure your husband is pleased too. Most new fathers act as if they're the only men to ever have children."

"I couldn't help but overhear," Marina said, stepping forward. "Are you designing a nursery?"

Valentina turned. She was even prettier up close, with large dark eyes and a warm smile.

"I'm designing the whole house." She gave a small laugh. "It's too big for us. It was a wedding present from my parents. And now with the baby . . ."

Marina took a card from her purse.

"My name is Marina. I work at the gallery on the corner, a short walk from here." She gave her the card. "If you need art, I'd be happy to help."

"Valentina Murano." Valentina held out her hand and smiled. "I'm sure I'll take you up on it."

Marina took the booties to the counter and waited while the salesgirl rang them up. It felt awkward not to buy anything, and she needed time to compose herself.

Something about Valentina had seemed familiar, and as she stood there, she realized what it was. The pearls around Valentina's neck resembled the pearls Alba had worn to the dinner party at the Adamos'. They were distinctive— pink and quite large. They couldn't belong to anyone else. The idea of Carlos giving Valentina his mother's necklace made Marina feel even worse.

"Are you all right?" Renata asked when Marina returned to the gallery. "You look as if you've seen a ghost."

"I'm fine." Marina set her purse down. "I'm not used to the South American sun, that's all."

"It's only spring; wait until next month, when our summer starts," Renata counseled. "The sun in the southern hemisphere is so bright; I have to wear a hat all the time. The long days are glorious. My husband and I used to drive in the countryside to visit the estancias—the ranches where they run cattle and livestock. We'd stop at a roadside cantina and eat steak and drink wine." Her eyes dimmed at the memory.

Marina tried to concentrate on Renata's words, but all she could think about was Valentina. It was all too much. Carlos had married a girl he just met. And he was about to become a father.

"You seem pale." Renata interrupted her thoughts. "Perhaps you should take the afternoon off."

Marina turned her attention to Renata. She couldn't afford to lose her job.

"I can't, I have so much to do," Marina replied. "I found a painting by Giovanni Paolo Panini for a client."

Panini was part of the neoclassical school in Rome. The painting was expensive, but the client didn't mind; her husband owned a copper mine.

Renata studied Marina appraisingly. Marina

was glad she had accepted the new wardrobe from Belle. Renata always noticed Marina's outfits.

"I knew you'd be an asset to the gallery," she said.

Renata left early to visit a client. Marina was standing at the cash register when she heard the bell above the door.

"I hope it's all right," Valentina said as she entered, glancing around. "If you're about to close, I can come back tomorrow."

She had changed into a red dress that showed her still-slim waistline. A pair of gloves was folded over her handbag.

"I was going out to dinner and thought I'd stop by here first," Valentina said.

Marina stepped out from behind the counter. "It's not too late at all. I'm glad you came."

"I've had terrible morning sickness. I'm almost four months, and it hasn't gone away," Valentina confided. "It starts in the morning and lasts all day. Some days I don't have the energy to get dressed until the afternoon."

"Drink warm milk with honey for the sickness," Marina volunteered.

Valentina glanced at her. "I hadn't thought of that. Do you have children?"

Marina shook her head. "No, but my friend has a baby. She was terribly sick for the first few months. Don't worry, you'll feel better."

"I hope so," Valentina said. Her smile widened. "Thank you for the advice. Somehow, I had the feeling when we met that we'd become friends."

Marina led her through the gallery, pointing out different paintings that might suit her home.

"Do you have any favorite artists?" Marina asked when they were seated in the little sitting area. Marina poured a glass of lemonade for Valentina and offered her a plate of cookies.

"I don't really have my own taste." Valentina flushed. "I lived with my parents until I got married recently. I never paid attention to the paintings."

Valentina seemed like an anxious schoolgirl instead of a new wife who was about to become a mother.

"How about your husband?" Marina inquired. "Does he appreciatc a certain style?"

"I never asked him," Valentina said, shrugging her shoulders. "He's Swiss, from Lugano. We haven't known each other long." Her eyes sparkled. "I always expected to marry a boy I grew up with. But we fell in love and . . ."

The weight that had been pressing on Marina's chest threatened to crush her. She took out a notepad and pen, then leaned forward and started to write.

"Why don't we start with the size of the rooms," Marina suggested. "Then we can choose some paintings."

The phone rang at the gallery the following afternoon. Marina picked it up.

"This is Valentina Murano," a female voice said. "Could I speak to Marina?"

"This is Marina."

"Marina! I've had terrible morning sickness all day. I can't come into the gallery," Valentina continued. "I wondered if you could come to the house."

"You want me to come to your home?" Marina asked.

She was elated that her plan was working. But she hadn't expected to have the opportunity so quickly.

"If it's too much trouble, I understand," Valentina said hastily. "I thought you could look at the rooms and tell me what pieces would work."

Marina clutched the phone. What if Carlos was there? But she didn't have a choice—she had to go through with it.

"Yes, of course," she spoke into the receiver. "I'll come when the gallery closes."

Marina climbed the steps to Valentina's house. She had brought a small bunch of fuchsias as a gift and carried a small package under her arm.

Valentina answered the door herself in a floral dress with a round collar.

"These are for you." Marina handed her the flowers.

"That's so thoughtful. I'm so glad you came," Valentina said, taking the flowers and ushering her inside. "Your visit forced me to get dressed. I've been in a robe all day."

"I brought you some honey for your milk," Marina said, handing her the package. "It will help your morning sickness."

Valentina's face brightened.

"Thank you." She set it on a table. "Let me show you the house, then we'll have tea and you can give me your thoughts."

The downstairs had a living room and dining room with high ceilings and wood floors. A sunny kitchen and a breakfast room with French doors faced the garden, and there was a study and an elegant powder room. Upstairs, the master bedroom suite had a king-size bed and a sitting area. Marina didn't look too closely. She didn't want to see Carlos's slippers next to the bed, his shaving kit on the counter in the bathroom.

Valentina showed her the room that would be the nursery. It was large but empty, except for a daybed pushed against a bay window overlooking the garden.

They returned to the living room to talk. "I've never decorated a house," Valentina said, sitting on a sofa. "When I was a child, my parents bought me a dollhouse. Even then, I wasn't sure what the colors should be," she admitted. "I thought all girls' bedrooms were pink."

Marina sat opposite her. Floor-length mirrors rested against the walls. The room was dominated by a marble fireplace.

"It's a beautiful home," Marina reflected. "The perfect backdrop for art."

"Do you think so?" Valentina asked eagerly. "It was very extravagant of my parents. They've been so good about everything: the marriage, the honeymoon, now the baby."

"Most parents want their children to be happy," Marina replied.

"I am happy." Valentina beamed. "But it's been such a whirlwind. I've only known Federico several months."

Marina kept her voice even. "Federico is your husband?"

"Yes." Valentina nodded. "We met at the Jockey Club."

Marina looked perplexed and so Valentina explained.

"The Jockey Club is the oldest private club in Buenos Aires. You don't have to ride horses to belong; they also have tennis courts and a swimming pool. Women aren't members, but we're permitted in the dining room. . . ."

She twisted her hands. Marina noticed her engagement ring, an emerald flanked by diamonds.

For a moment she thought of the cameo ring

Carlos had given her, sitting in the drawer of her bedside table at the pensione.

"I'm sorry." She turned her attention to Valentina, who had trailed off. "You were saying women aren't allowed to be members."

"It's silly, but I never minded. And I'm glad I went to dinner with my parents, or I would never have met Federico. He was sitting at the bar, and he smiled at me." She stopped, embarrassed. "I'd never felt like that before. As if the room was empty and we were the only ones there."

"I know what you mean." Marina nodded. A sharp pain pierced her chest and she brushed it away.

"I feel foolish talking about it," Valentina continued. "Federico came over to our table and said hello." She gave a little laugh. "He acted so familiar that my father thought we were old friends.

"We'd known each other only a couple of months when he proposed. He was so nervous. I told him from the minute he smiled at me, there wasn't a chance I'd refuse." She sighed dreamily. "My parents wanted to wait and have a big wedding. But Federico doesn't have any family and we thought . . ."

Her expression changed and Marina wondered if Valentina was hiding something.

"Anyway, the wedding was perfect. The ceremony was in the small chapel at the Parroquia de San Miguel Arcángel and the reception was at my parents' house. We honeymooned in Uruguay, and now we're here." She took a deep breath. "With this big house and a baby on the way."

"How old are you?" Marina asked curiously.

"I'm almost twenty-one. Federico is twenty-five; I was worried I was too young for him. He said my youth and beauty are what he loves about me." She blushed furiously. "He says the sweetest things."

Marina shifted on the sofa. She kept her gaze firmly on the coffee table.

"I'm sorry, I'm doing all the talking. I haven't let you say a word about art," Valentina apologized. "I'll make tea and biscuits. Then you can give me your suggestions."

Valentina walked to the door. She turned and smiled.

"I'm glad you came. It's the first time all day I haven't felt sick," she said. "Maybe you want to wander around, get a sense of the house while I'm in the kitchen?"

After Valentina left, Marina glanced around the living room. The sparse decor left no place to hide anything. She walked down the hall to the dining room. The sideboard drawers were empty and the drapes were simply hemmed.

At the end of the hall was the study. She scanned the bookshelves. There was a set of encyclopedias and a few romance novels.

It had been Carlos's idea to hide Ludwig's pistol behind the books in Bernard's library.

She slipped her hand behind the books. There was nothing. She kept feeling along the shelf and her hand ran into a square object. She removed the other books and took it out.

Her heart raced and she turned it over carefully.

It was a book of sketches. The drawings were so old, they were thin as spiderwebs. The signature in the corner read Sandro Botticelli. She handled the book gently; she didn't want the pages to disintegrate.

Marina couldn't believe the sketchbook wasn't in a safe, or at least inside a locked drawer. Perhaps Carlos worried that Valentina might wonder why he was keeping secrets from her if she came across a safe or a lock without a key.

She slipped her hand again behind the books. There were two more bound books. One was a book on Italian grammar by Leon Battista Alberti. The date scrawled inside said 1439. The last book was large and square. This one she recognized, and her heart gave a small leap.

It was Titian's diary. Inside the cover was the portrait by Verrocchio, exactly where she had placed it. Surely Carlos had opened it and seen it there. Yet he never returned it to the Uffizi. Marina's heart contracted and waves of anger and hurt overwhelmed her. Carlos had known how important the painting's return had been to her; that's why she had agreed to switch it with the fake.

Thankfully her satchel was big enough. She quickly slipped the diary inside and replaced the books on the bookshelf. She couldn't simply take everything; she and Luc had to legally retrieve the items. Even so, Marina found it difficult to leave them behind.

Botticelli's sketches should be in Italy, where they belong, she thought to herself. *Not hidden behind a bookshelf in Argentina so that Carlos can profit from them.* Marina forced herself to leave the study.

Valentina was coming back from the kitchen as Marina entered the living room.

"Over the fireplace is a perfect place for a large painting," Marina suggested, hoping Valentina hadn't noticed her leaving the study. "I have a few things in mind."

Marina leafed through the gallery's catalog and pointed out the paintings that would work. Valentina hovered over the catalog, her smile growing wider.

"I love your ideas," she said when they finished. "Especially for the nursery. They say babies don't notice their surroundings. But I want our baby to have the best start in life."

"Your baby will be greatly loved," Marina said absently.

"I feel so fortunate." Valentina sipped her

tea. "These days, women want careers, but I've always dreamed of being a mother. Federico is going to be a wonderful father; he already sings to the baby."

Marina stood up. The afternoon was drifting into evening; Carlos would likely be home soon.

"I should go," she announced.

Valentina walked her to the door and kissed Marina on both cheeks.

"I was dreading filling the walls, and you've made it so easy," Valentina said. "I don't know how to thank you."

Marina sat on her bed at the pensione. Her head felt heavy and her throat was parched.

Valentina was so young and sweet. Marina wondered if Carlos was in love with her. What did that say about his relationship with Marina? Carlos had given her the cameo ring and sworn he was in love with her. Yet he hadn't contacted her when he arrived in Buenos Aires. There had to be a reason. Perhaps he sent a letter and she never received it, and when she didn't answer, he thought she had moved on. Things like that happened all the time because of the war. Couples were separated simply because they couldn't find each other after the war ended. Yet that didn't explain why he stole the diary and the Verrocchio portrait. She still couldn't come to terms with that.

Marina opened the box with the cameo ring. She thought of other times when she had needed strength. When Nicolo betrayed her. When she switched the Verrocchios at Captain Bonner's quarters. But those times hadn't felt like this, as if her heart would crack open.

CHAPTER TWENTY-SIX

Buenos Aires, November 1945

The following morning at the gallery, Marina was so nervous she could barely concentrate. She checked her bag three times to make sure Titian's diary was still there.

She called Luc on her lunch hour.

"I have some things to tell you."

"Already? I'm intrigued," he replied. "I'm tied up this afternoon. It will have to be tomorrow—or it could be this evening." He paused, and she could almost hear the smile in his voice. "That is, if you'll have dinner with me."

She was too anxious to wait until tomorrow.

"I suppose dinner would be all right."

"Try to sound a little more excited," he said good-naturedly. "I can pick you up if you like."

"You don't need to go to the trouble," she said. "Give me the address of the restaurant and I'll meet you there."

"Café Miguel in San Telmo," he answered. "You know, you're quite unusual. Most women in Buenos Aires aren't so independent."

She smiled into the receiver. "I'll take that as a compliment."

• • •

San Telmo was the opposite of Recoleta's refined sophistication. The cobblestone streets were so narrow that Marina had to get out of the taxi and walk the rest of the way. The restaurant was as casual as the Alvear Palace was elegant. Marina felt overdressed in a scoop-neck blue dress with a pleated skirt. There was one room with an open grill and a rack of dusty wine bottles. Families chatted noisily around tables and the windows were open to the street.

Luc stood up when she entered. He was dressed casually in a sports coat and linen trousers.

"You could have told me what to wear," she said, glancing at the next table. The men had their shirtsleeves rolled up, and the women wore simple dresses and flat shoes.

"And miss out on seeing you in such a pretty dress?" Luc grinned. He glanced at her high-heeled pumps. "I haven't seen shoes like that since I left Paris."

Her shoes were lizard skin with pointed toes.

"I'm surprised you noticed a woman's shoes when you were only sixteen," Marina returned, sitting opposite him.

"My mother worked in a department store after my father died," Luc explained. "I thought you'd like to experience Buenos Aires like a porteña. San Telmo is the oldest neighborhood in the city. It's been here since the seventeenth century."

"A porteña?" she repeated.

"It means 'local,'" he explained. "The porteños are the heart and soul of Buenos Aires. Recoleta and San Nicolás are full of Europeans who arrived in the last sixty years. They made their money in the mines. The porteños provided the labor. I like to support them when I can."

San Telmo reminded Marina of Trastevere in Rome. Trastevere didn't have the elegant shops or grand palazzi of other neighborhoods, but there was an energy one didn't find elsewhere.

"I do like it," she said, smiling. "And I'm hungry. I haven't eaten all day."

Luc pointed to the grill. Platters of sizzling meats stood on the counter. There were bottles of spices and plates of sliced vegetables.

"Miguel's is a traditional parrilla restaurant," he said. "Parilla means 'grill' in Spanish. There are a few ways to order your steak. Vacio is a boneless cut from the cow's belly. Matambre is a flank steak that's stuffed with cheese and vegetables. Personally, I prefer entranas. It's very tender, and perfect with a side of chorizo."

"You eat meat as a side dish as well," Marina said, laughing.

In Recoleta, the restaurants served a variety of foods. Many of the dishes were Italian and Spanish.

"Argentina is the land of the cow," Luc reminded her. "Porteños eat meat with everything."

Marina's face clouded. She pictured her father standing in the kitchen over a pot of spaghetti. He had insisted pasta should be served at every meal. At lunch, he ate tagliarini with olive oil and grated Parmesan. Dinner was spaghetti or lasagna in a red sauce.

"Italians are passionate about their pasta. The night my father died, I had stopped to get anchovies for his pasta sauce. He was an art dealer. He was hiding a Jewish artist in our basement." Her voice caught. "German officers shot them. If I had come home sooner, I could have saved him."

"Or you would have been shot too," Luc said quietly.

"He didn't confide in me about what he was doing. I would have helped him. Perhaps things would have turned out differently."

"I had a good friend in Paris, François," Luc said. "François was Jewish. In 1940 he wrote and said his parents were thinking of immigrating to Argentina. It took me two months to reply. I was twenty-one and busy." He paused. "I never heard from him again. I learned later that he and his parents were sent to a concentration camp. I doubt they survived. If I had written sooner, offered to help, it might have made a difference."

Marina was silent. She ran her hands over the tablecloth.

She hadn't planned to tell Luc about helping

the partisans, but now it all spilled out. How she arrived in Florence and felt she had to do something to make a difference. Carlos asking her to value the artwork. The precious art that passed through her hands.

"Carlos did so much for others," she said. "He was determined to do his part to win the war."

"It sounds like you did a lot too," Luc replied.

Her mind went to the last night of the German occupation in Florence. The bridges being blown up, people trapped and unable to leave. The fire that raged for days, so much of Florence and its history left in ruins.

"It never felt like enough," she said soberly.

They ordered steaks as Luc told her about himself. His mother lived in nearby Palermo; he ate dinner there once a week. He had a younger sister whom he adored, and he enjoyed swimming and dancing.

"I used to be a good dancer, but I don't have time anymore. Since I started my own firm, I'm at the office late every night."

"One day I want to open my own art gallery," Marina said. "It's all I've ever dreamed of."

"I'm sure it will be a great success." Luc eyed her appreciatively.

The waiter set down their plates. Luc showed Marina how to cut her steak so it didn't lose its juices.

"I've been talking about myself," he said,

sipping his wine. "What did you want to tell me?"

Marina told Luc about Botticelli's sketches and the book of grammar by Alberti that belonged to Levi, Luc's client.

Luc leaned back in his chair and whistled. "I can't believe he still has the book of sketches; it must have been too difficult to sell. Even I know anything by Botticelli is worth a fortune. Wait until Levi hears the news," Luc said eagerly. "He'll be so happy."

Marina put down her fork. She glanced at Luc nervously.

"There was something else behind the books," she began. "Something that's very important to me."

"I don't understand," Luc frowned.

She told him about the Verrocchio. How it ended up in her possession, and her original plan to return it to the Uffizi Gallery.

"I felt so terrible when it disappeared," she finished. "I thought I'd never get it back."

"You were trying to do what you thought was best," Luc consoled her. "It wouldn't have done any good inside a German officer's safe-deposit box in Switzerland."

Marina was grateful that Luc felt that way.

"I'll help you send it back to Italy," Luc offered. "The organization will make the arrangements; you'll get a reward."

"I don't want a reward, I only want it to be displayed where Italians can enjoy it." She fiddled with her napkin. "First I want to ask Carlos about it."

Luc's brow creased into a frown.

"Why would you do that?"

Marina thought carefully, trying to work out how to explain.

"Carlos knew how important it was to me that the Verrocchio was returned to the museum," she stumbled. "I want to give him a chance to explain himself."

"Botticelli's sketchbook and Alberti's book of grammar are still on the bookshelf," Luc reminded her. "What if Carlos disappears with them before I can legally retrieve them? I have to provide written proof that they belonged to Levi's relatives. Then I can go to Carlos and demand their return." He deliberated. "Or Carlos might realize that the diary and the Verrocchio are missing, and that he's in danger of being caught. He fled before, what's to stop him from doing the same thing now?"

"Surely he wouldn't do that. He's married, he's expecting a child."

Luc spent a long time before answering. He toyed with his wineglass.

"You really were in love with him, weren't you?"

Marina's eyes flickered. She gulped her wine.

"Yes, I was. And he loved me. I thought I

knew his character." She hesitated, determined to believe her own words. "Carlos helped many people during the war; he deserves a chance to prove himself."

"If you say so," Luc agreed haltingly. He ate a piece of his steak. "Carlos is very lucky. He doesn't deserve you."

After dinner, they stood on the sidewalk. The street was crowded. Couples strolled hand in hand, and music drifted from an upstairs window.

"There's a nightclub in Plaza Dorrego," Luc suggested. "We could watch the tango."

Marina looked up at him. He looked so handsome and she was tempted. It had been a long time since a man had made her feel like this.

"I thought you had to work late every night," she reminded him.

"We have been working," Luc countered.

Marina gave a small smile. She was imagining things; he was just being collegial. And anyway, she had promised herself that she wouldn't start seeing him because they worked together.

"I'm tired, maybe another time," she said coyly.

Luc's face fell and she felt slightly guilty.

"You can see me to a taxi," she offered. "It's impossible to walk on the cobblestones in these heels."

The next morning, Marina called Valentina from the gallery and said she had some photographs of paintings to show her. She had to find a way to see Carlos. He would probably be home for dinner. Marina would be there when he arrived.

"Marina, please come in," Valentina said, opening the door.

Valentina wore a smock over her dress. Her hair was held back by a scarf.

"I'm a mess. I've been painting the nursery." She smiled. "I haven't had so much fun since art class."

"I didn't know you took art classes." Marina followed her inside.

"Only a class for beginners, but I know how to hold a paintbrush. Come upstairs and give me your opinion."

They went upstairs to the nursery. One wall was covered in wide strokes of yellow paint.

"My mother would be furious if she knew I was going to paint the nursery myself. She has staff for everything." Valentina laughed. "I'm enjoying myself so much."

The evening light streamed through the window. A crib stood in the corner, and Marina recognized the rocking horse she had seen at the baby shop. Suddenly she imagined Carlos holding his baby, his emerald-green eyes soft and full of love.

She put her hand out to steady herself.

"I love it. The yellow makes the room so bright," she managed to say. "You've done so much in one day."

"It's the milk stirred with honey." Valentina beamed. "My morning sickness is much better. Let's go back downstairs, and you can show me the photographs of the paintings."

They sat in the living room and Marina took out a set of loose photographs. The paintings Marina had chosen were modern abstracts with bright colors and different shapes.

"I narrowed it down from the paintings you liked in the catalog. The paintings themselves are quite large; we'll have to choose the frames. I was thinking gold and silver downstairs, lighter colors in the nursery and master bedroom."

Valentina brought out coffee, and they talked about Marina's ideas for the nursery.

It grew late, and Marina wondered if Carlos was coming home soon. Perhaps he was away on business.

"I should go," she said eventually. "I'm sure you want to change clothes before your husband arrives."

"Federico doesn't mind what I wear." Valentina set down her cup. "He's so sweet; he says I look beautiful in anything. Every morning he kisses my stomach and says he can't wait to meet the baby." She sighed happily. "I'm so lucky. I never knew marriage could be like this."

"What does Federico do?" Marina inquired.

"I'm not sure what he was doing when we met, but my father owns a paper mill, and now Federico works for him. My father thinks he'll go far; he's very good with people."

Carlos hated working in his father's lumber business. Now he was working in a similar job for Valentina's father. Marina wondered what happened to his dreams of being an artist after the war.

"I'm sure he'll be hungry. I don't want to intrude." Marina stood up.

As she gathered her folio case, the front door opened. Footsteps sounded in the hallway.

Suddenly Carlos was standing in front of her. Her heart pounded so fiercely she was certain he could hear it. His hair was cut short, and he wore a blazer and tie. But he was as handsome and boyish as when she last saw him.

His mouth opened in astonishment. He was about to say something when a cloak dropped over his features.

"Valentina," he said instead. He kissed his wife on the cheek. "You didn't tell me we had company."

"This is Marina. She works at an art gallery. She's helping me choose pieces for the house."

"You didn't say anything about it," Carlos said shortly.

"I wanted to wait until we had finished."

Valentina blushed. "Marina has been so helpful. She even brought me honey to help my morning sickness."

"It's my fault. I shouldn't be here," Marina interjected.

Carlos glanced from Valentina to Marina. He walked to the sideboard and poured a glass of Scotch.

"Valentina has so much to handle with the new house and the baby," his voice was careful. "I'm glad she has someone to count on."

Valentina showed Carlos the paintings and told him Marina's suggestions. Marina tried to concentrate. All she could think about was how she could find a way to talk to Carlos alone.

"I'm interested in art too." Carlos turned to Marina. "Perhaps I could come to the gallery some time."

Marina handed him her card.

"It's around the corner. Please stop by." She got up and smoothed her skirt. "It's late—I really should go."

Carlos stood and smiled, and she was reminded of how magnetic his smile was. How warm and alive it used to make her feel.

"You mustn't leave," he urged. "Please, join us for dinner."

"Do stay," Valentina encouraged her. "I cooked today. The roast is too much for two of us."

Marina shook her head. She was tired, and her

head throbbed. She couldn't possibly endure eating dinner with Carlos and Valentina.

"No, thank you, I have dinner waiting at my pensione." She turned to Carlos. "It was nice to meet you, Federico."

Valentina walked Marina to the door. She leaned forward conspiratorially.

"Sometimes Federico is aloof with strangers, but I could tell he was pleased." She squeezed Marina's arm. "Thank you for everything you've done."

Marina strode along the sidewalk. The night sky looked so different here. In Tuscany, the stars seemed far away, high above the hills. In Buenos Aires, the stars were right above her. As if at any minute they would shower down in tiny silver flecks.

The evening breeze picked up and she wrapped her coat around herself. The pain was as raw as the first month after Carlos had left. It had been almost impossible to sit across from him this evening, to chat and nod politely.

She had to give him a chance to explain. She hoped he would contact her soon. Her heart couldn't take much more of the strain.

CHAPTER TWENTY-SEVEN

Buenos Aires, November 1945

For three days, she heard nothing from Carlos. Marina was afraid she had made a mistake. She didn't return Luc's phone calls, and she avoided seeing Valentina. She was certain Valentina could hear the anxiety in her voice when they spoke on the phone.

At night, she sat in her room and recalled the good things about Carlos. He became a partisan because he wanted to make a difference. He couldn't spend his days delivering firewood while so many people were being murdered by Hitler and the Nazis. And he had been so kind to Eli. Eli looked up to Carlos as if he were some type of Italian god.

And there was Belle. Belle had known Carlos for years. She wouldn't have encouraged their relationship if Carlos couldn't be trusted.

But no matter how she tried, Marina couldn't dismiss the suspicions from her mind. Carlos arranging for her to have dinner with Captain Bonner. Ludwig's missing pistol. Bernard telling Marina about seeing Carlos and Captain Bonner talking in Florence.

• • •

The bell above the gallery door sounded as Marina was about to take her lunch break.

Carlos entered, wearing an immaculately tailored tan suit. His shirt was crisp and white, and his shoes were polished to a high shine.

"Marina, it's nice to see you again," he said formally.

Marina flinched. It felt so odd for Carlos to speak to her, as if they didn't know each other. She glanced at the sitting area where Renata was talking to a client.

"Is there something I can help you with, Señor Murano?" she inquired.

Carlos moved closer.

"I need to talk to you. Let's go to lunch."

Marina didn't want to sit across from him at a restaurant. But they couldn't talk at the gallery.

She shook her head. "I don't want to eat lunch with you."

"Then where shall we go?" His voice was impatient.

Marina studied the paintings on the wall. They gave her an idea.

"We'll go to the National Museum of Fine Arts," she decided with a smile.

The National Museum of Fine Arts was on a wide street in Recoleta. It was smaller than the Uffizi Gallery in Florence, and it didn't have the lush gardens of Villa Borghese in Rome. But it was still beautiful, with rooms full of Renaissance paintings. Marina recognized a Bernini and a statue by Donatello.

They sat on a bench in the courtyard. A willow tree shaded the cobblestones.

"I was afraid I'd never see you again," Carlos began. He ran his hands through his hair. "You're even more beautiful than I remembered."

He seemed nervous. She had never seen Carlos nervous before.

"It's been almost two years," Marina said.

"Valentina told me how you met," he went on. "At the baby shop. It was such a coincidence."

"Your wife is lovely," Marina cut in. "I like her very much."

"Marina, let me explain." He turned to her. He was so close she could see the smooth planes of his cheekbones.

"No, let me go first," she interrupted, moving away.

She took Titian's diary with the Verrocchio from her satchel and showed it to him.

Carlos's expression changed. His brow creased.

"Where did you get this?" he demanded.

"Where you hid it," she said crisply. "Behind the books on the shelf in your study."

"I don't understand. What is this about?" He jumped up.

Marina took a deep breath. She told him everything. About her decision to come to

Argentina to work with Luc and help recover stolen art.

"I wanted to give you a chance to explain before the Verrocchio is returned to the Uffizi," she finished.

Carlos paced around the courtyard, then sat back down and took Marina's hand.

"You can't know how much I missed you and how much I miss Italy. It's as if I were forced to shed my own skin," he said earnestly. "For months I longed for the hills of Tuscany. I dreamed about the garden shed at night, holding you in my arms and seeing the moonlight stream through the window."

Marina pulled her hand away. She inched down the bench, away from him.

"I don't want to talk about that." Her voice was cold. "I want to know why you stole Ludwig's pistol and books. Why other priceless books are hidden in your study. And why you kept the Verrocchio for yourself when you knew how important it was to me that it be returned to the Uffizi."

He nodded. "All right. I'll tell you."

Carlos stood up and for a moment he was the charming young man in Desi's living room once again, peering out from behind a pile of firewood. She willed herself not to think about that. She crossed her arms and listened.

"Captain Bonner approached me one day; it

was after the raid on the house in San Gimignano. One of the prisoners had given him my name. He wasn't part of the partisan network but somehow he knew about me and what I was doing. Captain Bonner had already met you at Villa I Tatti, and he was very impressed with your knowledge and with what Belle told him about you." Carlos paused and glanced at Marina. "He said he would forget what he had heard if I arranged for him to meet you. He was obsessed with collecting art, and he wanted your expert advice. He didn't want to ask Belle to approach you. She wasn't very friendly when he called on her; he was afraid she'd turn him down."

Marina's blood went cold. She could almost feel the color drain from her cheeks.

"So you set me up?" she asked in horror.

"I immediately said I wouldn't dream of it," he assured her. "But he kept pressing me. He threatened to search my parents' house, to throw me and them in prison." Carlos stopped. "He said I'd be tortured. I finally agreed. It was the only way to keep my parents and the partisans safe. I convinced myself that Captain Bonner only wanted your opinion on art, so you weren't in any danger. Then you told me about the Verrocchio, and I couldn't resist. Anyone who's seen what I had as a partisan knew that anything could happen during the war. Keeping the Verrocchio could be my ticket to freedom. It wouldn't be missed. Few people knew it still existed. Then more safe houses were being searched, and I got frightened. I decided it was time to disappear. I used Ludwig's book collection to pay for my false papers and my ticket. I didn't have time to get my own gun. I had left it at a safe house by accident. I took the pistol in case I ran into trouble."

"Your parents have money," Marina interjected.

"My parents keep everything—money, jewelry—in a safe."

"Except for your mother's pink pearls," Marina said absently. "Valentina was wearing them on the day we met."

"I knew that when I arrived in Argentina it could be months until I found work. The Verrocchio would be hard to sell. It would have to be a buyer I trusted, someone willing to overlook its provenance." He put his hands in his pockets. "Then I met Valentina, purely by accident. She was so sweet and innocent. . . ." He hesitated. "I thought it would be a pleasant flirtation. She got pregnant, and I had to marry her." Carlos's voice became urgent. "You have to believe me. Valentina is in love with me, and I'm very fond of her. But I never felt anything for her like I feel for you."

Marina remembered thinking Valentina was hiding something. The wedding happened so quickly because Valentina was pregnant.

"I want to know about the Botticelli sketchbook and the Alberti grammar book that belong to Luc's client," she snapped.

Carlos sat down again. He bowed his head.

"The books were hidden in the ceiling of the villa in Oliveto Citra that was being used as a deportation center. The family had been put on a train and sent east. I knew they weren't coming back."

Marina remembered Carlos telling her about the three centers in Tuscany. She felt slightly dizzy.

"So you stole them?" She turned to him in disbelief.

"Was I supposed to leave them for the Germans?" He was suddenly angry. "Partisans did that kind of thing all the time. How do you think there was enough money for guns and food?

"It was better that I used them to start a new life," he continued. "I never stopped thinking about you. I couldn't send you a letter from Italy. The war was still on, and I could get caught or put you in danger. When I arrived in Buenos Aires, I wasn't in any position to ask you to join me. I wanted to get settled first, sell some more of the books and find a job. Then I was going to send you a ticket. Nothing has changed. I love you more than anything in my life."

Marina turned to him angrily. He had told her

everything she needed to know and revealed his true character. Carlos could be charming and kind, but he would always put himself first.

"Even if I believe you, everything has changed. You betrayed me with Captain Bonner; you risked my life. You took things that weren't yours to take. And now you're married and your wife is expecting a baby."

"I was always going to tell you the truth," he claimed. He stroked her cheek. "Now you know everything. We can leave Argentina. We'll go to Rio de Janeiro or Caracas. We can leave the Botticelli and the books for Luc's client. We'll sell the Verrocchio and buy a villa in the hills. You can open an art gallery, and I'll paint." He took her hand. "It will be the life we dreamed of."

Carlos leaned forward and kissed her. For a moment, she was too surprised to move. Then she jumped up. Her hands trembled and her heart was pounding.

"How dare you!" she spat. "After all we went through together. You begged me to help the partisans. I put myself in danger by switching the Verrocchio with the fake. You let me go back to Captain Bonner's apartment a second time. If he discovered what I was doing, I would have been shot." All the anguish and fear that had been bottled up inside her rose to the surface. "And how many times did you shower me with gifts and prepare me dinners?" Her eyes filled with tears and she blinked them away angrily. "Then you disappeared without a word and turned up a year later as a married man."

"When I saw you in my living room, it was as if I had been given another chance. Valentina's parents will take care of her and the baby. In time, she'll find someone else to marry. She'll forget all about me," Carlos explained.

His eyes lingered over her. He spoke slowly, as if every word was a caress.

"I can't live without you, Marina," he said softly.

Marina turned away. She stood and walked in small circles.

"We all did things during the war we didn't expect to. The war is over now, and we have to take responsibility for our actions. Your signet ring was found on the body of a partisan killed by a firing squad. I was devastated. Why didn't you try to contact me in all that time?"

"I sold the signet ring, I didn't know what happened to it." He shrugged. "Even if I had known, I wouldn't have reached out to you," he admitted. "Hitler knew he was losing; the Nazis were conducting retaliations on partisans throughout Italy. I was on the run; it would have been too dangerous to contact you. And as I already explained, once I arrived in Argentina, I met Valentina almost right away. . . ." He looked at Marina plaintively. "There wasn't time, I got swept up in everything. I'm sorry, I made a terrible mistake."

She glanced at her watch. Her lunch hour was almost over.

"I'm going back to the gallery. This afternoon you'll deliver the books hidden in your bookshelf to my pensione. In return, I'll make sure Luc doesn't go to the authorities."

Carlos's face brightened. He rubbed his hands eagerly.

"It's fine, we don't need the money," he said. "Valentina's father gave me a car. I'll pack tonight. We'll leave tomorrow."

Marina shook her head.

"No. Enough children lost their parents during the war." Her voice was cold. "You will stay and take care of your new family."

Carlos took a long time to answer. She thought he would try to argue. But then something shifted. When he looked at her, his eyes had their old twinkle.

"Valentina is fond of you. She'll invite you to dinner parties," he said. "How will we behave when we know everything about each other?"

Marina smoothed her skirt. She gathered her purse.

"You'll pretend we just met. You're quite good at that." She started walking away, then turned around. "There was a war, after all. In some ways, I didn't know you at all."

· · ·

Marina went to Luc's office the next day after work. The secretary wasn't there, and the door to his office was open.

"Marina, come in."

She took a folio from her bag. "These are for you."

Luc leafed through the grammar book. He glanced at the sketches by Botticelli.

"These are magnificent," he breathed.

"These are only sketches of his early work," she replied. "They're nothing compared to the completed paintings. Once, my father took me to Florence just to see *Primavera* at the Uffizi. I walked on a cloud for days."

Luc studied her thoughtfully.

"Art is very important to you."

"More important than anything. It's not just paint and brushstrokes on a canvas. It's the artist's heartaches and dreams."

"I never thought about art like that. I'll have to pay more attention next time I visit a gallery."

He flipped through Alberti's book on Italian grammar, then leaned back in his chair and smiled at Marina.

"This is wonderful. Levi will be pleased."

She reached into the folio again and took out Titian's diary. She placed it on the desk.

"The Verrocchio is inside. The diary and the painting have been together through so much; I didn't want to separate them. You'll make sure the Verrocchio is returned to the Uffizi?"

"You have my word," Luc promised.

Marina sat back in her chair. For a moment she felt a sense of loss. The Verrocchio had loomed so large in her memory, it was hard to part with it. She knew she should be happy. There was so much during the war that she hadn't been able to accomplish, but at least she was able to do this.

"I've decided something," Marina said. She shifted uncomfortably on the chair. "Renata has been talking about giving me more responsibilities at the gallery. Perhaps, when I save enough money, she'll consider making me a partner. I think I'm going to make that my full-time position; no more searching for lost works on the side. I hope you understand. And I hope I'm not leaving you in the lurch after you took the time to hire me." She took a breath. "It's just too painful. Since the war began, everything in my life has revolved around loss and the past; it's time I start looking toward the future."

Luc couldn't keep the disappointment out of his eyes.

"I understand how you feel. At some point the war must end for everyone," he acknowledged. "I'll miss working with you."

There was a small twinge in Marina's chest. She wondered if she would see Luc again.

"I'll miss working with you too."

Luc stood up and walked to the window.

"Carlos doesn't deserve you," he said suddenly.

Marina shut the image of Carlos out of her mind.

"Carlos's child deserves a father," she said levelly. "He's no concern of mine any longer."

CHAPTER TWENTY-EIGHT

Buenos Aires, February 1946

Marina stood in front of the mirror in her room at the pensione. It was a Saturday in late February. Luc had invited her on a picnic.

It had been three months since she stopped working for him. He had called a few times in the first month and invited her to dinner. Each time, she declined. She needed time to get over Carlos, and she wanted to devote all her energy to the gallery.

Marina worked long hours, learning more and more about South American art. She accompanied Renata to private showings and attended receptions and auctions. At one auction she went to alone, she fell in love with a painting by an unknown artist and bid more than she thought Renata would be comfortable with. The next day, she told Renata and offered to pay the difference. The painting only hung on the gallery wall for two days before it was snapped up by a client for double what Marina had paid. Renata took her to lunch to celebrate. Marina vowed to trust her own instincts from then on.

She even stayed friends with Valentina. She never went near the house, but she and Valentina met occasionally for lunch. Afterward, they browsed in the dress shops or picked out baby clothes. Valentina admired Marina's knowledge and sophistication, and Marina enjoyed Valentina's bright personality.

On the weekends, Marina explored the city. She visited La Boca, where the buildings were painted in vibrant turquoises and yellows, and the streets were filled with paintings by local artists. Renata took her to the opera at Teatro Colón and to watch the polo matches at Campo Argentino de Polo. Sometimes, Marina missed a man's company, but she kept telling herself she wasn't ready. And even if she were, after the first month Luc stopped calling.

But then they had run into each other by chance, and now they were going for a drive in the countryside. She realized she missed him. Luc was warm and easygoing, and she felt she could trust him. Besides, it was only a picnic; perhaps he asked her only as a friend.

Elena's voice called up the staircase—Luc was waiting downstairs. Marina wrapped a colorful scarf around her hair and grabbed her bag.

Luc looked very handsome in a yellow V-neck vest and white trousers. His hair was almost golden from a summer of Argentinian sunshine and his arms were tanned.

"Marina," Luc said as she came downstairs. "It's nice to see you. I almost didn't call you; I was afraid you'd be too busy."

"Luc Feron afraid of calling me," she said, laughing. "That doesn't sound like the Luc I know."

"It's different now, I'm not your boss," he replied. His face broke into a smile. "My mother was upset you quit before she could ask you to Sunday lunch."

Marina followed Luc outside to his car, and they drove out of the city. The countryside was green, and the air smelled sweet and fragrant. They passed waterfalls and rushing streams and Marina thought how different it was from Tuscany. The landscape was wild and new. There was none of the European history: hilltop villages that had been the same for a thousand years, ancient churches that had been there as long as the Romans.

Luc glanced over at her. "You look much too serious for someone going on a picnic."

"I was thinking about the differences between Italy and Argentina."

"I like it here, there's a hunger," Luc reflected. "People want to work hard and build good lives for their families."

They drove farther until Luc turned onto a road shaded by plane trees. In front of them was a colonial-style house. Beside it was a barn and another building with small windows and a shingled roof.

"Where are we?" Marina asked. "You didn't

tell me anything about where we were going."

"It's an estancia." Luc jumped out and opened Marina's door. "That's Spanish for 'cattle ranch.' It's owned by a friend of mine. They have three hundred acres, and cows and horses. Fifty years ago, visitors used to arrive by stagecoach and stay overnight. The guests were fed steak and wine, and the gauchos regaled them with stories of life on the ranch."

"Gauchos?" Marina said.

"Argentinian cowboys." Luc took her hand. "Come, let me introduce you to Santiago and Amelia. They'll tell you all about it."

Santiago and Amelia were in their midthirties. They had two children: a ten-year-old boy named Juan and an eight-year-old girl named Maria.

Marina was amazed by the grassland that stretched for miles. There was a lake where travelers used to cool off after their journey. The gauchos had their own dormitory with a huge kitchen and a parlor for relaxing.

The best part of the ranch was the main house. It reminded Marina of Villa I Tatti, with its spacious rooms and elegant furnishings. There was a library filled with books about local history and the ranch's past, and a living room bathed in sunlight. Marina pictured the living room at Villa I Tatti and Belle entering in one of her outrageous outfits and asking Marina about her day.

Lunch was served in a long dining room with a

timbered ceiling. They ate empanadas filled with beef and cheese and drank a red Médoc wine as delicious as the wine from Desi's vineyard.

"You have a wonderful place," Marina said, tasting the side dish of grilled eggplant.

"The ranch has been in Amelia's family for decades," Santiago said.

"When I first came to the estancia, I never thought I could live here. I grew up in Buenos Aires. I was going to be a banker like my father," he went on. "Now I couldn't imagine doing anything else." He reached over and squeezed his wife's hand. "Sometimes, love leads you where you least expect it. It's part of the adventure."

After lunch, Luc and Marina strolled by themselves beside the lake.

"I've never been anywhere like this," Marina said. She felt warm and happy from the wine. "You told me we were going on a picnic."

"I wanted to surprise you." Luc grinned. "And we are going on a picnic." He held up a basket. "Amelia packed a blanket and chocotorta for dessert."

Luc spread the blanket on the grass. Marina sat down and Luc sat near her, his long legs stretched in front of him.

They ate cake and talked about Luc's work and Renata's gallery. Luc was so easy to talk to. Before Marina knew it, two hours had passed.

"We should go soon," Marina said eventually. "I have an event this evening."

It would take them a while to drive back to the city, and she didn't want to be late for the art showing she was attending.

Luc covered the last piece of cake and put it back in the basket.

"Santiago and Amelia loved meeting you. They said I should act fast or some young gaucho will find you."

"What do you mean?"

"I picked up the phone to call you a dozen times in the last two months. Each time, I put it down. You had made it clear you weren't interested."

"Interested?" she repeated.

"In seeing me again," Luc prompted. "I like you, Marina. I have since the first day you came into my office."

"You said you didn't have time for things like dinner and dancing," she reminded him. "You were too busy working."

"One makes time for the things that are important," he reflected. "I'd like to make time for you, if you'll give me the chance."

Marina gulped. Luc did have feelings for her. Perhaps she could allow herself to admit her feelings for him. Luc was different from Carlos, different from Nicolo. She wasn't sure how she knew; it was something about the way he talked to her. And he had waited patiently all these months. He hadn't forgotten about her; he was just waiting for her to heal. Something stirred inside her, like the opening of a window, and she took a deep breath.

"I'm certainly not going to run off with a gaucho, if that's what you're afraid of," she said, laughing. "I'm not much of a horseback rider."

Luc's voice softened. He touched Marina's hand.

"I'm serious, Marina. You're bright and lovely," he ventured. "I don't know if you plan on staying in Buenos Aires. But if you do, I want to be part of your life."

Her mind went to the past. To Nicolo, whom she believed she would love forever. To Carlos and the heady excitement of their joint cause.

Was she ready to find love again? How could she be sure Luc wouldn't break her heart?

The war taught her that nothing in life was guaranteed, that each day was too precious to waste. If there was a chance at happiness, she had to take it.

"I'd like to see you too." She nodded.

Luc moved closer and kissed her. The kiss wasn't long, but his lips were warm as she kissed him back.

"We'd better go," Luc said when they parted. "If we don't leave soon, Juan and Maria will come out to show us a magic trick, and you'll never get back in time for your cvent."

They hugged Santiago and Amelia goodbye, then drove back to Buenos Aires. Marina felt different: light and buoyant, like on New Year's Eve in Rome before the war, when she used to stay up to watch the fireworks.

Luc pulled up in front of the pensione. He turned to her.

"I was wondering if you'd like to go to dinner tomorrow night."

"On a Sunday night?" she asked.

"It doesn't have to be anything elaborate," he assured her. "I know you have work the next day, and so do I. We can go to a nice restaurant and not stay out too late."

The sun was setting over the Metropolitan Cathedral and the clock tower. She was reminded of the light in Rome. How St. Peter's Basilica had been bathed in the golden light that attracted artists to the city for centuries. There were other places and other kinds of light. Some of them were just as beautiful.

"We don't have to make it an early night," she said. There was a twinkle in her eye. "I don't have to be at the gallery until ten a.m. on Monday."

Luc leaned forward and kissed her. He wrapped his arms around her, and his embrace was sure and welcoming.

"In that case, wear your dancing shoes. You can't live in Buenos Aires and not learn how to tango."

ACKNOWLEDGMENTS

First, thank you as always to my incredible agent, Johanna Castillo. She makes me a better writer every day and I'm so grateful.

Thank you to my incredible team at Atria: my editor, Kaitlin Olson; Falon Kirby in publicity; and Raaga Rajagopala in marketing. A huge thanks to Fiona Henderson and Anthea Bariasmis and everyone at Simon & Schuster Australia. I'm a lucky writer!

Thank you to my children, Alex, Andrew, Heather, Madeleine, and Thomas. And to my daughter-in-law, Sarah, and especially to my granddaughter, Lily. These stories are for you.

ABOUT THE AUTHOR

Anita Abriel was born in Sydney, Australia. She received a BA in English literature with a minor in creative writing from Bard College. She is the internationally bestselling author of *The Light After the War*, *Lana's War*, and *A Girl During the War*. She lives in California with her family.

A GIRL DURING THE WAR
ANITA ABRIEL

This reading group guide for *A Girl During the War* includes discussion questions, ideas for enhancing your book club, and a Q&A with author Anita Abriel. The suggested questions are intended to help your reading group find new and interesting angles and topics for your discussion. We hope that these ideas will enrich your conversation and increase your enjoyment of the book.

TOPICS & QUESTIONS FOR DISCUSSION

1. " 'Art was as necessary to my father as oxygen' " (page 47). What is/was the significance of art for Marina and her father, both with regards to their knowledge and expertise as well as their emotional connection to it? Find more examples in the book to support your answer.

2. "She thought about Bernard's clandestine trips to Switzerland and about the envelope on Desi's dressing table. The war was every-

391

where. Even the people closest to her were hiding something" (page 110). Almost every main character at this point is or was keeping some secret from Marina or someone else. What are some of the other secrets? How have they affected Marina?

3. On page 143, we see Marina remembering looking through her mother's jewelry when Belle offers her own jewelry collection for Marina to borrow from. What are other ways that Belle assumes a maternal figure after the absence of one in Marina's life?

4. On page 89, we read that "Marina had told Carlos she didn't want her father's death to have been in vain," and on page 149, Carlos says, " 'I suppose that's also why I joined the partisans. To my parents, I'm a failure.' " Apart from defending their country and protecting vulnerable Jewish people, what were the other, more personal emotions behind why Marina and Carlos found themselves a part of the resistance?

5. Take note of the metaphors that Marina uses to describe the war: "as if [the war] were lurking behind the silver drapes, settling itself on the table next to the soup bowls and butter plates" (page 61), "the war seemed

to settle over her as if it were fog covering the hills, filling her chest like a terrible cold" (page 95), and " 'like the snow on the hills during the winter—it can't last forever' " (page 166). She likens the war to an unwanted guest, a physical ailment, and a seasonal precipitation reoccurrence. What do you think this expresses about the role of the war in Marina's life?

6. " 'None of us see exactly who we are when we look in the mirror,' " Marina tells Carlos (page 155). How does this foreshadow both of their destinies and their roles in the resistance?

7. Carlos, Marina's neighbor and new love interest, often reminds her of her former lover, Nicolo. What are the similarities and differences between them and the role they play in Marina's life? How did Marina's experience with Nicolo affect her ability to trust people? Has anyone else in Marina's life broken her trust?

8. Compare the letters from Vittorio to Marina (pages 22–24) and Peter to Desi (pages 173–175). What are the parallels of their experiences and those who are left to mourn their absences?

9. Discuss how Ludwig and Gerhard as Germans play unique roles in this story and the fight for Italian liberation. Can relationships ever fully transcend identity and nationality? Why or why not?

10. In chapter 3, Belle and others engage in a debate over choosing between love or beauty for the rest of your life if you had to do so. What do these two things represent in the beginning of the novel with regards to the lives of its characters? What do they represent closer to the end of the novel? Do the characters' answers stay the same as the story progresses?

11. When first introduced, Eli is fourteen years old, toeing the line between youthful innocence and adolescent awareness. How do these simultaneous identities capture the full range of emotions and experiences that the Italians and Allies feel under Nazi occupation?

12. Months after the fall of Hitler and Mussolini, Marina grieves the destruction of parts of the city she had grown to love and the hundreds of civilians who were killed in the process. Desi comforts her by saying that " 'that's what memories are for. So that our loved

ones never die' " (page 305). How do the characters use memory as a way to celebrate what they once had and reconcile what they have lost?

ENHANCE YOUR BOOK CLUB

1. " 'Our time is fleeting, while a painting brings joy for centuries' " (pages 62–63).

   " 'Can you imagine if bombs were dropped on the Vatican, the Duomo in Florence, St. Mark's Basilica in Venice? It would be the end of two thousand years of civilization' " (page 115).

   "Marina thought of the priceless artwork at the Uffizi in Florence, at Villa Borghese in Rome and the Doge's Palace in Venice. The thought of losing them to the Germans made her stomach turn" (page 151).

   A deep underlying fear for many of the characters in *A Girl During the War* is the seizure of precious Italian art and the destruction of revered Italian architecture by occupying German forces. Approximately eleven years after this novel was set, there was a global convention in The Hague, Netherlands, on how to protect cultural property during wartime. Research an example of cultural theft/destruction during armed conflict within the past century and explore the impact it had on civilian populations through figures, anecdotal stories, and any other useful information.

2. Whether it's the curfew that kept them from staying out late or the rationing that prevented large dinners (page 119), we see how life after the Germans arrived was very different for Italians. Take note of the differences in life before and after the arrival of the Nazis, however big or small, as described in the novel to paint a full picture of what the German occupation was really like. See how this compares to real-life firsthand accounts from Italian survivors of World War II.

3. Italians are known for their expansive and globally revered cuisine, as depicted in *A Girl During the War*. Discuss how meals and food play a central role in Marina's life, old and new. Research the cultural and historical significance of food in Italy, especially during times of political turmoil.

A CONVERSATION WITH ANITA ABRIEL

Q: What inspired you to choose Florence as a setting for *A Girl During the War*?

A: I visited Florence when I was young, and I was amazed to find so much history in one city. Florence has centuries-old paintings and sculptures and architecture by the most famous artists and architects in the world. Lately, I've thought about what would have happened if more of those things had been destroyed during World War II—what would we have been left with and how would Florence be seen by future generations? That's when I started doing my research.

Q: How does Marina differ from your previous protagonists, Lana (from *Lana's War*) and Vera and Edith (from *The Light After the War*)?

A: Vera and Edith were both real people (my mother and her best friend). Marina and Lana are fictional characters, but both are very much products of the time in which they live. Marina and Lana are both strong women who have experienced terrible tragedy. Marina feels younger to me than Lana. She comes of age and experiences love for the first time during the war. Those experiences together change her in many ways. They make her grow from being a girl to a woman.

Q: How much of *A Girl During the War* is factual and how much is fiction?

A: The characters of Marina and her father, Vittorio, Desi and her family, Carlos, and Sara and Eli are fictional, but Bernard, Belle, Gerhard, and Ludwig are all real people. Villa I Tatti is a real villa that is now owned by Harvard University. And the main event—the Germans blowing up the bridges—and Gerhard only being able to save the Ponte Vecchio are factual.

Q: After losing the only family she knew, Marina forms a new community in Florence, continuing the strong themes of interpersonal relationships that determine the destinies of your characters. What inspired the creation of this world and these characters to support Marina?

A: In Europe during the war, people had to band together—it was the only way to survive. In Northern Italy, especially after the German occupation, many Italians found comfort and food and companionship by forming small groups.

Q: As the child of Holocaust survivors, how do you approach writing non-Jewish characters who serve as allies to the vulnerable Jewish community during WWII?

A: It was difficult at first. Most of the stories I heard as a child from my parents were about

Jews helping other Jews. But the more I have researched, the more I realized that many people from all nationalities—including some Germans like Gerhard and Ludwig—also helped the Jews. Humanity existed in many different quarters.

Q: How did you go about researching the partisans of Italy? Was it difficult to find accurate information about this prolific and heterogenous movement?

A: I read everything I could on the subject. It's difficult to know if details are completely accurate since many of the partisans' activities were clandestine by nature, but I did the best I could.

Q: What is something you want American readers to take away from stories about the Holocaust and the movements of resistance around it?

A: I want readers to know just how terrible the Holocaust was, and yet that at the same time, there was always hope, always beauty, always people ready to celebrate life. That doesn't go away just because there is a war.

Q: Do you have a next project in mind? If so, what is it?

A: I'm still in the early stages, but soon!

Center Point Large Print
600 Brooks Road / PO Box 1
Thorndike, ME 04986-0001 USA

(207) 568-3717

US & Canada:
1 800 929-9108
www.centerpointlargeprint.com